D0583240

The Book of Mordechai

and

Lazarus

THE HUNGARIAN LIST

GÁBOR SCHEIN

The Book of Mordechai

TRANSLATED BY ADAM Z. LEVY

Lazarus

TRANSLATED BY OTTILIE MULZET

LONDON   NEW YORK   CALCUTTA

SERIES EDITOR

OTTILIE MULZET

Seagull Books, 2017

Originally published in Hungarian as *Mordecháj könyve* (2002)
and *Lázár!* (2004)

© Gábor Schein, 2002, 2004

English translation of *The Book of Mordechai* © Adam Z. Levy, 2017

English translation of *Lazarus* © Ottilie Mulzet, 2017

ISBN   978 0 8574 2 441 9

British Library Cataloguing-in-Publication Data

A catalogue record for this book is available from the British Library.

Typeset by Seagull Books, Calcutta, India

Printed and bound by Maple Press, York, Pennsylvania, USA

CONTENTS

The Book of Mordechai

TRANSLATED BY ADAM Z. LEVY

It is said of Rabbi Zusha of Hanipol that in his youth he heard the future in the whispers of the trees. Then there was Nachman of Breslov, who could not sleep in his newly built house; among the fresh boards he felt as though he were lying with the dead. He heard voices as well but not those of the future. And after his first night in the house, he woke his wife and three sons at dawn with great shouts, Fire, he screamed, though the house had not yet begun to burn; he waited until they were all outside before he set it ablaze. What was it that Rabbi Zusha's trees whispered? And what was it that the boards of Rabbi Nachman's house said, the ones which stood charred by morning facing the prayer house? Of this there is little we can know. Where our story begins there are no forests, nor are there fields, and even if there were, our protagonists would not hear the words of the trees, if they still speak at all, if Rabbi Nachman had not been the last one to hear their voices, having burnt out the words within them once and for all.

Our story begins with a silent wooden object and does not leave it. But we will never glimpse this silent object, it will remain hidden until the end by an oilcloth cover, under which receipts, shopping lists, notices and letters have been slipped. When P. sat down beside the oilcloth cover, for the silent object is in fact a table, he felt the way the orange floral pattern and the poison-green stripes stretching between the flowers stuck out a little here and there. Further in on the table, there stood a lemon-yellow plastic bowl, with discarded paper in it, and beyond that a patterned metal box, filled with buttons and sewing needles. Waiting for P. in the other chair was an old woman in a synthetic violet wrap decorated with floral print finer than the tablecloth's and with several pins stuck just above her breast on the right and left side, a green measuring tape around her neck. When P. sat down, or, rather, when he lowered himself into the backed chair aged a deep brown, the old woman immediately butted the book that lay open before her on the tablecloth with her thick, stumpy fingers and, half-turning her head to the young man sitting beside her, said, 'Here, read!'

The book, which the old woman brought out from the back room, her daughter had got in 1953, more precisely, according to the inscription, on 19 May 1953, on the occasion of her bat mitzvah. On the left side of the yellowing, heavy pages was the Hebrew text, on the right the Hungarian, and accompanying the story were the black-and-white impressions left by the copperplate engravings. The translation was the work of Leopold

Blumenfeld and, as paging through the beginning revealed, the Leaders of the Pest Israelite Women's Association's high regard for the Scripture enriched the literature of Hungarian Scripture with this book.

Leopold Blumenfeld, who will have a role in our story not only with this translation but also with the foggy memories that have survived him, and who, though he was long since dead in those days, will remain with us until the end; he was born on 6 July 1869, four days shy of one hundred years before P. In Berlin, Leopold Blumenfeld was a student of the famous Rabbi Sigmund Jampel, with whose letter of recommendation he read the Book of Esther for the first time on his return home to Turócszentmárton on Purim in 1896. Two years later, he was invited to stay by the same congregation which, thirty years later, when they could not keep a rabbi any longer, made P.'s great-grandfather one of its leaders. Leopold Blumenfeld remained a bachelor all his life. His only passion, which not one of the surviving anecdotes about him fails to mention, was his usual afternoon walk. In warm summer weather or winter frost, he was often seen with his friend, the village doctor, who perhaps was one of P.'s ancestors, walking on narrow earthen streets lined with sumac trees in the vicinity of the synagogue. As for what they spoke about, that no one knows. In truth, the doctor only went to temple with his daughter and his rather homely wife on the New Year and the 'day of the fast', otherwise he kept himself at a distance from his friend's practice. Leopold Blumenfeld, who was famous for the fact that, in place of lengthy sermons for the new year, making due instead with a short story here and there and by way of explication adding merely, 'My dear brothers and sisters, and this was word for word the truth,' the Leopold Blumenfeld, who that year, when he stood for the first time before his congregation, leaning against the wooden balusters of the bema and glancing around with a look full of significance, said to his followers in a temple orator's raised, sonorous voice, 'Once, the emperor asked for Rabbi Gamliel and said to him, "I know what your God is doing, and I also know where he is." With this Rabbi Gamliel gave a deep sigh. The emperor asked, "Why do you sigh?" And the rabbi answered, "One of my sons went out to sea. I miss him and would like it if you could tell me where he might be." To this the emperor said, "How should I know, Rabbi?" The rabbi then smiled and said, "You don't know what is happening on this earth, how then could you know what is in the heavens?"' And Leopold Blumenfeld's congregation waited in vain for an explication of the story. After a short silence held for effect, quietly, practically in a whisper, all he said was, 'My dear brothers and sisters, and this was word for word the truth,' and turned around, stepped down from the raised platform of the bema and sat back down in his throne-like place beside the covenant.

The green measuring tape hung down from the old woman's neck onto the table. She always fastened the bound bouclé and the woolen sections with the pins stuck in her wrap so that she got the back of the sweater, its sleeve or its front, by drawing around the well-worn outline with sharp pieces of soap, and by cutting off the unneeded parts along the lines so the sections would stay together. The difficult part—finishing the necklines and making the buttonholes—only began after this. Now, however, there wasn't a word about it. Her thick, short pointer finger waited under the first letter, unwilling to bargain, while P. looked searchingly at his grandmother to see whether it was really from this book that he needed to read. But his grandmother was unwilling to notice the hesitation. She had been given the task of teaching the child to read that summer. So P. dropped his head towards the old woman's hands; for a moment he was amazed by the softness of her wrinkles, and then, on that page, where the writing was in Hungarian, he tried to read out the first words. But right away he ran into the sort of words which, even on a third attempt, he did not succeed in deciphering. At this the old woman, like a piano teacher who taps out the beat with a conductor's baton on her pupil's head, began to read the first paragraph in his stead, coming down on every other syllable: 'And-it happ-ened in-the days-of A-ha suer-us . . .'

And it happened in the days of Ahasuerus—the Ahasuerus who reigned over a hundred and twenty-seven provinces from India to Ethiopia. In those days, when King Ahasuerus occupied the royal throne in the fortress Shushan, in the third year of his reign, he gave a banquet for all officials and courtiers, the administration of Persia and Media, the nobles and governors of the provinces in his service, to display the vast riches of his kingdom and the splendid glory of his majesty. The royal festivities lasted half a year: hundreds of cows and bulls were slaughtered, fat sizzled and crackled, round bread baked all day on the hot stone slabs and sweet royal wine was consumed by the barrel. The king hosted every man and his son in Shushan, regardless of age. Barefoot or in sandals, in white linen robes, as was customary for celebrations, young and old flocked to the gardens of the king's palace; they were all fed well and many became drunk. The king was also in good spirits from the wine. And on the morning of the seventh day, he ordered his servants to bring out Queen Vashti in her royal crown to display her beauty to the peoples and officials.

Reading time came in the afternoon, when the day's sweaters were ready and the last customer, whose waist, hips and arms needed measuring with the green tape, had gone. In the mornings, when the day had just begun, before a large mirror standing in the corner, the old woman combed the few long, silver strands of hair that remained on her head after the devastation of an illness twenty years before. Later, still in a nightgown, she adjusted the inside of her wig so it would not chafe, and closing her eyes, pressing her lips together, she placed it on her head, her eyes remaining narrowed, so that she could put it in place, from either above the ears or in front of them, and tucked the remaining strands of her own hair into the thick brown wig. P.'s grandfather meanwhile brought in coffee and hot pastries, put them on the table covered with the floral-patterned oilcloth and said, Fresh from the baker's, which meant he had just taken them out from the oven—when you bit into one, the warm cakes melted right there on your tongue.

The servants returned to the gardens of the royal palace with their tasks unaccomplished. The king was greatly incensed, and anger burnt within him. He asked the sages and the astrologers close to him, Carshena, Shethar, Admatha, Tarshish, Meres, Marsena and Memucan, the seven ministers of Persia and Media, what should be done to Queen Vashti according to law for failing to obey the command of the king. And Memucan declared in the presence of the king and the ministers: Queen Vashti has committed an offence not only against Your Majesty but also against all the officials and against all the peoples in all the provinces of King Ahasuerus.

The small porcelain plate in which his grandfather brought in the pastries each morning was covered in grey, thread-thin scratches. The centre of the originally white plate had turned completely grey, though the flowers on its rim remained a bright pink, their leaves a poison green. P. spent a large part of the day with his grandfather. Together they went to the store for yarn and thread; they used a large suitcase for carrying home the thread, which had already been treated somewhat with paraffin, but before the sewing could begin, especially if the thread had sat for a while in the closet, one needed to run it through again on a piece of paraffin with the help of the little spindle machine they had at home.

The day's spinning was like the repetition of stories. 'Listen, my son, do not betray the wisdom of your father or the teachings of your mother.' We do not know whether Leopold Blumenfeld still believed in the unity of the mothers and their sons, for at that hour, when the Torah had been given to Israel, the mothers and their sons were still together. We who live among the boards of Rabbi Nachman's charred house do not know whether Leopold Blumenfeld had already recognized the silence that encircles us. He surely must have suspected something. For the stories and objects did not all go quiet at once but, rather, in their subtle turn, one after the other, and who knows when the fire went out, the one which began to burn out the words within them. And since then what we hear as silence is really just a frenzy of voices. The speech of the dead is a flickering flame, and it all began with that fire. Leopold Blumenfeld could hardly have heard this speech as we do. Otherwise, perhaps he wouldn't have told the following story to his congregation in one of his new year's predictions: 'Once a Persian paid a visit to Rabbi Hillel and asked of him, "Teach me the Torah." So the rabbi showed him an aleph and said, "Say that, aleph." But the Persian asked, "Who can guarantee that this is really an aleph? Maybe someone would say that this isn't an aleph." The rabbi then showed him a bet but the Persian answered as before. The rabbi shouted at him and angrily dismissed him. The Persian, however, did not let the matter drop and went to see Rabbi Samuel and asked of him, "Teach me the Torah." So the rabbi showed him an aleph and said, "Repeat after me, aleph." But the Persian asked, "How can I be sure that it's really an aleph?" At that moment the rabbi grabbed hold of the Persian's ear. And in pain, the Persian shouted, "Ow, my ear! Ow, my ear!" And Samuel asked, "How can I be sure that this is really your ear?" The Persian, still in pain, answered, "Everyone can see that this is my ear." The rabbi then let go of the Persian's ear and said, "Just as everyone knows what's an aleph and what's a bet!" The Persian's mind was put at ease and the rabbi taught him the Torah.'

So that P. would learn not only to read but also to write, since one amounted to little without the other, the old woman found it best to dictate the hard-to-read passages for P. to write out in a blue, spiral-bound notebook, carefully articulating each syllable, just as a teacher takes dictation at school. At first all this accompanied a smaller sort of suffering, the most painful part of which, out of sheer exhaustion, P. hardly even felt, as the old woman underlined every mistake twice with a red pen and made him write down the correct sentences on the other side. His head was buzzing but he believed that this was really the only way to learn to read well.

P.'s mother remembered nothing of her bat mitzvah. Probably several of them all at once were led in white dresses before the covenant; with a great theatrical movement, the rabbi extended his arm above the girls and blessed them, then they said a prayer, which in all likelihood they had practised for days. Only weeks later did the old woman reveal to her daughter in passing which book she had begun to teach P. from.

Until that point, if her daughter asked whether they were reading, she said, Calm down, as though the questioning were already a bother; by the end of the summer, her son wouldn't just be reading the book, he'd be singing it. For the moment, however, P. read in stops and starts. Though the old woman became more patient from day to day, allowing P. to stumble on the longer words for a third time and keeping her piano-teacher hand still, P. nevertheless felt it there on his head and saw in the letters the tapping of the old, thick pointer finger.

While the nobles, sages, astrologers and advisers to the king were drafting the edict against Vashti, the queen, locked up in the women's palace, entertained her servant girls; they danced and played their instruments. When King Ahasuerus' anger subsided, he thought of Vashti. He was reminded of the pleasantness of her touch, the pleasantness of her voice. But the king's servants said, 'Let beautiful virgins be sought out for Your Majesty. Let Your Majesty appoint officers in every province of your realm to assemble all the beautiful young girls at the fortress Shushan, in the harem under the supervision of Hege, the king's eunuch, guardian of the women. Let them be provided with their cosmetics. And let the maiden who pleases Your Majesty be queen instead of Vashti.' The proposal pleased the king and he acted upon it.

At the beginning of the book, there was an odd dedication: 'To Mordechai, who raised an orphan girl.' The dedication could only have been written by Leopold Blumenfeld, who summed up the book's contents further down: 'It is the nature of truth to triumph; it is the nature of evil to be defeated. Everything that stands in the way of a basic moral order falls away, even with miracles and divine intervention. This is why the book does not mention the name of God even once.'

His fate, to say nothing else, spared Leopold Blumenfeld from having to doubt the triumph of good and the defeat of evil. In July 1914, when Leopold Blumenfeld had a heart attack during a Friday-night service and died in the small room used for common celebrations, where his body was laid, that fatal shot had already been fired in Sarajevo; but the emissary of the emperor and of the royal authority in Belgrade had not yet delivered the ultimatum to the representative of the Serbian government in which Vienna later declared that, while it had tried to be forbearing with respect to the nationalist agitation ruling in Serbia, on the basis of the open glorification of the perpetrators of recent outrages, it felt compelled to submit itself to the demands of events, still calmly and soberly weighing the circumstances and not giving up the virtue of forbearance. And so up until his tragically sudden death,

Leopold Blumenfeld believed firmly in the sturdiness of a basic moral order, but the fact that he suspected the coming of terrible times could not have been proven better than when in his last prediction for the new year, in the autumn of 1913, he tested the good humour of his congregation: 'It once happened that a Jewish girl ended up in the captivity of the Greeks. A Greek man took her and in his house she was raised. One night, however, an angel appeared before the man in a dream and advised him to turn his servant girl loose. But the man's wife said, "Don't let her go." So the angel came again and threatened the man: "If you don't send her away, you won't see a third morning." The man's heart was torn but he could do nothing else and sent her away. He wanted to see, however, what might ensue and followed the girl in secret. When the girl had already been on the road for a long time, she grew thirsty and stopped at a well to drink. As she gripped the edge of the well, a snake materialized before her and landed a fatal bite. The girl's body floated there in the water. The Greek went down after her and buried her. When he arrived home, he said to his wife, "You see, the father in heaven is angry with his people."' And before Leopold Blumenfeld had stepped down from the raised platform of the bema with his usual slow, slightly clumsy steps and gone back to his throne-like chair, in a sad, quiet voice he said, 'And again, my dear brothers and sisters, it will word for word be like this.'

By this time P.'s grandmother was also sitting there in the temple, but since she was only two years old, and taking into consideration the evening hour of the service—she was probably dozing beside her mother—Leopold Blumenfeld's words hardly could have returned to her thirty-one years later when those same people were herded up and driven from the Bácsalmási ghetto to the train station in groups of forty. Standing before the platform, P.'s great-grandfather asked permission from one of the officers whether he could look for his daughter and granddaughter. In the meantime, they had begun to fill the cattle cars. There was room for sixty in each. As soon as one was filled, they opened the next. When it was P.'s grandmother's turn in line, she had already stepped onto the ladder of the wagon into which the first part of the group had disappeared, but her father grabbed her by the arm and snatched her away. Without comprehending, she turned back and said, This is the one, get on here. But her father had already stepped in front of the next car since he had reservations about the cantor of Szabadka, who was the wagon leader of the car she had chosen. And the train was later split at precisely this point. The first car was directed to Auschwitz; the one which they had boarded went on to Austria. Of course no one could have known this at the time. And as a result, P.'s great-grandfather was very angry at himself simply because the cantor of Szabadka, who bothered everyone with his unbearable talent for being in the know, had switched places with their wagon leader at the last minute before departure.

As for why Leopold Blumenfeld dedicated his translation to one of the main characters of the book or why for that matter he wanted to call such unusual attention to Mordechai, P. did not concern himself with this for the time being. There was already something at the beginning of the story that bothered him. The drunken king's order was really an ultimatum, which would cause him, no doubt, to lose Vashti. If she were to satisfy him and step into the garden of the king's palace, which was prohibited for a woman, that single covetous glimpse would have inflicted a deadly wound. And by refusing him, she brought doubt upon Ahasuerus' unshakeable order.

For generations, the old woman's family lived on the production of vinegar in Leopold Blumenfeld's former town. In the basement of the house, the vinegar was made in two-metre-high wooden tubs. The tubs were filled halfway with cobs of corn, birch shavings could also have been used, and later the cobs were pickled with vinegar. The tubs stayed like this for two or three weeks. The fermenting vinegar was a yellowish colour at first, then by degrees turned white. Meanwhile, every month or so, a delivery of pure alcohol arrived from Pest that the excise officer had denatured, that is, made undrinkable. From this alcohol, with a two-handled trough, fifteen litres needed to be poured every day into each barrel. Every two hours, they let out the same amount of vinegar from a tap underneath; later, they poured it back in from a bowl. Then in the evenings, twenty to twenty-five litres of clear vinegar could be let out from the barrel with which they pickled the peasant's and store owners' peppers. But since the time for pickling peppers ran from July till October, they could only seriously count on sales then, even though the alcohol needed to be paid for year round. Every year they opened a large notebook in which they wrote, months in advance, who had ordered vinegar for when and how much, and when it came, they got exactly that.

P. did not know all this, nevertheless the taste of vinegar had seeped into his childhood. On Saturday mornings, his grandfather ceremoniously marched into the bathroom, bathed and whitened his hair with vinegar. Coming out, he wrapped his undershirt around his head and tied it so that it wouldn't slip. Meanwhile, under his bathrobe, the belt of which always wanted to come undone, you could see his old, hairless chest, his stomach swelling out like a drum. Half an hour later, he took off his undershirt, dressed, his face fresh, his hair a greyish white.

This was the way P. imagined the Benjamita Jew who lived in the city of Shushan and whose name was Mordechai son of Jair son of Shimei son of Kish. He had been exiled from Jerusalem in the group that was cast from the city with King Jeconiah of Judah, which had been driven into exile by King Nebuchadnezzar of Babylon. He was foster father to Hadasah—that is, to Esther—his uncle's daughter, for she did not have a father or a mother. The girl was shapely and beautiful, and when her father and mother died, Mordechai adopted her as his own daughter. Each time P. came across Mordechai's name, he thought of his grandfather, perhaps because the yellowing pages had a similarly sour smell as his hair had on Saturdays. He did not suspect that with this very thought, he was giving credence to Leopold Blumenfeld's dedication.

Already several months after the war, P.'s grandmother felt with great certainty that her husband was not going to return. There were some who had seen him on the Russian front, while to her knowledge he had been taken to Birkenau. As she later said, she was all alone with a bad nasty child and needed to start everything over from the beginning. Suitors came to the house, a lawyer from Mélykút, a trader from Baja, but the old woman did not find any of them reliable enough to be a father to her daughter and refused them all 'flat out'. Then in the first days of March '47, as soon as the cold grew mild, P.'s great-grandfather took to the bed. His temperature shot up. The old woman led the vinegar production alone, negotiated alone with the traders and the peasants, and soon it turned out that her father, whom she for ever called *apus*, had leukaemia. When the sickness was sufficiently advanced and caused him unbearable pain, the old woman went into her father's room. They spoke of what she needed to do. Her father had a friend, a young man from the congregation, a fruit trader, whom he played cards with regularly, and he asked P.'s grandmother what she would say if this young man were to propose. The old woman was amazed; until then there had never been a word about it. A short time later, the young man proposed, or, rather, didn't quite propose, but it was clear that he had come for that reason and the old woman did not refuse him; he became P.'s grandfather.

The morning always passed quickly. After lunch, you could sit at the spinning machine undisturbed and watch as the thread ran through your fingers, grew thick, and the spindle filled with thread, the material slowly running out from the brown paper bag. The spinning machine that they had at home was a new purchase. For the most part, it was not so different from an electric motor that could be made to work with a pedal. The motor turned an arm, which wound the paper or plastic spindle. If the material did not need to be run through with paraffin, P. turned on the motor mounted on the edge of the dresser for a moment here and there; it was nice to watch it as it turned, even when it was empty, and listen to its sound. The sewing machine itself was a modern marvel. It was simple and easy, though one might not call it beautiful, not like the old table-mount Singer sewing machine which stood beside the mirror. The almost arabesquely intricate, wrought-iron pedal drove an inch-thick leather V-belt, which turned a wheel laterally, and as the pedal spun and shook faster, the needle clacked wildly above, punching holes in the air.

In the inner room, facing the large front door, a picture hung in a plain, gold-coloured frame. A dark-brown- or black-haired girl with braids looked down seriously from the picture, not smiling, in a frilly-necked, pressed dress, her braids bound with silk ties. P. knew that this was his mother, not much older than he, but the picture only began to mean something to him much later, in adulthood, once it had long since been lost in moves and renovations. The old woman, soon after P.'s grandfather was kicked out of the party, and the council had taken away their vinegar operation and their house since it was too big, and told them to pack their things and leave town by the end of the week, one of the first things the old woman did, once they had moved to Pest with the help of friends, was dress her daughter up nicely and take her to the very same photographer on the Ring Road to whom she took her grandson thirty years later. The picture was framed there in the shop and hung between two lacquered dressers on the wall of the inner room.

When the king's order and edict were proclaimed, and when many girls were assembled in the fortress Shushan under the supervision of Hege, guardian of the women, Esther was also taken to the king's palace and pleased the eunuch; he took a liking to her and quickly provided her with cosmetics and rations as well as with the seven maids due to her from the king's palace.

The camp where the family ended up was situated on the border of a small city named Mistelbach, not far from Vienna. Together with Strasshof, it was officially part of Mauthausen, but in truth there was no connection between the two facilities. Certainly no one was directed there and there was no knowledge of whether a single transport had carried its passengers from Mistelbach to certain death. The camp lay at the edge of a forest; a half-metre-wide stream, which flowed directly in front of the gate, made up one of its borders. The grounds were surrounded by a fence as well, there were guard towers; the guard regiment, however,

consisted of only twenty to twenty-five Austrian soldiers. The camp was nothing more than a great vegetable garden, at the end of which, on both sides of
the main street, called the *alle*, four identical barracks
had been erected in visible haste. Considerable space
remained between the barracks, where washing was
done on Sundays. Of the four barracks, three were designated for families, which here, in contrast to those at
concentration camps—the news of which had reached
them as well—could remain together. The fourth barracks housed single men whose relatives had ended up
elsewhere, for the most part at Mauthausen or Birkenau.
A group of the camp's eighty or so adults gathered in
the evenings in the men's barracks to pray. In each of
the barracks, to the right, as you stepped inside, stood
an iron stove. On the opposite side, families slept on
raised wooden bunks. P.'s mother and grandmother lay
directly next to the stove, above them the relatives
from Baja. The adults worked in the neighbouring
fields and gardens during the day, the young children
were entrusted to the older ones, and with one or two
of the elderly they stayed back at the camp.

In the afternoon, Leopold Blumenfeld liked to
walk in the Catholic cemetery. The path took him
between doleful angels, crosses, broken columns and
family crypts. The grass in all directions was carefully
weeded. Usually arriving several minutes before him

was a woman in a black headscarf, who, hunched over for at least an hour each day, snipped scissors beside her husband's grave. They never greeted each other. It was acknowledged with silence that they had come for the relief of their own private burdens.

There, at the beginning of the book, was P.'s mother's old name. According to this, she still went by her father's name in '53, a name which later was never allowed to be uttered. P.'s grandfather for ever remained jealous of him, because he had preceded him, because he was only second, because none of it would have been as it was had her first husband not been killed in a labour or concentration camp. For years after their marriage, he still tortured P.'s grandmother: if one day her first husband turned up, and he really could picture this crazy scene, what would she do—send him away?

The window of the Budapest apartment to which the family moved in '51 opened onto a church. P. liked the bell's resonant ring, and when he was headed home with his grandfather, as they passed behind the church, it was nice to see the house's tall, brown gate. On the corner stood a short tree. His grandfather's hands completely covered his own, and when they had gone further than the tree, he was the one to press down on the copper latch. The afternoon's reading and dictation, however, caused P. greater pain from day to day. That summer, like every summer, heat poured over the city. Until late at night, houses and bodies emanated the heat, everyone was sticky with sweat, the humidity weighing down directly on people's nerves; the air stood still. All day in the big room, the cloth window shades were let down and the thick, yellowing pages absorbed the wetness of one's hands. The passage between the Hebrew pages and black-and-white impressions made from the copperplate engravings was tiring and hopeless.

Mordechai meanwhile had told Esther not to reveal her people or her kindred. He bore the name of the patient god Marduk, the patron of Babylon, who tamed the old, wild gods, created man and gave life to Nabu, the god of writing. Mordechai was a Babylonian. He could not have been among those tens of thousands whom Nebuchadnezzar exiled from Jerusalem with King Judah, for by then three generations had already passed. He was childless and a widower, and the two greeted him in a single moment: his wife was unable to give birth to their child and nothing could be done to save her. As the years passed, Mordechai became increasingly rich. And when his uncle died, he took his daughter Esther into his care, who also got her name from Babylon. Ishtar, woman of the gods, queen of the kings, saw the depths, descended, and there was no more love on earth.

The bells always rang out very suddenly. Two bells could be heard at once, the shades snapped up, the sound of the bells streamed into the room, storming past the armchairs, the round table and the large green pullout bed, bumping into everything, noisily tumbling into the hall, barely fitting through the doorposts; and out there it turned the colours of the linoleum from green to grey, green to grey, the hallway ringing out, like the path of a labyrinth; and as it arrived at the turn, you could hear the bronze cracking, as it then made it quietly to the door; the broken pieces needed to be avoided until evening.

Leopold Blumenfeld might not have been right after all. Not when it came to morality or the nature of truth—we cannot have any proof of that—but, rather, as to why the name of God does not figure into the book. Of course for the same reason that Mordechai advised Esther not to speak of her origins. For if someone were to come forward as a Jew, it would be uncomfortable for everyone. It is better to keep quiet. Why should a person say anything about himself or God?

Night passed slowly. P. lay awake between the two old bodies. The duvet was heavy and soft, much heavier than the comforter that was the norm, and, as he later thought back on this, it was mainly this great softness and the bright pink of the covers that made the extreme closeness between these two bodies hardly

bearable. His grandfather wore light-blue linen pyjamas and snored with an open mouth. The duvet had
slipped down one of his legs, and his pyjamas were
rolled up to his thigh. P. tried not to touch him and
inched over to his grandmother. Her bald, excoriated
head made an impression in the pillow, and the few
grey strands of hair, which had not fallen out, clinging
to her scalp, travelled down to the bottom of the
impress. As was his custom, P.'s grandfather awoke at
dawn. Leaning on his elbow, he sat up with great difficulty; with his feet he searched around the bed for a
time, then, having found what he was looking for, he
shuffled out in green, rubber slippers to pee. He came
back and, from a plastic cup half-filled with water that
he kept on a dark-brown nightstand beside the bed,
took out his false teeth and did not go back to bed. P.
adjusted his position and slept in peace until morning.

Every single day, Mordechai would walk about in
front of the court of the harem to learn what was happening with Esther. But as each girl's turn came to go
to King Ahasuerus, twelve months passed according
to the law of the women. For six months they were
treated with oil of myrrh and for six months with per-
fumes and women's cosmetics. And it was after this
that one of the girls would go to the king. She would
go in the evening and leave in the morning for a second
harem in the charge of Shaashgaz, the king's eunuch,

guardian of the concubines. The girl could not visit him again, unless the king was fond of her and summoned her by name.

On Friday afternoons, the old woman laid out three candles on an aluminium tray. Two in a single candleholder, one on its own. She couldn't stand being even one minute late. As soon as the time came, she knew when, she lit the candles, and if the flame began to flicker in the wick of the third she quickly, unintelligibly mumbled over them what was required and, with her two palms, brought the light to her face. Then she relaxed, she did not concern herself with the candles any more, at least not until the following evening when she scraped out the hardened wax from inside the candleholders and rinsed out the tray in the sink.

And as P.'s mother saw her son with the old man and woman her memories began to return. She thought about what happened increasingly in vain; she could not expect the old woman to understand anything. What it was like, for example, when she got fed up with her daughter's constant bloody noses at the camp, and that she always wanted to be by her mother's side. Of course it was also difficult for the old woman not to have any idea who from her family was still alive and who was not, but how then, for this very reason, could she have tied a bundle to her daughter's back and sent her as a four-year-old to find herself another mother.

And where was she supposed to find one—in the camp or among the Austrian peasants?

In that heat it was best to stay put. P. was bored for hours on end. The lowered yellow shade, at the edge of the window, allowed in a strong ray of light that broke brightly through the glass showcase. The few objects, a white porcelain statue of a nude woman made in the style of the Greek nymphs, the candleholders, the silver trays and the other mementos brought back from travel destinations nearly burst from the light contained within the glass. P. lay on the bed, looking at the flowers on the wallpaper, tracing their outlines with his pointer finger; he would have liked to but could not fall asleep.

When it was Esther's turn—daughter of Abihail, uncle of Mordechai, who had adopted her as his own daughter—to go to the king, she asked only for what Hege, the king's eunuch, guardian of the women, advised. And Esther won the admiration of all who saw her.

The inmates of the camp rarely left its gates. When they did, they crossed the stream at a footbridge at the corner of the fenced-in area and, proceeding along the highway to Vienna, the guards led them to the nearby seeding garden by twos in an orderly line. The trip hardly required more than a quarter hour. They were met at the entrance to the garden by the project leader.

The thirty or thirty-five able-bodied inmates worked together with four women. The women showed them neither contempt nor interest, nor were they curious to learn their names. They explained what needed to be done; if the inmates did something wrong, they instructed them how to make it right. Since a majority of the inmates understood German, they did not run into problems organizing the work. The apportioned amount did not allow much time for relaxation, but no one would have called them unfair. Caring for the gardens, preparing the flowerbeds, spreading and ploughing the dung required a lot of attention. Since the inmates had not been exposed to this sort of work before, in the first weeks accidents were known to happen. On one occasion, for example, P.'s great-grandfather and two other men, in the storage room next to the shed, tried rolling a long beam a little more in one direction when a rusty nail tore into his palm. He was running a fever by evening. He had sepsis.

Once a week a few old friends came over to visit his grandparents. After the war, in '51, in '52, they all moved to Budapest from the same village; there couldn't have been any of them left. They came in the afternoon, the doctor's daughter, the shopkeeper, one of the old suitors, and recounted until late in the evening the names and stories which on each occasion emerged slightly differently; new additions occurred in them, new pieces of information were authored together. On the basis of these stories, one could have put together the story of a little city that had never existed, a map on which each street was called something slightly different each day. Talk was full of the dead. And as they spoke, while evening overtook them on the brown, floral-patterned armchairs, it was visible in their faces that this was the only thing in which they took absolute pleasure: they hardly even noticed the passing of time.

Esther was taken to King Ahasuerus, in his royal palace, in the tenth month, which is the month of Tebeth, in the seventh year of his reign. The king loved Esther more than all the other women, and she won his grace and favour more than all the virgins. So he set the royal crown on her head and made her queen instead of Vashti. And the king threw a great banquet for all his officials and courtiers.

Say someone were to board a train car, the direction of which he does not know. He gets on the next car and avoids the worst of what's to come or, instead, points his life down the path of certain death. He decides for himself, he takes a step, but the result of this decision and this step is not revealed until much later. Just as it is also not revealed until much later that someone somewhere has already written a letter, making this step possible, without his knowledge. Kaltenbrunner, director of the Reich Main Security Office, granting authorization by expedited courier on 30 June 1944 to Blaschke SS-Brigadenführer, the mayor of Vienna: 'Dear Blaschke, For the special reasons you mentioned, I have ordered that several evacuated shipments be directed to Vienna/Strasshof. This will involve four shipments, with approximately 12,000 Jews, that are to arrive in Vienna in the coming days. Past experience suggests that these shipments, according to our estimates, will contain approximately thirty per cent (in the current case, around 3,600) able-bodied Jews, who can be drawn upon for the work in question, with the condition that they can be returned at any time. Providing a well-guarded, closed work space and secured camp-like relocation is the obvious and absolute precondition for the release of the Jews. The wives of those Jews unfit for that kind of work, and their children, who are to be kept together in preparation for the purposes of a special mission and who are, therefore, to be removed on a certain day, must also be kept during the daytime in the camp overseen by the guards. I hope these deliveries offer some assistance to you in realizing your plans, which are of the utmost importance. I remain, Heil Hitler, your Kaltenbrunner.'

He proclaimed a remission of taxes for the provinces and distributed gifts as befits a king. The next day, however, the virgins were gathered and again taken away by Hege, under the supervision of the guardian of women.

On the way home, P., holding his grandfather's hand, always loudly counted his steps. The store was 416, the newspaper shop was more than 700, and on top of this were the 42 stairs. High up on the gate of the house was an opaque pane of glass, the wrought-iron bars in front of which shaped like flower stems. Where the bud diverged, the four-cornered iron thickened from the soldering. Walnut-sized patches of fungus lined the bottom of the pane in the broad frame. The door opened inward, turning with great difficulty on its hinges. Behind it the air was always cooler.

Time, as far as we are concerned, has gone quiet. Perhaps at some point the speech of the dead, the light, which is called the light of origin, could have addressed the world, just as it could have addressed the future. But seeing as this speech to us is silent and the objects that circle us are silent, Leopold Blumenfeld could not have seen anything either, not from the future or the past. For the light, in which Adam saw the world from one end to the other, which also shone for David while he sang, and in which Moses saw everything from Gilead to Dan, drew back into darkness, the depth of which only the eye adjusted to the dark can gauge. For this reason, Leopold Blumenfeld spoke before his congregation with his eyes closed, as though he were witnessing an apparition, considering every word of the meeting between Rabbi Yose and the blind man:

'Over the course of his life, Rabbi Yose thought of the meaning of the words contained in the scripture: "You shall grope at noonday, as a blind man gropes in darkness." Well, did it really make much of a difference to a blind man, asked Rabbi Yose, whether it was light or dark? One day, however, on the way home, he came across a blind man carrying a flaming torch in his hand. He asked, "My son! Of what purpose to you is this torch?" And the blind man replied, "When I hold the torch people can see me and warn me if there is a ditch or a bush of thorns in my path." Rabbi Yose smiled and said, "My son, today it is you who have taught me."'

On the side of the house facing the street, on the corner where the road curved in the direction of the synagogue and the brick church built in 1834, P.'s great-grandfather owned a watchmaker's shop, which stood in the shade of a sumac tree even more tangled than the others. In the store, down the three steps past the glass door with the little bell, the same unpleasant, sour smell greeted customers in winter and summer. cuckoo clocks and wall clocks stood on the shelves. The most beautiful was the delicate, gilded work of a jeweler. Its pendulum waited behind four bone-coloured alabaster columns to start measuring the time. Just the same, P.'s great-grandfather only wound the clocks if the customer seemed serious, and he could tell right away, as the person stepped into the shop, the bell ringing above the door, whether the customer was serious or not. With the magnifier over his eye, he especially liked to fiddle with the little springs and toothed gears. His favourites were the Swiss pocket watches guarded in the drawer of the counter. If an acquaintance stopped by, he was happy to chat with them. He was a friendly man but everyone still kept him at a distance.

Meanwhile, Esther, whom Ahasuerus named queen in Vashti's stead, still did not reveal her kindred or her people, as Mordechai had instructed her. It is known from other accounts that when the king began to interrogate her, Esther was by no means silent and instead answered, 'I am queen, daughter of kings.' Later she added, 'Was it not because of her pride that you saw to Vashti's ruin?' To this the king replied that he did not intend for Vashti's ruin, he was following princely advice. But this hardly could have happened. Esther would have been foolish to say this to the king.

For P.'s mother, no memory of her father remained. The old woman once took out a photograph and, pointing to the man in the white suit standing at the edge of the frame, intoned the name that meant: everything could have turned out differently. Even in '48, many people were coming home from Russian and western prison camps, so when P.'s grandmother declared her husband and her husband's parents dead

at the district count with the proper inheritance pro-
ceedings at the beginning of the year, there was still no
way of being sure that one day they might not come
back. And as this was customary at the time, several
months after she married, according to P.'s great-
grandfather's dying wishes, the news spread through
Mélykút that her first husband had returned home. For
days the family lived in unspeakable fear. They themselves did not dare to pass through Mélykút, they asked
a friend to go in search of him, to ask around to see if
there was truth to the rumour. P.'s grandmother and
great-grandfather imagined, with differing visions,
how the meeting would play out, what might happen
if he had become unrecognizable, what might happen
if he was just as he had been before and wanted to kiss
his wife, who was no longer his wife, or whether understanding the situation he would be satisfied with a
handshake, or if he would lay claim to what was his or
recognize in a gentlemanly manner that his place was
no longer here but, rather, in memory. He should have
had the good sense not to come back. And how could
they prepare P.'s mother for all this? It would be cruel
to greet her father like a stranger; if she greeted him as
he deserved, it could not be undone. However, it soon
came to light that there was nothing for them to fear.
There had, in fact, been someone who returned to
Mélykút with the same name as P.'s grandfather, his

blood relation, but only the names were the same and thankfully he was not the one.

By the middle of summer, the reading was going much better for P. The piano-teacher fingers sometimes rested for long minutes on the tablecloth's patterned flowers, and if a need for them did arise, it would have been enough to raise them a little, but if they had already moved, they did not miss the opportunity to go from letter to letter across the offending word. The writing, however, proceeded with the same tiring anguish. On the pages of the blue spiral notebook, under the lurching lines, the number of red underlines had hardly decreased, the struggle against omitting and interchanging letters seemed hopeless. It also turned out, meanwhile, that P.'s grandmother did not remember the story well herself. It was news to her that after Esther had ended up in the harem, she could not meet with Mordechai and that her own origins were not known.

Behind the fortress Shushan, the sun was setting. A reddish light veiled the plateau that rises suddenly on the banks of the river, a hot, parching brilliance that tired the eyes of the person coming from a distance. These few minutes turned the city into a reflection of the sun, an empty, expressionless face glowing wildly, and burnt the columns facing the sky, quivering above the water, as if a memory of themselves. At night

Mordechai sat near the Lion's Gate, watching as the guards checked the returning envoys, solicitors, peasant carts and grain carriers. Visible beneath their helmets were Persian, Egyptian, Syrian and Lebanese features. Several steps from the guards, so as not to be heard, two members of the palace guard, Bigthan and Teresh, were speaking. Mordechai did not understand the entirety of the two guards' conversation but he did make out the king's name. Bigthan and Teresh were confidants of Haman, the leader of the inner-palace guard. Mordechai sensed something was afoot in the palace. He notified Esther of his suspicions and Esther relayed the message to Ahasuerus.

The train on which P.'s family travelled was directed from Bácsalmás to Kosice. There they separated the wagons headed for Auschwitz. For the remaining five days, they were held in the outer part of the Kosice freight yard. Once a day, someone was allowed to get off the wagon to walk to the train station accompanied by four guards and bring back water for those in the wagons. Since the head of the transport was not prepared for such a long delay, no food was given to the prisoners. Fortunately, though P.'s grandmother had not brought money with her, since her father had convinced her not to, saying that only trouble would come of it, he put in his pack on the morning of their departure a two-kilogram loaf of bread from which the family ate twice a day until the waylaid trains were set on their course from Kosice. No matter how well they rationed their portions, however, they still managed to go through the bread within two days remaining before the two cattle cars slowed into the farthermost track in Mistelbach.

Rabbi Sigmund Jampel, whose student in Berlin was Leopold Blumenfeld, translated the Book of Esther himself in 1907. The interesting thing about his translation was that in one place, without changing the original text, he made a choice that diverged fundamentally from the usual translations. Spurred on by his master's example, Leopold Blumenfeld went one step further and, by arranging the letters of the Hebrew text from an unquestionably hard-to-understand sentence in a way that departed from the original, namely, by inserting one letter, a surprising but correct-seeming reading was attained. When Ahasuerus has Vashti taken away, he sends a letter to every province in his kingdom, to every people in its own script, that every man should wield authority in his own home. The original adds that every man should speak 'in the language of his own people'. Leopold Blumenfeld corrects this section by arranging the letters to read that every man 'shall say what suited him'. Doesn't all this prove that writing, which is a stronger chain than that of chance, can be broken and repaired with reason? And if this is possible, why is it nevertheless the case that the weaker chain, if we try to break it and repair it with reason, still proves harder to change?

After breakfast, P. and his grandfather went out together to do the shopping. At the vegetable seller's they bought potatoes and onions, and at the corner store, milk, bread, coffee and rolls. They paid, and before they left the store, they went up to one of the two coffee grinders set up behind the checkout, and while the door opened, closed, creaking unceasingly, his grand father poured the contents of the silver-coloured bag under the spout, and shaking the machine, began to grind the coffee. In the store, a delicious coffee smell always hung about the checkout. When the last coffee bean had run through the machine, his grand-father first delicately, then a little harder, started tapping and hitting the side of the machine so that more of the coffee would come up and, finally, with the little cardboard tab originally folded over the bag, he swept up the dirty coffee grounds from the plywood under the machine. If he did a good job of it, he could scrape together more than the ten decagrams.

And in the seventh year of King Ahasuerus' reign, the armies of Persia and Media suffered a terrible defeat at Salamis. In all likelihood, the king never had a wife named Vashti or Esther, who sat on the throne. As for the many books to be written, however, as the sage says, there is no end.

At dawn, the stripe of light that appeared under the door of the main room was a signal, the first sign of departure. When the old woman opened the door and P.'s mother could finally get out of bed, the rugs, the covered-up armchairs and the hibiscus standing by the window appeared quite different in the semi-dark than they did in the day. They all spoke quietly and moved without making a sound, hurriedly packing up the last of their things, as though they no longer had a place in their own apartment.

The day's required reading and the writing that followed dictation always soured the afternoons. The whole thing didn't take long, though. But since P. had sensed from the beginning that the now ritually repeated scenes—his grandmother taking out the book and, opening it, placing it on the floral-patterned table-cloth—had a purpose other than practice, he was incapable of getting lost in the story, even if it interested him more. From his grandmother's strictness, he understood that what he read and what he then wrote down with great difficulty pertained to her in some way, while at the same time he also had the foggy suspicion that it did not exactly contain the meaning his grandmother had in mind when picking this book to bring out from the back room.

And after Ahasuerus investigated the matter and found it to be true that Teresh and Bigthan had been planning to incite rebellion in the palace, the two were impaled on stakes, and this was written into the BOOK OF RECORDS at the insistence of the king.

P.'s great-grandfather lay sick in the camp. The old woman sat up with him for a week as his progress under the effects of the medicine provided by the Mistelbach hospital did not improve. One day, once he had already begun to recover, he dreamt something from which he could not free himself for the rest of his days. He was going through the village cemetery, where he would later be buried, but there were no names on the gravestones. In the middle of the grey stones covered in holes was a Cohenite hand, according to custom, engraved with a rose or a palm tree, and the two letters which mean 'Here lies buried'. But not a single stone revealed who it was. P.'s great-grandfather stopped before one of the gravestones. He wanted to pray but could not remember the words of the Kaddish. He stood there for a while, then bent down, looked around for stones before his feet and placed three instead of one on the edge of the grave.

What could the Book of Records have been? Was it a real book? And if it were, was it simple or showy? How was it decided what needed and what might be written in it? And who was able to take it in his hands? What kind of trials did the person to whom the king entrusted the Memory of Babylon need to endure, and was it possible to leave the palace and give up the king's quiet gardens after that? Was it enough that someone began to write and read the book, and believe that there was time, believe there was memory?

On one occasion, in the seeding garden, several men were ordered over to the end of the property: they needed to fill in a great ditch. The pit began to rise with brown, wet earth. It grew higher. Already it was almost halfway filled. The pile of damp soil grew and grew. They put down their shovels. There were some who took off their hats, sometimes they hit the heads of their shovels against the grass to clean them. P.'s great-grandfather bent down to scrape off the earth that clung to the head of the shovel. Then they resumed filling in the ditch. A short young man from Mélykút, who lived in the single men's barracks, noted, 'We are like gravediggers.'

Some time afterwards, King Ahasuerus promoted Haman son of Hammedatha the Agagite; he advanced him and seated him higher than any of his fellow officials, so he could have his fill of power. All the king's courtiers in the palace gate knelt and bowed low to Haman, for such was the king's order; but Mordechai would not kneel or bow low.

When the old friends met, again and again they told each other how someone had been freed, how someone had unwittingly avoided the worst. The stories were always the same, and from the sentences, even from the words, it was possible to know where they were, where they had left something out, where someone had cut in, where the other had continued, and during all this the war was not called a war but a storm. Full of good cheer, they crossed over into the rich, unspeakable lives of the dead.

Climbing the short ladder left in the pantry, P. once found on the top shelf a jar of crystalized honey. The colour was that of stone-hard caramel, and through the glass you could see the yellow grains of sugar coming apart with a few bubbles of air. The vignette on the top shelf had become completely dirty and damp. Above the red outline, however, it was still possible to read what was written in similarly red letters: MIXED HONEY. With great difficulty he succeeded in unscrewing the aluminium top of the Mason jar spotted with dust. He raised the jar to his nose. He smelt it but did not note any particular fragrance. With his left pointer finger, he carefully tested, then scraped a bit at the surface of the thick honey. On the top, it was completely hard; below, slightly softer. He got a small amount from the soft section on his finger and brought it to his tongue. It was smooth and much sweeter than anything he had ever tasted. He felt each grain of sugar as they dissolved in his mouth. P. quickly climbed down from the ladder so that if his grandmother suddenly came in, he wouldn't need to explain, and he hid the jar in the back corner of the lowest shelf. Before he had gone through the whole thing, he often made trips to the pantry to eat the sugary honey. It felt as though he were stealing something, the only thing in an apartment where even the furniture emitted an unpleasant, sour smell that had been getting sweeter over time in secret.

And the courtiers began to ask Mordechai why he had disobeyed the king's orders. When they spoke to him day after day and he would not listen to them, they told Haman, in order to see whether Mordechai's resolve would prevail, for he had explained to them that he was a Jew.

Leopold Blumenfeld—whose sentences P. scrawled so bitterly into the blue spiral notebook after reading them and hearing them dictated in the rhythm of his grandmother's old, raspy voice—on one occasion spoke before his congregation about an enormous cliff somewhere in Bukovina; an underground path came to the surface, which would lead anyone who dared to the Holy Land. Though it was clearly visible where the path went from the cliff, Christians were not allowed to travel the path, not for anything in the world. God himself guarded the path for Israel in both directions, depending on which was necessary, and he reserved it for times of need, for even the roe deer have their shelter. Leaning against the wooden balusters of the bema, Leopold Blumenfeld said all of this in a temple orator's raised, sonorous voice, like a story, like a legend, the truth of which he himself did not believe but whose meaning he held in high regard. To all this he added, 'This, my dear brothers and sisters, was word for word the truth, for God tests man and deer alike, each in his own way—a broken pot still leaks, even if one does not give it a try.'

The letters rested uncertainly on the lines of the blue spiral notebook. Sometimes they leant too far to the right, sometimes too far to the left, as though after a long period of wandering, they were still wearily staggering towards a faraway destination. That summer, P.'s grandparents received a postcard from an old relative. The picture was of a bleak yellow land-scape, the barren, infertile mountains cut through with chasms and the grey angry water covered in fog between the mountains. This was the blind navel of the earth. Dead soil, dead water, on the banks of which no grass grew and in which certainly no fish lived. This land carried the world's oldest people on its back. As though they had wandered to the ends of the earth, far-ther each time, from captivity to captivity, multiplying, dying, being born, they finally came back to the place where they had started, but in the meantime the earth had grown older, and they had grown older, too. As he sat beside the table and looked at the picture placed there on the floral-patterned cover, for some reason P. saw his grandmother in it, as she crossed the road without her wig, with her few stands of grey hair, immersed the cup into the greyness, and when she tasted it, she realized that the cup was not filled with water but with stinging vinegar.

In the end it was not Esther but Mordechai who broke the oath of silence. He could not say that he was not a Jew and he could not keep silent. For even silence is like speech: you come from one side and you know what you are, you come from the other and you've suddenly lost your bearings.

On Saturday morning, P.'s parents took him home. The next afternoon, his father established himself in the bathroom; he filled the tub, settled in, placed a book and an assortment of nail clippers beside him on the washing machine, turned on the radio and dozed off. The water slid up and down his chest, forming waves in time with his breaths. One hour later, P.'s mother went to him and washed her husband's hair. When she had washed out the suds for the second time, she pulled out the plug; you could hear the sucking sound of the water as it swirled down the drain, and, squatting by the now open door, P.'s father washed himself off in the shower. He raised the showerhead before him and, with eyes closed, he sprayed his mouth and face with water. Towelling off, drying his hair and shaving followed. Steam had fogged up the mirror. When he was finished, he walked naked into the room, wrinkled from his stomach to his groin. P. was always amazed how this enormous body could be supported by such thin legs.

The pictures were guarded in a metal box that could be locked with a key in one of the lower drawers of the dresser. In one, P. was perhaps four or five years old and held in his hand a large bent cane, taller than himself. He stood before a tree, looking past the swamp with a serious face, as though he had been held up from his wandering when the camera clicked. A bush could be made out several steps behind him; it was probably autumn since it had no leaves.

But perhaps it was not in vain that the book said that Mordechai was sent from Jerusalem in exile, together with Jeconiah and King Judah, even if it was impossible. For captivity and silence can also be a person's home. By the time Esther had become queen in the fortress Shushan, there were already those who spoke often of Jerusalem, the ruined city, which would one day have a nation built on its ruins. And there were those who became living swords, saying, 'The end is near, the end is near, it rises against you, here it comes. The end is coming for you, citizens of the nation, the time is coming, the day is near, disorder and no cries in the mountains.' Mordechai considered this a half-witted prophecy, a crazy rant. God was more power-fully present on the city's ruins than every word and hope, and by now invincibly so even for Marduk's impressive army: the ruined city was the mockery of the ages, and God's brilliant laughter.

But Haman disdained to lay hands on Mordechai alone; having been told who Mordechai's people were, he plotted to do away with all the Jews, Mordechai's people, throughout the kingdom of Ahasuerus.

When P. read this, the thick, stumpy fingers moved beside his arm, but the old face did not turn in his direction, they were both focused on the book. And on the next page, the drawing depicted Haman as an ugly, bearded old man, with bulging eyes and a crooked nose, the evil visible plainly on his face.

One could access the old house where P.'s mother and grandmother once lived by a fifteen-metre-long corridor that opened onto different rooms. Decorative stones covered the lower part, which could be mopped easily; its two sides were made of glass. One part of the L-shaped corridor received sunlight in the morning, the other in the afternoon, and if it were really hot, they let down the blinds. The blinds were raised and lowered depending on how much they wanted to block out the sun. A small bench stretched under the longer side of the glass wall; in the afternoon, on the way home from school, you could study or play there. At the end of the corridor, you could get to the kitchen through a glass door. And from here you could access P.'s great-grandfather's room as well. Unlike the others, his room looked out on the street.

One of the most exciting things was when P., while his grandmother was working the machine and his grandfather had disappeared into the kitchen, could rummage through the drawers under the glass credenza in the room. He found badges, used batteries, trade-union-member booklets, medals attached to red silk triangles in little plastic boxes, pens, filled notebooks and, in a discarded box of chocolates, all kinds of pieces of wire, candy wrappers and, on one occasion, he came across a top among half-empty medicine vials, a four-sided wooden top; there was neither colour nor writing on any of the four sides.

What was the root of Haman's evil? The Agagite people, of which he was one, were just as scattered across the Persian states as the Jews, and they also lived by different laws. But when hate is released, it creates a path for itself, like a storm covering the land in darkness—does it matter what its source is? To us, Haman has no face, but then again neither does Mordechai. We see only the storm as the sky becomes full of wrath, mountains of black clouds sweep over the land, it will be dark, and the first bolt of lightning will cleave the darkness with a startling crack and its message will be: 'Everything is possible!' And everything does happen. Leopold Blumenfeld dedicated the book to Mordechai but he could just as easily have dedicated it to Haman. Their faces are the storm itself, the glint in their eyes, the lightning, but can the person have a face who sees all this, writes all this, reads all this, who is living; compared to them, can that person be an invented figure?

P.'s great-grandfather was the prayer leader at the village synagogue. He had a place in the bench in front of the bema, where P.'s mother could sit beside him. Before they went out in the evening on Fridays, after the candle lighting in the glass corridor, there, where the rocking chair also stood, the old man, by then deathly ill, ceremoniously blessed his grandchild, extending his large, gnarled palm above her head, and in a raised voice, recited in Hebrew: 'The Lord bless thee and keep thee; the Lord make His face to shine upon thee and be gracious unto thee; the Lord lift up His countenance upon thee and give thee peace.'

In the first month, that is, the month of Nisan, in the twelfth year of King Ahasuerus, *pur*—which means 'the lot'—was cast before Haman concerning every day and every month, until it fell on the twelfth month, that is, the month of Adar.

The Austrian peasants occasionally gave the inmates of the camp onions, potatoes, grey bread, and in the evenings allowed them to collect twigs and sticks on the land behind the farm that they could use for fires at night. Already by January that year, the worst of the weather had arrived. At night someone always needed to sit by the stove to feed the fire, stir it, aerate it; light glowed from behind the little iron door, the others slept covered in coats or blankets. Everyone was exhausted by ceaseless rain. The wheelbarrow constantly slipped and the ditches around the barracks filled with water. Many times in the morning they found dead rats in them. The mud soon found its way into the barracks, it soaked through the blankets, the cover overhead sagged under the weight of the water, and time did not seem to want to pass.

Sometimes, a pigeon flew onto the windowsill. It took one or two steps in front of the window, stopped and cocked his head. P. tried to figure out what the two pigeon eyes could see on either side of its walnut-sized head, the red of the roof tiles, the sill and the grey of the eaves, the yellow blinds, the sun, and how did it arrange all of this in a single picture? And did the pigeon see him? Did it know that there was a person, a child, watching it?

From the age of two, P.'s mother regularly took to the bed. Her fever shot up and only with great difficulty could the help of cold wraps, a cold bath and other remedies bring it down. Everyone dealt with her in a way that is customary with a sickly child, one who remains a constant problem, who requires special care, though circumstances permitted this less and less. Perhaps for this reason, she felt much later that she had to pay off an insurmountable debt to the old woman; at the same time, she wanted to spare her, not of her own weakness but, rather, of what she saw increasingly clearly now, that so much of everything had been ruined, so much of everything had been done wrong. It was good to see her mother strong and without doubts, for who knows if things would have been better otherwise? It is true that the years left the old woman strong; many things can be justified looking back.

And Haman then said to King Ahasuerus, 'There is a certain people, scattered and dispersed among the other peoples in all the provinces of your realm, whose laws are different from those of any other people and who do not obey the king's laws, and it is not in Your Majesty's interest to tolerate them. If it please Your Majesty, let an edict be drawn for their destruction, and I will pay 10,000 talents of silver to the stewards for deposit in the royal treasury.'

Often not a single customer stepped into the watch-maker's shop for days at a time and a watch in need of fixing rarely ended up in P.'s great-grandfather's hands. Nevertheless, there was always a guest in the store. In the middle of the shop stood two worn-out armchairs upholstered a golden brown, and between them an inlaid little table. He preferred the one closer to the door. In the other chair always sat one of his old friends, who regularly spent the morning or afternoon at the shop; there was always something to talk about. But still the business wasn't all loss. Once a month, a wholesaler came out from Pest with a buckled leather briefcase with ever-impressive pieces. He always left only as much as had been sold from the inventory. Then the store was nationalized in '48. Not even the armchairs were spared. P.'s great-grandfather was no longer alive by then and hardly any of the men who had chatted away the mornings and afternoons were left. The police did not allow anything to be taken from the store. The group leader ordered his men to set and wind the cuckoo clocks, the wall clocks, the grandfather clocks and the Swiss pocket watches in the drawer. It was absurd, after all, that no clock in a watchmaker's shop should work. And this was how it happened that behind the closed door and lowered blinds, the clocks started measuring the time.

The old woman worked the whole morning at the sewing machine. First, the padlock needed to be set under the carriage that passed over the needle bed, that is, to see that the needles ended up next to one another in the grooves and determine how taut the sewn piece should be. The short- and tall-legged needles needed to be set in place with the hooks facing downward, so that, as the carriage slid over above them, they would duly rise, the thread would catch and then, from underneath, they would join the thread to the then-bound piece. While the pattern emerged on each piece, the padlock needed to be set several times or a new colour needed to be attached to the carriage on a different thread guide, making sure to attach only as much thread as necessary for the pattern. As the knitted piece grew a few centimetres underneath and the thread-thin metal-toothed comb, in which the first knots formed, separated from the needle bed, weights were hung on the lower part of the material, but this wasn't enough to ensure that the resulting work would not tear or have holes. Patiently and evenly, the carriage needed to be guided back and forth.

Consider the suffering of Haman the Agagite, who for our purposes has no face, who suffers not from his own doing—he being the perfect servant, the servant of his unrealizable ambition—but from ambition itself, since he was never able to attain the command over others that he sought. Like Mordechai, Haman, whose face for our purposes cannot be a face, was the son of a small despised people, who, as a result of his ambition, was reduced to ceaselessly proving the baselessness of this disdain while hating those similar to him with a similar vehemence; he should have despised himself as a Persian, since that was precisely what he could not become. Haman's face itself was hatred, his face itself was the storm; in truth he was amazed by death and mania, that which his ambition could not control, and when he put the throne above all of Ahasuerus' subjects, death and mania became master of the land.

When P.'s grandfather was kicked out of the party, he could not find work for six months. He searched high and low, many places would have had a need for him since he understood how to run a business, but no one dared to hire him. If the local party secretary, the one who had turned him out, signed his card, saying that the party was in support of his employment, there wouldn't have been any problem, but the secretary refused. Then, six months later, a new party secretary landed at the head of the party's local branch who did not know him, and, within ten minutes, had signed the paper. After this, until '57, P.'s grandfather professed to be a sympathizer, a Bolshevik beyond the party line.

While he sat beside the oilcloth-covered table and, bent over the book, deciphered what was written, P.'s concentration flagged for a moment here and there, beginning to slip between the lines, from the Hebrew text to the Hungarian and back, always lower and lower, stopping only before falling from the book itself, to his grandmother's hand. The ring, which had remained from the watchmaker's shop, where they also sold gold, formed a deep impression in the old woman's finger.

And the king removed his signet ring from his hand and gave it to Haman, son of Hammedatha the Agagite, and said, 'The money and the people are yours to do with as you see fit.' And on the engraving that this section illustrated, Haman was pointing at the wailing Jews off in the distance with his right hand and, with his left, at the gold cane resting in the king's lap.

When she was three years old, P.'s mother received a doll from one of her uncles. The doll had golden-blond hair. She tied a cloth hat to its head and outfitted it with a yellow, crocheted jacket. She played with it for a few weeks, then forgot about it; she preferred to sit around where they produced the vinegar or in the watchmaker's shop. Months later, when the doll materialized again, she made it walk, played with it in the corridor, took it out with her behind the cookhouse, where she first built it a home, then, fiddling for a while with a piece of wire, bore a hole in the place of each eye.

Leopold Blumenfeld's last story, after which he said the same blessing to the congregation as the one said by P.'s great-grandfather to his granddaughter in the glass corridor each Friday, was itself a mystery. It was about time, which still needed to pass before David's son would arrive. Rabbi Jose ben Kisma was asked one day by his students, 'When is the coming of the son of David?' The master answered, 'I won't say, because then you'll ask me to give a sign of the truth of my words.' The students, however, promised not to ask for a sign. Then the master said, 'If this wall gives way here and it is rebuilt, if it is destroyed and then again rebuilt, if for a third time it is lying in ruins, then when the stones are put back, the son of David will come.' Nevertheless, his students wanted a sign that his words were true. And the rabbi asked, 'Didn't you promise not to ask me for a sign?' His students acknowledged, 'Yes, we promised, but still we'd like it if you could give us a sign.' And the son of Kisma answered, 'The source of Panias' water shall turn to blood, the water from which the Jordan flows.' And the water of the source turned to blood at once. Not long after, when Jose ben Kisma was on the verge of death, he asked his students to bury his coffin good and deep, since there would not be a tree in Babylon to which anyone other than Persians would tie his horse, and there would not be a coffin in the land of Israel that would not be used as feed for the Medians' horses.

On the thirteenth day of the first month, the king's scribes were summoned and a decree was issued, as Haman directed, to the king's satraps, to the governors of every province in its own script and to every people in its own language. The orders were issued in the name of King Ahasuerus and sealed with the king's signet. And written instructions were dispatched by the couriers to all the king's provinces to destroy, massacre and exterminate all the Jews, young and old, children and women, on a single day, on the thirteenth day of the twelfth month—that is, the month of Adar—and to plunder their possessions. The text of the document —which was to be treated as law in every province— was to be publicly displayed to all the peoples, so that they might be ready for that day.

From the wall of the staircase, the oil paint was peeling, coming off in pieces. As P. ran his hands across it, his palm facing out to feel the cold, the paint chips on the outside of the bone-coloured plasterwork often got under his nails, sometimes only a little, sometimes much deeper. It was a sharp, sudden pain.

And the couriers went out posthaste to every province of King Ahasuerus' great kingdom, far past the Euphrates, so that the news would arrive without delay and be treated everywhere as law. And as Ahasuerus sat down with Haman to feast, beyond the Ishtar Gate, the decree travelled beyond the city of Shushan, after advancing along the processional road lined with gardens and palaces, which led from Marduk's sanctuary to the limits of the forbidden city. And as the news spread along Shushan's narrow streets, people began to whisper at the fountains; many agreed with Haman, many were afraid and did not dare to speak. And Mordechai knew what happened. Mordechai tore his clothes and put on a sackcloth and ashes. He went through the city, crying out loudly and bitterly, until he came in front of the Lion's Gate. There he sank down against a stone. The afternoon sun drew one side of the gate into the shade; the other shone with improbable brilliance.

In 1953, the celebration of Purim, the fourteenth day of the month of Adar, on which calm was restored to those endangered by Haman's cast of fate, the year when P.'s mother took from the rabbi's hands on her bat mitzvah Leopold Blumenfeld's translation, with which the Leaders of the Pest Israelite Women's Association's high regard for the Scripture enriched the literature of Hungarian Scripture, that year, the celebration of Purim fell on the 1st of March. Winter had made the sudden turn to spring. In the synagogues, the Book of Esther was read out in the evening and morning. And the following day in Moscow, a certain man was in the throes of death. His right leg and right hand had gone stiff, he lost consciousness and the ability to speak. Everyone was awaiting further developments.

From day to day, the newspapers reported on the state of the diagnosis of a by-then-speechless, paralysed

Stalin, with awkward, dispassionate precision. Beneath the diagnosis, the signatures of the members of a medical team featuring professors of neurology and internal medicine figured prominently: 'On 4 March, at two in the morning, the state of J. V. Stalin's health is increasingly critical. Significant difficulty breathing observable: frequency of breaths has reached 36 per minute, breathing rhythm is irregular with more protracted breaks. Pulse accelerating, as high as 120 beats per minute, full arrhythmia: maximum blood pressure 220, minimum blood pressure 120. Body temperature 38.2 degrees. Hypoxia observable in connection with breathing and circulatory issues. Impairments to cerebral functions have at present spread. At this time, the treatment measures aimed at restoring the patient's vital functions will continue.' Beside the doctor's report one could read the condolences of the Hungarian Communist Party Central Commission: 'Our father, our teacher, our people's truest friend, the great comrade Stalin is ill. The heart of the Hungarian workers beats there at his sickbed, pounding together with the heart of the mighty Soviet people. Our people, too, during these difficult days are displaying the greatest togetherness and unity, fortitude and vigilance, and are redoubling our efforts to carry out the demands of our great five-year plan, and for the construction of socialism, and are gathering even more tightly around our communist party and our government.'

On the fourteenth day of the month of Adar, the royal decree was rescinded. No hands were laid on the Jewish people; they won back their freedom in Persia, save for the capital, Shushan, where freedom would have to wait another day. And it was read in the synagogues on this day: When the king's orders had reached every province, Esther's maidens and eunuchs came and informed her of what had happened. And the queen was greatly agitated; she sent clothing for Mordechai to wear, so that he might take off his sackcloth, but Mordechai did not accept them.

News of Stalin's death appeared in the newspapers on 7 March 1953. The previous day a gardener from a collective farm made this statement in the party's daily paper: 'I've lived to see a lot in life but I have comrade Stalin to thank for my true calling. And for that I also call him "Our Father". I know that even he loves fruit trees. In a film, I saw a gesture of his, made with the tenderness and care of a good gardener tending to a blossoming tree. It also occurred to me that he teaches: we must raise people, we must prune back their faults to strengthen the noble sprouting of the spirit just as a good gardener cares for her favourite fruit trees. Crying has dried out my throat. I've never felt as I do now how much he loves us, simple people, village women. It is not possible to describe with words how we love him— but I know that Comrade Stalin must know.'

On that day, Wednesday, on which news of Stalin's death was announced, at ten or eleven o'clock in P.'s mother's school, as in every similar institution across the country, the children were led out to the school-yard. The classes stood in pure silence beside one another, facing the high brick wall that separated the schoolyard from the building of the prison next to the school. The principal and the vice principal stood in front of the wall; there was no table or stage before them, as at other assemblies or celebrations. The principal cleared his throat and, summoning strength in his voice, announced that comrade Stalin had died. He did not need to keep order; everyone stood silently at attention. Then the principal directed the return to the school by class. Through the narrow, unpainted door, up the stairs, all the way to the classroom, where every-one needed to stand by her desk, other times singing 'The enemy ambushed us and crushed us' as they marched; now, however, the girls went up quietly; only the pebbles grated under their feet; it was visible on the faces of the adults that they did not know how they themselves should behave.

And Esther summoned Hatach, one of the king's eunuchs, and sent him to find out from Mordechai what had happened and why. Hatach found him in the square in front of the king's gate. And Mordechai told him all he knew; he even told him the precise amount

63

of money that Haman had offered to pay into the royal treasury for the Jews, for their destruction.

P. read and wrote all this as though it were a terrible tale, a frightening legend, which he did not believe for a second to have happened. Not only because he was used to there always being truth in the books he read or in those read to him, even though what was written was never true in itself, but also because he vaguely sensed the implausibility of Haman's hatred. And indeed. Only the beginning and end point of Haman's hatred are certain, the affront to his ambitions and the decree for mass murder, but in light of what followed, there should have been something between the two points, a simple deed—at the very least, a slap in the face—which would have presented him with an unalterable choice and which would have been the deciding factor in whether the impediment, which stretched inevitably between the beginning and each ensuing manic plot, could be avoided or not. But how can one slap a face that is not there? Haman's hatred still existed. The old woman's piano-teacher severity made this clear, confined as it was to the daily writing and reading tasks, but one could still feel that it had more to do with the book. But the book, which necessarily deprived its main characters of their faces, could not explain this hatred. It was up to P. to make the hatred real and inscribe in his memory what P.'s grandmother had vaguely but more decidedly hoped for. But to do so, P. needed to give some portion of his own features to Haman, that is, from the face of an eight-year-old boy, to make the son of Hammedatha detestable. In Haman's place, P. should have done what would have united beginning and end; he should have slapped Mordechai, who raised an orphan girl.

On the way home from picking up thread, P. and his grandfather always took a little detour. They arrived at a park, where standing at the top of a few stairs was a statue, a steel wheel erected on a stone block and, behind it, on similar blocks of stone, all sorts of castings, turbine screws, train tracks, pieces from the pillars of a bridge. This park was the border of the morning. The metal heated up in the sun, the poplars filled the air with white bits of fluff. Other days, they went the way to the playground. On the edge of the grounds, retired men, disabled men, work-shy men played chess and hands of *ulti* all day. Women couldn't join in. In front of each player lay a handful of money—fillérs, one-forint coins, two-forint coins, even five-forint pieces too—and behind them stood the vigilant onlookers, who never dared to wager much but who were still just as furious over the cards that were dealt as the owners of the piles of coins themselves. P. and his grandfather were never allowed close to any of the tables. While the hands were being played, the stubbly, distorted faces of the men focused silently, only sighs and suppressed groans could be heard, then when the red seven struck, suddenly everyone had something to say. Fold, draw, 1,400 red *ulti*, double, renounce, block, forty down, straight run, a clean pass—these were the sort of words that one could learn there.

And Mordechai gave Hatach the written text of the law, which had been proclaimed in Shushan for their destruction, to show Esther, inform her and instruct her: go to the king, appeal to him and plead with him for her people.

After the war, the village where P.'s family had at one time lived was full of men whose children and wives did not come home. P.'s mother was practically smothered by the affection of these men; they embraced her, greeted her with kisses if they met. She was skeptical of them and sensed that in their sudden declarations of feeling they were searching for the dead. Her new father was also mourning, not a child or a wife but his parents. P.'s mother behaved insolently towards him, with a coldness that lasted for a long time. She did not address him, and did not come to call him father. She watched him and scrutinized him as only a child can. She felt that he needed to stay faithful to the dead, and her best friend affirmed this view, a girl who, after her father, too, did not return home—

her mother did the same as her own, marrying again in '48—on one occasion, whispering behind a stable, the girl said with resoluteness in her voice, you only get one father. Six or so months later, when she was coming home from school with the very same friend, she spotted her mother's new husband on the far side of the street. He was walking under the acacias; they noticed each other almost at the same time, and right then the man set off towards her, hurrying across the street. When he came up to them, P.'s mother found herself unexpectedly hugging the man's waist.

An old level turned up in one of the drawers. The water had become yellow in the short copper tube, the two ends soldered shut, and on the top, under the three little windows, the air bubbles floated back and forth. If you tipped it left, the bubbles floated right, if right, then the bubbles floated back. P. set the copper base of the level against every wall in the apartment. The bubbles almost never settled at the centre. Other times, raising the copper tube to his eyes with two fingers, he studied how the air moved at even the slightest movement, and no matter how carefully he tried, he could not get them to keep still even for a second.

Leopold Blumenfeld's true legacy was not Rabbi Gamliel's wisdom, Rabbi Samuel's belief or Rabbi Jose's shock but was instead a promise that they were all a part of and which, over time, became a threat:

'One of Rabbi Simeon ben Jochai's students felt one day that he had forgotten everything he had ever learnt. In tears, he rushed to the grave where his master lay; as he cried there bitterly, he fell asleep. In a dream, he saw his master, who instructed him: 'Put three stones on me, and I will come to you.' The young man found someone who could make sense of the dream and explained what had happened. The dream-reader then said, 'If after every paragraph you study, you repeat three times what is written, what you have forgotten will return and stay with you. If one's sword is nicked, one needs strength to sharpen it.'

And Hatach went to Esther and delivered Mordechai's message. And Esther sent him back to Mordechai to tell him: All the king's courtiers and the people of the king's provinces know that if any person, man or woman, enters the king's inner court without having been summoned, he will be put to death. Only if the king extends the golden sceptre to him may he live. And Esther, meanwhile, had not been summoned to visit the king for the last thirty days.

But is it possible to live without forgetting? Doesn't a degree of dreaming and dreamlessness, of infinite repetition, already somehow mar a life? Isn't Rabbi Simeon ben Jochai's student digging his own grave with his tears, the one who cries at his master's headstone? Then again, is it possible to live without memory? Isn't the person who builds himself the strongest house the one who builds it upon a grave and holds the stones together with his tears? This is how we should speak, in a language that does not exist, so as to ask Leopold Blumenfeld: Rabbi, what does the story of Simeon ben Jochai's student mean? But the thirty-three stones of memory cannot elicit an answer. For we ourselves are preparing his grave with our book, we are placing above it the stone which reads 'here is hidden', and only before the grave is finished will we have the chance to speak.

Mordechai knew that no one was allowed to see the king without an invitation. He did not know, however, what it meant to step within the exceedingly high walls, to walk down between the arrangement of Marduk and Nabu's bull-headed lions, as though each of them were asking if you really dared to take a chance in coming there, and even if the golden scepter that ended in an ivory fist showed benevolently down from the height of the marble staircase, how difficult it was to break the silence of the empty room with mere words and complaints. And this empty, silent room was the heart of the kingdom where, with a single movement, mistaking or neglecting even the simplest cues could cost the entrant his life and the extermination of an entire people. Esther had become queen in vain; she never knew the cues, for one face held their answers,

Ahasuerus', whom she did not even see when he came to her bed. Above her breast, a curtain of thick fabric came together; she could merely feel it as a strong, powerful male hand touched her thigh, her stomach.

Until the dissolution of the order, P.'s mother was taught in first grade by nuns, strict, good-hearted old women. The Jewish children did not go to school on Saturdays and did not take part in the religious instruction during the week, but the nuns tried to ensure that they did not feel left out. They were as much a part of the class as anyone else. On one occasion, one of the nuns, in place of the day's lesson, took the class to the village's Catholic church, which faced the synagogue, to explain why things were the way they were and what they meant. Above the labyrinthinely complicated, slightly faded but all the more impressive-looking altarpiece, a bearded old man was sitting on a cloud; he was looking down at what was happening below, where a beautiful and sad woman held a gaunt, tortured man with remarkably long hands in her lap, though he was not looking at her but, rather, at something above, not at the old man. And beside the woman, other women stood crying, chubby babies playing harps or without instruments floated around them in the confused scene, while on one side disfigured bodies lay on the ground, and on the other, as though these bodies were about to rise in a nice arrangement. The nun explained everything clearly and calmly, yet everything was still unclear. It later turned out that P.'s great-grandfather had watched stonily from the door of the watchmaker's shop as the class marched into the church, and at home he beat his granddaughter in horror for not leaving the line.

If we ourselves are preparing Leopold Blumenfeld's grave with our book while the book itself is not completed, we cannot consider him among the dead. But just the same, we cannot consider him among the living, for at the beginning of our story, no matter what we make of the beginning, he certainly was dead. Our heroes could have searched for his grave in the village's Jewish cemetery; had they done so, however, they would have found nothing more than an unreadable, worn piece of stone, grown over with ivy and weeds. But we also need him, we would also like to keep him at our side, even if silently, for he has guided us this far through the maze of stories and memories.

It was night, the city Shushan was at rest. But even at that hour the acrid smells from the carpenters' streets wafted in the air. In the courtyards of certain houses a thick glue was cooked in enormous vats from the bones of hens and slaughtered cattle. The bubbling glue, which constantly needed to be stirred in the vat so as not to burn, started out a greenish colour, then yellowed, and when it was done, became completely clear.

Mordechai watched countless times how the carpenters made the glue, the smell of which stuck to their skin, their hair, and the dried glue spattered between their fingers. Esther was far from him. She was confronted with silence, which for a long time had floated around her like a fog. So when Hatach appeared and reminded him that no one was allowed into the king's inner court without permission, Mordechai answered, more angrily than necessary, and sent a message to Esther: She should not imagine that she would be spared on account of her place beside the king, moreover, should deliverance come to the Jews from elsewhere, surely she and her father's house would perish.

Inside, beside the spinning machine, a radio stood on the linen cabinet. It was the size of a small chest, its side varnished, the brown fabric on the speakers pilled, and one could play the piano wonderfully on the bone-coloured buttons. If it was turned on, the names of the cities began to light up in turn above the buttons—Paris, Luxembourg, Munich, London—and one could hear all different languages spoken, men and women in all different voices. If the radio was turned on, the spinning machine would not work; it was all static, anyhow, what you could hear them saying from Munich or London.

When P.'s father and mother decided to get married, their parents were against it, though perhaps they should have stayed silent, for one evening they tried to dissuade their daughter, who became visibly more determined as a result but in truth was herself more uncertain. They said, all right, the young man's handsome, serious and clearly honest, it's not an issue that he's divorced. But he's coarse and crude. No one can ever be right but him. And in the thirty years that followed, P.'s grandfather noticed nothing else in him but this. Later, in the hospital, several days before his death, when he was beginning to fade, sleeping or muttering for the most part, P.'s grandfather said that they had always been right for each other. But what does it mean when someone seeks acceptance going back half a lifetime in a dying man's words?

And Esther's answer, which Hatach took to Mordechai, went like this: Go and bring together all the Jews in Shushan, begin a fast in my name, do not eat or drink for three days, night and day; my servants and I will fast soon thereafter. Then I will go to the king, despite the law, and if I must die, well then I will die. And Mordechai left and did as Esther had instructed.

There is no one, however, who could lead us through the maze of our story. Leopold Blumenfeld, whom, if silently, we would like to keep at our side, is not a person and not even a shadow; he does not speak to us in a hoarse voice because of the long silence, for we summoned him here and we are keeping him here in the pages of the book. He does not know our paths. We don't allow him to go ahead of us, we don't want to follow him. He came from the opposite direction, the one in which we might nevertheless be headed, down the paths of the labyrinth but facing back, in a crab walk, so that its paths to death, which he walked right down, might be for us paths to life. For he fled just as we fled Rabbi Nachman's burning house, at another time, in another direction, only for the both of us to meet again in a place unknown to both of us on 19 May 1953.

And in the book that P.'s mother received that day, a commemorative page has survived. The twenty-third psalm is written in Hebrew and Hungarian on it, the one sung at bar and bat mitzvahs and funerals. The two texts, however, are different. On the left side of the page, the Hungarian translation, as though it were depicting a meeting, duplicates the last lines of the original: 'Thou anointest my head with oil, thou anointest my head with oil, my cup runneth over, my cup runneth over. Only goodness and mercy shall follow me all the days of my life. I will dwell in the house of the Lord. For ever and ever, for ever and ever!'

And on the third day it came to pass: Esther changed into her royal gown, went into the inner court of the palace, and stopped within the house of the king.

Ahasuerus was sitting on the royal throne. And when he caught a glimpse of Queen Esther, he found her appearance charming.

P.'s father and mother had already been living together for nine years when he was born. He had had an older brother, his mother at least thought he was a boy, but after a few weeks she needed to get an abortion. P.'s mother was brought into the operating room on a flat stretcher, the nurse strapped up her legs; the doctor had entered in the interim, a tall man with glasses, whom she had already seen in the hallway; he came over to her, tying a green cap around the nape of his neck, and when he was ready he asked the patient lying before him whether she was feeling all right and said with a feigned, slightly exaggerated informality, rest assured, there was no reason to be scared, everything was going to be fine.

One of P.'s first memories was of the hallway in his grandparents' flat. Under the four-metre-high ceiling a little bit of light loomed, an oblong, yellow glass chandelier, on which dust had collected. Green- and black-patterned linoleum covered the hallway; thin grey stripes ran across it at the fittings.

Since the old woman started knitting—this began sometime in the mid-sixties—P.'s grandfather was in charge of the housekeeping. He shopped, he cleaned; the kitchen fell under his jurisdiction. As a result, the kitchen was constantly 'covered in oil', as the women in the family said, the utensils and the plates were never properly cleaned, dried food of all sorts hardened on the glasses; filth made the red vinyl-covered kitchen stools sticky. Sometimes P.'s mother, refusing to take no for an answer, announced that she could bear the sight of it no more, and cleaned it, and after more than an hour's work, 'she had rid the kitchen of filth'. But in two day's time everything had become just as dirty.

And the king extended to Esther the golden staff. She stepped closer and touched the tip. And the king asked: Why have you come, Esther? What is your wish?

The blue spiral notebook was half-filled with lurching childish letters, full-bodied here, tapering off there. It was no use changing the letters written with the ballpoint; each soon started to run. P.'s finger became covered in ink. And since with the pinkie of his right hand he leant against the notebook again and again while writing, the lines became a little smudged, for which the old woman had not managed to scold him sufficiently. She said: 'Even cleanliness is part of writing.' At such times, she launched into long stories about how strict the nuns were with them, though with him it was different, since he was first in the class, and they knew he studied day and night.

In those days P.'s mother was terribly anxious. She worried whether P.'s father could bear the heat. It was impossible in winter to heat the company's office where he worked; the heater that he brought from home didn't help, and in summer it was too hot to stay inside; already by nine in the morning, the tar-covered roof was pouring out heat.

One evening, P. spied on his mother while she was bathing. He did not see her face, only her short, plump body as it leant slightly forward, and her soft stomach folding over unexpectedly thick, wet pubic hair. The water travelled in thin trails down the wrinkled hips, the thick thighs, and P. suddenly sensed that from the other end of the entryway his father was watching him: when P. half-turned in his direction, frightened what would happen now, his father went over to him, bent down and, smiling, picked him up.

And Esther replied: 'If it please the king, he shall come for a feast for Haman and the king.' And the king said: 'Order Haman to comply with Esther's wish.'

In '52, after they had moved to Pest, the old woman first sold goods at the market, then one year later, found work as a bookkeeper at the headquarters of the biggest state-run vegetable distribution company. After a few days it turned out that she had an amazing understanding of bookkeeping, which was no surprise, considering that at home, with the vinegar production, she had already been in charge of the revenue and delivery books. Now she needed to prepare the enormous monthly and quarterly accounting, the end-of-year balance sheets, and if someone had skipped over a line in the accounting or added up the totals incorrectly, she was asked to find the mistake. The columns and the lines needed to match up in each direction.

Thanks to an inoperable cataract, P.'s grandfather had long been blind in one eye, and with the other he saw only blurrily. P. did not know this, however, for a long time. His grandfather should have worn thick glasses a long time ago but he was not willing to do so, probably out of laziness, in the same way that he should have gone to the doctor. He also thought there were always problems with glasses, the bridge breaks, one loses them. As a result, he needed to learn the precise place of everything, in the apartment and in the street, so as not to miss anything and so that P. should not notice his blindness.

As a child, P.'s mother always scraped together the wax after the Friday candle lighting. Saturday's leftovers were signified at that time by a bluish flame. From a short silver gauntlet, pálinka was poured onto a palm-sized tray, P.'s great-grandfather said the blessings for it and lit it. Right away the flame ran the length of the tray, then burnt out, and only the aromatic smell of the burnt alcohol remained.

So the king and Haman came to the feast that Esther had prepared. At the feast, the king asked Esther, 'What is your wish? It shall be granted you. And what is your request? Even for half the kingdom, it shall be fulfilled.'

P.'s mother was full of guilt. If she made an observation that she could not help suspecting would provide her daughter with ammunition, the old woman sensed it right away and began to speak at length about how others could not imagine how much she had had to suffer—that she didn't eat for years, only potatoes and bread with plum jam, while P.'s grandfather came home at night, often for weeks at a time, and without even taking off his shoes, lay down on the settee, and already at dawn, needed to leave for the country. The old woman never liked the house in Pest. She said it was filled with bugs and mice, she was simply unable to root them out, they came up through the drain, they climbed in from the pantry, and she set out traps in vain, she covered the foot of the wall with poison.

When they taught P. to swim at Lake Balaton, his mother stood in a shallower part, his father several metres further out. He swam between the two of them, there and back between his mother and father, not yet with proper strokes; when he got close, they extended their hands to him. The sun shimmered brightly in the reflection of the lake, the grey water entered P.'s mouth, his nose, and he felt as though despite all his efforts he would not go forward. When he swam towards his father, his father always kept taking a step or two back without his knowing; he would almost reach him, but not quite, one more stroke, one more, one more, he knew that with his feet, if he stopped, he would no longer reach the cool sludge, and his mother shouted from behind, very good, very good, keep going, though she could see that he was afraid.

'My wish,' replied Esther, 'my request—if Your Majesty will do the favour, if it please Your Majesty to grant my wish—let Your Majesty and Haman come to the feast which I will prepare for them.' And Haman went out happy and lighthearted. But when Haman saw Mordechai in the palace gate and Mordechai did not rise or even stir on his account, Haman was furious.

One of the suitors, the lawyer from Mélykút, tried to win over P.'s mother by constantly offering her money for chocolate and ice cream. The old woman, who at that time was considered an intelligent and attractive widower, naturally did not suspect a thing, but neither did she have any plans for the handsome, well-to-do lawyer. The man who showed her open interest could not expect much sympathy in return.

On the way home on Wednesday afternoons, P. and his grandfather stopped by the betting place—at the entrance was a large, green metal drum, and on it a four-leaf clover—and bought two tickets. Then at the newspaper stand, in order to enlist some expert support, they bought a *Sportfogadás*, which contained everything one needed to know about the team playing on that day: what results they had achieved in previous rounds, whether they had any injuries, whether someone needed to sit out the match because of a booking and how the relationship stood between the coach and players. After lunch they meticulously laid out the newspaper on the oilcloth cover, weighed the odds, took into consideration the possibility of surprises, conferred and, going line by line, wrote in their bets. They each filled out their own tickets.

And that day, Haman's friends came to see him. He told them about his wealth, his many sons, and all about how the king had promoted him and advanced him above the officials and the king's courtiers. 'What is more,' said Haman, 'other than the king, Queen Esther did not invite anyone else in the kingdom to her palace for a feast but me, and so tomorrow I will again sit beside the king. But all this means nothing to me while that Jew Mordechai sits in the palace gate.'

And here in the book, a page-length drawing followed. With outstretched arms and eyes raised to the sky, Mordechai knelt before the royal castle; he was larger than the bastion-like columned palaces but he did not cry out; he looked like he was waiting fixedly, mouth open, to see whether something would come from the sky.

As for who thought what about whom and who had reason when to take offence: In truth, this was most interesting, but there was always more one wanted to know. For example, when P.'s grandparents lent the young couple a larger sum for the down payment on their first flat, whether they really asked for it back a week later and, if yes, whether they asked straight out or only hinted at it, which may have been mistaken for the former. Or that several days before he had really told the old woman, when she needed accompanying somewhere, that he couldn't stand the whole thing any longer, he was filing for a divorce, what will be with the child will be, the visiting rights would be determined as they would. In any case, when the old woman went home and called her daughter in tears to see whether they were really separating, and if not why her son-in-law would say such things to her, it turned out that they had never said a word on the subject. Well, they were constantly saying words on the subject, but they both preferred what they had to divorce.

P.'s grandfather had a black briefcase with a pouch, from which, if unbuckled, the cold smell of onions flowed as if from an enormous mouth. With this brief-case, which always ended up in the pantry, they went to the market twice a week. The road there ran beside a playground. Long ago the paint had peeled off the jungle gym, rust in many places had eaten through the grey metal; from the uppermost boards of the platform, known as the spaceship, the boards were giving way, and the sun burnt its grey, out-of-place tin dome. People selling flowers sat at the entrance to the market. They sold marigolds and roses in plastic buckets, the stems tied tightly together in tens. And there they sold brooms, glazing brushes, wooden spoons. A knife grinder worked by the market gate; the stone was mounted to his bicycle and driven with the pedal. Further in on low tables, brown bacon, spareribs, smoked thighs oozed grease. At the butchers' shops pink kidneys, hearts in plastic containers, claret-brown livers, beautiful pork chops, thin flanks of pork, thighs, red undercuts and purple legs cooled; thinly textured white cloths protected them from the flies and the butchers chatted intimately with the customers from behind a fragrant curtain of sausages. At the vegetable sellers' the yellow paprika stood in piles, the edge of the leaves on the heads of cabbage were burnt black, above the long poison-green cucumbers the potatoes were turning brown. And there were apples and apricots, too. A few tomatoes had split open at the edge of the case, the sweet-and-sour juice under the skin ran over the wood, and you could see the small green seeds.

There was also an old man at the market in a dull brown overcoat selling carrots, root vegetables and potatoes, who looked very much like Haman, as he was depicted in the book. He had the same crooked nose, bulging eyes, untrimmed beard, and when P. saw him he felt ashamed.

Then his wife Zeresh and all his friends said to him, 'Let a stake be put up, fifty cubits high, and in the morning, ask the king to have Mordechai impaled on it. Then you can go happily with the king to the feast.' The proposal pleased Haman and he had the stake put up.

When P. was born, his grandfather started collecting stamps. Stamps of Olympians, astronauts, football players, the Soviet–Hungarian friendship stamps, flowered ones, ones with animals, blocks and series, everything that the post office put out each year. In a small, lined school notebook he recorded precisely the names of the blocks and series, the value of each issue, and how much their value had grown according to the annual philately book. With his large, calligraphic letters and numbers, he kept up a careful a system of double-entry bookkeeping, to which P. was also drawn, after a time. Together they went out to the Philately Society at 7th November Square; together they buried themselves in the annual book and often took out the albums, too, straightened the corners of the stamps, reattached the cellophane if it came undone somewhere; they looked at the astronauts, the butterfly wings and the cover of the album in which P.'s name was inscribed.

P.'s father often came home late; sometimes even at ten they waited in vain. At such times his mother immediately thought of the worst. She began calling the ambulatory service, the police, paced back and forth in the room, stopped for a moment by the open window and angrily stared out at the street, then started her pacing up again, and meanwhile asked her son what he thought, did he think something was wrong.

In the town's muddy streets, white-flowered acacias stood in a row. For weeks in spring, the sweet smell of acacia hung above the houses, moved into them, the rooms, the beds, too; for several days, people woke up to and fell asleep to the smell of acacia, then the petals began to fall from the trees, the wind blew them onto the verandas. And it was on a day like this, with the trees dropping their flowers, when, with bags and bundles prepared well in advance, they were ordered to the ghetto. In many places in Bácsalmás, there were not acacias but plum trees planted in front of the houses. It was strange that they did not grow in the garden but there in the street.

We, however, do not see these white-flowered acacias. Just as we do not see the sumac tree that stood before the entrance to the watchmaker's shop; neither do we see those plum trees, with their plentiful branches, which lined the road leading to the ghetto. And the acacias could have said how Leopold Blumenfeld walked in the afternoons to the Catholic cemetery, whom he met, whom he greeted; and presumably, that sumac would have something to say that might concern us, too, the one which listened for decades to the ringing of the door to the watchmaker's shop. If these trees were still there today, and the words had not been burnt out within them, as though lightning had struck their branches, our path would be straight and our every step an opening.

That night sleep deserted the king and he ordered the BOOKS OF RECORDS to be brought. And it was read to the king.

Both of P.'s father's ankles were purple with varicose veins. They frequently flared up; at such times he needed to soak them in standing water. Later, after a thrombosis, he went around in rubber socks in the worst heat; the damp, brown socks lay there on the chair's wooden armrests each evening. P.'s father said that all that running around in military boots ruined his ankles, that is, after '57, the three years served in the armed forces. He was eighteen then; after basic training, he joined had the party.

The stamp collecting came to a sudden halt. One day, a close relative came to visit P.'s grandparents.

They showed off the albums, with the blue vignettes on their covers. Not long after, when P. and his grandfather brought out the collection and went through to determine, as was their custom, where the corners needed to be reinforced, where cellophane needed to be reattached, they were distraught to see that one of the astronaut blocks, commemorating the coming together of the Soyuz and the Apollo, was missing. They searched every possible place, rooted around the table, emptied out the bookshelf, but it did not turn up. After that they never turned to the stamp collection again. They did not forget about it, but they did not speak of it.

And when the servant in whose care the book had been placed began to read from the book, one entry in particular caught the king's ear: one day Mordechai, a Jew, had denounced Bigthan and Teresh, two of the king's eunuchs who guarded the threshold, who had plotted to do away with King Ahasuerus. 'What honour has been conferred on Mordechai for this?' the king inquired. And the king's servants replied, 'Nothing at all has been done for him.'

At some point, P.'s father had worked with horses. This was very difficult to imagine, though he really did work as an agriculturist beside a horse farm, and, what's more, he supposedly had his own horse, too, a mare named Muki, with which he even set out for the

Hungarian championships in show-jumping. But since P. only knew him as a hundred-kilo man, who tired easily and moved clumsily, he ultimately felt that the idea of his father at some point on the back of a horse, flying above gates and water pits, belonged to legend, when, in fact, it was the truth.

In '44, when the Germans came, the old woman could no longer go to Mélykút. The officers said to her mother-in-law that if they saw her one more time, they would lock her up for sure, there was enough of her kind there, so just watch out.

That summer the heat was unbearable. Over the course of a month, the same heat consumed the houses and dried out the air. The tired, weary hours passed slowly. It was only worth opening the windows late in the evening, but even then the curtain remained still.

And the king said, 'Who is in the court?' For Haman had just entered the outer court of the royal palace to speak to the king about having Mordechai impaled on the stake he had prepared for him. And the king's servants answered, 'It is Haman standing in the court.' And the kind said, 'Let him enter!'

When P.'s mother needed to have her tonsils taken out at the age of six, she was taken to the hospital in Baja. At least ten children were waiting for surgery in the corridor of the hospital. The surgical attendant always went up to the next one in line, gathered her with a smile, and ten minutes later had already brought her back. On the way there, every child screamed and cried. On the way back, in a daze from the anesthesia, they ended up in bed. P.'s mother was alone when it was her turn in line, and the attendant stopped before her. The old woman had noticed just beforehand that she had forgotten to bring pyjamas for her daughter and so she ran off into town to a relative. By the time she returned, her daughter was already lying in the hospital room. Several days later P.'s mother's fever shot up. They gave her X-rays, and it was then determined that her previous fevers had been the result of untreated tuberculosis, which had cured itself at the Mistelbach camp.

And Haman entered. The king said, 'What should be done for a man whom the king desires to honour?' And Haman said to himself, 'Whom would the king desire to honour more than me?' So Haman said to the king, 'For the man whom the king desires to honour, let royal garb which the king has worn be brought, and a horse on which the king has ridden, when the royal crown was placed on his head.'

Not long after P. was born, P.'s father gave up working as an agriculturist. In the last three years, he no longer needed to go out to the country. He worked in the Zugló district of Budapest at the Artificial Insemination Centre, where carefully selected bulls were mated, their sperm diluted, cooled in vials, put in thermoses, and once a day the quantity requested of that culture was sent out to Keleti or Nyugati Railway Station. A long evaluation period preceded the selection of the bulls. On the testing grounds, two dozen cows were mated with each one, and the young calves were then monitored over the course of two years while the male specimen rested. The bulls were only used for large-scale production if the breed-specific traits of the young calves were considered favourable. The hardworking railway men sent out the bull sperm containing the corrective traits to every part of the country on the morning postal trains, so that in the appropriate places the inseminators, who among the fertilizers themselves were simply called booted bulls, should receive the required dosages and, reaching the designated localities, fertilize the cows in heat. After a short time, however, P.'s father called it quits with animals. He did not do it of his own accord, it was his father-in-law who made the decision on his behalf, saying that it was absurd for him still to spend two or three days in the country when he had a child at home. In a word, his father-in-law spoke with a former colleague, who arranged a position for him at the Zöldért vegetable distribution centre by the following week. First, he would work as a salesman, but later, they would enroll him in a course for store managers. P.'s father later acknowledged that what had happened was for the best, but as for how far his father-in-law had allowed himself to intrude on his life and that he had taken measures on his own without asking, P.'s father could never forgive him for that.

Every other year, P.'s mother succeeded in securing vouchers to the company holiday home. She and P. took the train down together to Szabadi, where P. spent the whole day in the water and the sand, and his mother tanned herself in the sun. On one of these summer excursions, P.'s mother got a terrible burn. Fat blisters broke out on her skin, her neck and back were like raw meat. P. watched his mother as she examined herself in the mirror; she ran her fingers down the length of her neck, the part above her breast that the one-piece bathing suit did not cover. In tears many years later, she once told her son that she never liked her body and that she could not imagine that anyone could love it. Her breasts were not breasts, but two mounds ready to be torn apart, and her knee was as thick as a man's. She stood there by the mirror and, as she ran her hands along her lobster-red neck, he saw that it pained her.

And Haman said to the king, 'Let the attired and the horse be put in the charge of one of the king's noble courtiers. And let the man whom the king desires to honour be paraded on the horse through the city square, while they proclaim before him: This is what is done for the man whom the king desires to honour!'

And P., following the old woman's dictation, wrote everything down with a childish slowness, his bespectacled face bent over the paper. To his mind, the story could just as easily have ended here. Haman had unwittingly glorified Mordechai; he had dressed him in the royal garb himself and sat him on Ahasuerus' horse, signalling that his ambition had its sights on the heights of the throne and that this ambition had made him blind. But the story had not yet reached its close, since the royal decree, which stipulated that on the thirteenth day of the month of Adar, the Jews in every province of the kingdom were to be gathered and killed, had been taken by dispatcher from Shushan to every province in Persia, and the stake was now standing in the garden of Haman's house.

P.'s great-grandfather was a shareholding member of the local bank's board of directors. Since he lived close to the bank, and also since there was not always much to do in the workshop, he was always called in if, among the regular clients, a trader or, more rarely, an owner buying produce or for other reasons applied for a loan. The signature of two directors was required for disbursement. What most often happened at times like this was that he disappeared for two or three hours and the old woman stayed alone to look over the vinegar production and the watch shop. The family did not really see much money from the bank. But at that time in such a little town, it was still a big deal to be the director of a bank. Nevertheless, in '36, before he gave his daughter away in marriage, P.'s great-grandfather decided to sell his shares in the bank. They were bought by the lawyer from Mélykút, the one who after the 'storm' tried courting the still-young widow. From then on, they did not send anyone from the office over to the watchmaker's workshop if something needed to be signed once or twice a week. A year and a half later, the bank went out of business. It turned out that the bookkeeper had long been embezzling funds, larger and larger sums; and even if they did not give a voice to their suspicions, everyone was convinced in their own minds that P.'s great-grandfather had suspected something, that was why he had given up his shares and his seat on the board of directors at just the right time.

At the labour camp, the children were given half a litre of milk each day. The kapo of the barracks, however, a young man from the village, whom P.'s grandmother knew well before, over the course of a year stole that half a litre of milk each day, and only on the way home did it come to light what had happened. He went to the farm with a buckled jug to bring back the milk, but he did not tell anyone about it; he gave it all to his own son in secret.

'Quick, then!' said the king to Haman. 'Get the garb and the horse, as you have said, and do this to

Mordechai the Jew, who sits in the king's gate. Omit nothing of all you have proposed.'

When inflation grew out of control in '47, in the unhappy time of the *millpengő* and the *billpengő*, each morning at half past six, the old woman turned on the radio, listened to the news and quickly adjusted to the day's calculations. By seven-thirty, she was already standing at the market behind the table of fruit. All the merchants came to her—there were ten-something of them who asked for help understanding the daily price specifications. There was only one merchant who never came to her for that sort of thing. He became P.'s grandfather.

A good many years later, while looking through a book, P. found a description of the synagogue in which Leopold Blumenfeld told peculiar stories in place of sermons and in which P.'s great-grandfather led prayers over the two decades that followed. Building began on the prayer house that served as the basis for the synagogue in 1782, not long after several Jews settled in the town of mainly Serbs. The congregation was only founded in 1820; until then, a majority of the town's Jewish residents went to nearby villages to pray and only came back for Saturday holidays. Soon, however, they grew tired of nomadic life and built a synagogue for themselves. During the period of the community's expansion they even had a rabbi, the last being Leopold Blumenfeld, who could sit in the throne-like chair beside the covenant. Later this chair remained empty, the congregation could only afford a prayer leader. In the second half of the 1700s the first prayer room was built, which in 1825 was extended lengthwise by a third. At that time the ark ended up against the back wall, while the women's section was expanded in a U-shape. A simple portico with wooden columns extended from the side of the building facing the lawn. On the side that looked out on the street, adjoining the school, the only decoration was the roof's crenelated edge. The eastern side was finished with a spandrel encircling the Torah board. A bema surrounded by a wooden balustrade stood at the centre of the traditionally furnished little inner square. The stairs over the lawn led up to the organ loft supported by cast-iron columns. The carpentry work on the ark and the benches was simple. There was a Star of David in the light blue field with a white painted ledge where the walls met, with a two-lined inscription written in a circle, which said: 'The Almighty rules with mercy for ever and ever.' Between the two sides of the women's gallery, as if they had expanded the cover of a prayer book, the tablets of Moses were visible.

The old woman's thick, short fingers rested wearily on the flower-patterned tablecloth, like a piano teacher's, who during her student's endless repetition of the same scales, paying attention for a moment here and there, pipes up every so often to say 'How was that supposed to go?' or 'Let's start that again'; the old woman's thoughts travelled in a different direction entirely.

And Haman took the garb and the horse and dressed Mordechai and paraded him through the city square, and he shouted before him: This is what is done for the man whom the king desires to honour! Then Mordechai returned to the king's gate, while Haman returned home, his head covered.

On one occasion in the camp, when the siren rang out, P.'s mother fell down in fear and a vein burst in her nose. As often happens, the bleeding did not want to stop. But there among the inmates was the surgeon from the hospital in Debrecen, the first female surgeon in Hungary, who at that time had been in the hospital in Mistelbach to see patients. She stuffed her wounded nose with a tampon and had her lie down for the day. One after the other the tampons were soaked through. They constantly needed to be changed, but finally they succeeded in stopping the bleeding. P.'s mother lay there in the sun, she hardly got any air, she was suffering from the dried-out bits of the tampons and the scab, but since there was no work on this day—in Mistelbach the inmates were also given Sundays off—the old woman took out a wash basin from the barracks and did a wash above her. This moment was etched deeply in P.'s mother's mind. She lay there in the sun, the wound in her nose contracting, and listened as her mother rubbed down her clothes above her, as she submerged them, as she wrung out the water.

A fly always slipped in through the window that looked out onto the church. P. waited for it to come to rest, to land on the tablecloth or on the mirror or on one side of the dresser; he tried to catch it, cupping his hands, and if he succeeded in doing so, he brought it to the bathroom and carefully tore off its wings, a thick, white pus oozed out at the roots, and he made its struggling body swim in the sink. Then he took it out of the water and left it to dry and climb out; finally he trapped it again, and dropped it out of the window, under the yellow blinds.

The cemetery was next to the gypsy part of town. Once each year, the family got in the car and drove down to town where P.'s grandparents and mother were from. The Zsiguli stopped in front of the cemetery's rusty iron gate; stepping out, as if on a strange planet, they looked over the mud of the gypsy section, the roofs half giving in, the barefoot, dirty children, then entering through the gate they went by the mortuary, which was in a similarly dilapidated state, and among the broken gravestones, grown in with thick runners and ivy, they found what they were looking for. The old woman produced rags and brushes, brought water in a plastic bottle from the cemetery tap, and the two women began to scrub the black gravestone with Hebrew lettering that belonged to P.'s great-grandfather. When they were ready they looked for stones under the bushes, everyone placed one on the side of his grave, then they went back to the car, got in, casting another glance at the gypsy section; the motor began to rumble and they did not stop until they were home.

And at home Haman told his wife, Zeresh, and all his friends everything that had happened. And his advisers and his wife, Zeresh, said to him, 'If this Mordechai, before whom you have begun to fall, is a Jew, you will not overcome him—you will fall before him to your ruin.' While they were still speaking with him, the king's eunuchs arrived and hurriedly brought Haman to the banquet which Esther had prepared.

The old woman always called P.'s grandfather 'my husband' in front of strangers. There was no special show of respect in the way she said it, it simply expressed the fact that she had decided on doing so at some point and since then it stuck. P.'s mother never dared to ask the old woman—though she often thought about it—whether, in '48, when she had fulfilled her father's last request, or anytime later, whether she had felt for her husband what people call love or desire, and when she had picked a winner, since there were reasons for choosing each suitor, whether the thought of whose bed she most wished to hide in had played a role. But what interested P. more and more as the years passed was what his ageing grandfather felt knowing that he was still just the second. What could 'my husband' have meant to him?

If P. stumbled and tripped on the stairs, or fell from the tree, his father always said, It's not a big deal, my little soldier, by the time you're married you'll be fine. This on top of the wound did not sit all that well with P.; he felt his father did not take him seriously. For the moment he had skinned his chin, blood ran down his leg; marriage, on the other hand, was still a ways away, and the solider stuff was more a threat than a consolation.

Two years before P.'s mother's bat mitzvah, she began studying in the 'church'. This needed to be kept secret, even mentioning it in school was not allowed. The one-hour sessions were given on Sunday mornings in the upstairs prayer room by a retired teacher called Aunt Sári. Girls and boys together attended the class, all for the most part the same age. They read biblical passages, learnt to pray, memorized poems and short scenes. P.'s mother did not meet with any of them during the week. The other children all lived a few houses or streets away from one another; she lived in a different district. This was why no one came to visit when she later came down with pneumonia. At the time, they were preparing a short play at Aunt Sári's place based on the Book of Esther. P.'s mother watched the premier, which they had put together for parents and friends, in its entirety, from the second to last row. From the performance, she slowly took the long way home.

And the king and Haman came to drink with Queen Esther. And the king said to Esther on the second day of the feast as they drank the royal wine, 'What is your wish, Queen Esther? It shall be granted you. And whatever your request—even half the kingdom—it shall be fulfilled.'

After a time, P.'s mother and grandmother could not help but speak about themselves. They told and told their stories. And as the numbers grew, details beginning to repeat themselves, in explanation of and justification for all they could not change, P.'s father and grandfather were drawn into an increasingly wounded silence. But each man's silence was entirely different: P.'s father's was hurt and hopeless, his grandfather's filled with surprising aggression.

For those who knew them only from a distance, one might have thought that P.'s grandparents had hardly argued with each other over the decades. In truth, though they lived quiet, calm lives, at the most unexpected moments bitter feelings arose between them. Once during lunch, when the old woman began to go on again about how she wanted to move elsewhere and that dwelling on such things was undoubtedly tiring, P.'s grandfather suddenly stuck the ladle in the soup and started to shout. Soon old things came up. For two weeks after this they spoke to each other only if absolutely necessary. By the end, the old woman was already crying. P.'s grandfather did not let up, only for a time did he show her mercy.

And Queen Esther replied, 'If Your Majesty will do me the favour, and if it pleases Your Majesty, let my life be granted me as my wish and my people as my request. For we have been sold, my people and I, to be destroyed, killed and exterminated. Had we only been sold as bondmen and women, I would have kept silent; for the adversary is not worthy of the king's trouble.'

By the middle of July, P. had already learnt to read. Only rarely did he come to a halt before certain words or start to stumble, and even if he did, the old woman's fingers at such times remained still. This was the most boring, tiring part of the afternoon. And so one day P., gathering up all his courage, told his grandmother that he didn't needed to read the story all the way through, he could stop there, where all danger could still be avoided; the thirteenth day of the month of Adar had not yet come around. The old woman, however, clung to each word; she refused to end the day's reading and writing.

Somewhere north of Kosice the deported were put up for a night in an enormous stable. The smell of damp straw seeped into everything. It was already winter, families lay huddled together, and at dawn in the nearby city the sirens were ringing out. From somewhere deep in the forest the Katyushas began shooting the city. Everyone stood out before the stable and watched as the short stripes of light shot in beautiful arcs across the reddish near-dawn sky. For a moment it were as though the forest, in a pass on the hill, had burst into flames. It wouldn't have been possible to dream up something more beautiful.

And with this picture facing us, resting for a moment on our way, maybe we should set free the one whom we chose to accompany us. P.'s request, which could not have been directed at us, perhaps was made in Leopold Blumenfeld's name, since wasn't he the one who wanted to follow this path, and beyond the point where we now stand, with the forest still in flames at our backs, isn't it possible that he should be the seer? His strength might have brought him this far, passed on from Samuel, Jose, Gamliel and Rav; the thread only reached this far, the thread that began to ball up who knows where or when and the end of which Rabbi Sigmund Jampel placed in his hands in Berlin. But we still have a need for him. He is the blind man with the torch in his hands, and he also has a need for us to ready his grave, on which his name will be written, in which he can be at rest and no longer need to cross the paths of the world.

And King Ahasuerus spoke and demanded of Queen Esther, 'Who is he and where is he who dared to do this?'

P.'s father applied for membership to the party when he was a member of the security forces within the army. Later, he became the secretary of the local party offices and, in the early sixties, took part in the re-establishment of collectivization. He once noted on the subject that he had never lied in his life as much as he had then. Years later, however, when P. recalled the incident, he firmly denied that he would have said any such thing. But it was a fact that when P. was an adult, his father was unwilling to put a foot in the local party offices, which were located on a sloping street beside a barracks. At the beginning of every month, he sent his son down with his party membership book for a stamp. P. entered the basement of the building; rooms lined either side of the corridor. Not a voice passed through any of them. After a bit of hesitation he knocked, entered one of the rooms and, in a loud voice, said good afternoon, but there was no one there. At the end of the room stood a little bust of Lenin on a writing desk, above the door hung a picture of Karl Marx, Friedrich Engels and Lenin. P. peeked in the other room, that one was empty, too. He hurried home, his father tossed his party-membership book aside and said, If they want something from me they'll come.

Her theatrical peak was Károly Kisfaludy's comedy *The Suitors*. P.'s mother played the role of Máli, Captain Baltafy's daughter, whose heart neither Szélházy nor Perföldy nor Hősváry could steal, only Károly, Captain Batalfy's adopted child. 'Is this love or is it not / What I feel inside my chest? / And if it is not love / What feeling resides in my breast?' pondered the slightly plump-cheeked Máli, blushing at the table, lost in a daydream above her book; later, after she became convinced that it was in fact love she felt in her chest, and steadfastly withstanding every confusion in old Batalfy's, together she and the man she had chosen could finally be at peace; the curtain fell to great applause and a well-dressed man came up and kissed the plump-cheeked Máli's hand. 'Do you have any idea who that was?' asked Aunt Sári, her eyes following the man. 'Iván Mándy. Do you know who that is?'

And Esther said, 'The enemy is sitting here at the table. And Haman cringed in terror before the king and queen.'

The greatest summer was when P. and his parents got in their Zsiguli and travelled through Bucharest and Varna to the Bulgarian Sunny Coast. They stayed in a bungalow there; lunch was included. The tide brought in an unbelievable number of mussels, snails and pieces of tar, and going underwater in the shallower parts one could see them in the rippled sand. P.'s arms and feet moved slowly and easily. He tried to guess the distance the water had brought the shells to the shore. When he touched them, it was hard to believe that inside was a living creature. The mussels themselves were just like one of the pieces of tar. Then coming up to the water's surface, P. started to examine his arm. On his skin, in his hair, the water sparkled in the sun. The mussels that he had brought up on the other hand had lost their lustre, and two days later the snail shells that he had collected underwater emitted a rotten smell in the doorway to the bungalow, where he had left them out to dry.

Sometime in '53 or '54, on a spring day, P.'s mother succeeded in luring her parents to the movies. This was considered a rarity, since for the most part they did not go anywhere together. In the enormous theatre, which had previously been a gentlemen's casino, it was pleasantly warm and you could hear the whirring of the film in the machine. From the little window, specks of dust swirled in the expansive beam of light like a fan above the viewers' heads. The theatre was almost full. They were putting on a Soviet partisan film. When the film was finished and they left the theatre, P.'s mother was seriously moved. At times like these, she needed to walk ahead; if she had had a moving experience, she liked to be alone. She left and her tears flowed all the way home. Even as an adult, P.'s mother believed that a good film was one that made you cry.

And the king, in his fury, left the wine feast and went out to the palace garden, while Haman remained to plead with Queen Esther for his life, for he saw that the king had determined to destroy him.

On the seashore, P. was drawn to a sailboat pitched on the sand, on the side of which there was damage in many places. From there, he looked out on the water and watched as his parents went into it. His father had on a black bathing suit that stretched from the small, hardly prominent groin to the weal of his bulging belly and reached all the way up to his navel. Compared to the others on the beach, his hairless upper body continued from a surprisingly narrow chest to thin shoulders, but one could still tell that there was some kind of strength, which ageing, the clear signs of which already showed on each part of his body, would soon wrest from him. When his mother covered her bag and sunglasses with a towel, P. already knew how his father, leaning on his arm, would sit up, placing his left knee on the mattress, how with the other leg he would get himself into a half-kneeling position, then raising his butt, pull his legs under him to finally stand up.

It was winter, the beginning of December, and P.'s grandmother was preparing just then for the wedding of a friend. She had forgotten her purse out in the hall. Her daughter—later even she didn't know what made her do it—took out two forints. The theft became apparent right away, and a stormy string of insults followed the cover-up, with her saying, wasn't she ashamed of herself, now she was certain that she'd grow up to be nothing more than a thief. It provided a certain comfort to P.'s mother that her nose started to bleed during all this, and that she succeeded fairly well in soiling her mother's fur coat. After this, for punishment and edification, P.'s mother was locked up in the empty stable, no longer in use, and his grandfather, for the crowning punishment, as it were, attached a piece of paper to her hung-up coat, and wrote, 'I STOLE TWO FORINTS'. That was all fine, but P.'s mother needed to go to school for the St Nicholas celebration, she even had a ticket in the raffle. After about twenty minutes of confinement, they let her out but grounded her to her room. Her mother of course went out to the wedding, and P.'s grandfather waited around for his card partners. It wasn't possible to stay at home, though, what with the raffle ticket in her pocket, since there was always the chance that she could come away with the main prize. Luckily, there were still maids in the house at the time, who tended not to be very strict.

The paper was taken off the coat and they helped P.'s mother out the window. At the raffle the winning prize was a postcard. When she got home, the maids were lifting her back up in the same spot just when P.'s great-grandfather turned in the gate. He wouldn't have suspected anything, if one of the maids, in expressing her opinions about certain child-rearing techniques employed in the house, hadn't written on the other side of the paper, 'I GOT TWO FORINTS', and then fixed it back on the coat, facing out. P.'s great-grand-father saw the new writing and decided that it would be best to pretend that he was implacably angry with his granddaughter, and for a time did not say a word to her at all. But two days later, his health took a turn for the worse, and he was taken to the hospital. He died in the evening of Christmas, so his granddaughter, whom out of consideration they did not bring to the hospital, did not get the chance to say goodbye; instead, she only saw his coffin, which sat there for a time in the main room.

And when the king returned from the palace garden to the banquet room, Haman was lying pros-trate on the couch on which Esther reclined. And the king said, 'Does he mean to ravish the queen in my own palace?' No sooner did these words leave the king's lips than the king's servants covered Haman's face.

P.'s mother had almost made it to the water when his father got up to join her. From the way they were both walking, you could tell the sand burnt their feet. As they walked past the spread-out towels and umbrellas, they looked at everyone, especially those who looked about their age, and they made quick comparisons to themselves. It was not difficult to recognize the Hungarian families vacationing on the Bulgarian Sunny Coast and their circumstances back home, but they did not know how to behave before one another, here, abroad, stripped down to bathing suits, on the seashore, which was of course not the Adriatic. The Czechs or the East Germans, of whom there were fewer, drank beer in groups of ten or fifteen, broke out in loud bursts of laughter, and if they went swimming, practically took the sea by storm so that everyone needed to pay attention, their fat already being offered up violently to the waves. At such times the Hungarians hid even further under their umbrellas and already found it uncomfortable that the people lying next to them a few metres away on the well-known terrycloth towels from Slovakian stores understood what they were saying, in all likelihood they had even been listening, and now everyone had an opinion about everyone else.

Towards the end of the war, they began directing Jews from the Vienna region towards Teresienstadt, but detours constantly needed to be made since the front was advancing. There were some who succeeded in leaving the group along the way, they hid or were hidden. Among them a few hired themselves out as maids in the nearby towns, and there were some who stayed in Austria for good. Meanwhile, even in the last days before the German capitulation, many people perished. Every single person in a group of more than one hundred, which on 2 May, deviating from the path, spent the night in Persenbeug, was murdered the next morning at dawn by an SS squad in retreat. The families doing the farm work in the Gössling an der Ybbs camp, similar in size to the one in Mistelbach, met a similar fate. The SS officers surrounded the barracks and set them on fire. After the war the burnt bodies of twenty-three men, forty-three women and ten children were found among the ashen boards.

And Harbonah, one of the eunuchs, said before the king: 'A tree is standing at Haman's house, fifty ell high, which he prepared for Mordechai—the man whose words saved the king.' 'Hang him from it!' the king ordered. So they hung Haman from the tree that he had put up for Mordechai, and the king's fury abated.

In March of '48, several weeks after her second marriage, the old woman came down with influenza, which later became TB. Her father, who by that point had not quite a year to live, took her to Baja to see a pulmonologist, who said that her daughter had a hole the size of a green nut in her lung. When they arrived home, the town doctor came over for a visit. He was even willing to put it in writing that the old woman did not have a hole in her lung but, to ease her fears, still recommended that in four days he take her back to Baja to see a different lung specialist, and what he said would be the final word. Doctor Jancsin, since that was the doctor's name in the place they went, gave her an ultrasound from the right side, gave her an ultrasound from the left, but did not find a hole. Finally he said to his colleague that he was going to take an X-ray. And on the X-ray, in fact, you could see the mark of three bean-sized bright spots. Doctor Jancsin recommended a trip to the Mátra hills in the name of recovery. On the train on the way, the old woman began to complain, Doctor, you're aware of my situation, there's no way I can go to the Mátra. And she didn't go. The doctor recreated the Mátra for her at home. He wrote everything down precisely that needed to be done. The old woman spent the entire day lying in a lounge chair in the yard, received regular liver injections, and was not to get up until she reached sixty kilos. When she reached the requirements recommended by the doctor, P.'s grandmother shouted, 'Good God, even my underwear won't fit!' But the doctor replied, 'Would you rather be pretty or healthy?—you decide.' The old woman lay in the yard from March till July, almost feverishly, and by summer she had, in fact, put on a nice amount of weight. This was the beginning of her second marriage.

The sun was bitingly hot. After a time it was impossible to escape it; the yellow of the sand and the washed-out cloth of the umbrellas, when you looked back from the sea, nevertheless radiated a great sense of calm. In the final days P. almost lost his sense of time, he built a sandcastle on the shore the entire afternoon, enclosed it with little motes, dug tunnels and raised bridges with the help of small twigs; later, when salt and sweat covered his back, water rushed into the castle; it caved in with the coming of the waves, and he gave up on it as the tide pushed in towards the shore.

Leopold Blumenfeld in certain places made changes to the text. Haman did not originally want to hang Mordechai from a tree but to impale him on a stake. And the height of the stake was fifty cubits. But a cubit is approximately half a metre long, that is, from the stake on which the turn in the story hinges a rope is hung from a height of twenty-five metres. When Leopold Blumenfeld turned the stake into a tree, he lengthened it as well, writing as many ell in place of cubits, which measure seventy-eight centimetres in length. Thus, according to Blumenfeld, Haman rocked in the wind at a height of thirty-eight metres. The hanging ritual, unchanged for centuries, could not have been carried out at such a height. Haman's wrists were bound to his left thigh, a so-called chin-guard was attached to his head, as well as a system of straps which covered his mouth and did not allow movement of his chin, so that he would not disturb the quiet of the city with his shouts. A stool was placed underneath the stake and the noose set around his neck. At this point, the hangman's assistant pulled the rope through the pulleys from behind the stake while the hangman kicked out the stool from under the victim's feet and, with a swift movement, twisted Haman's chin to the side, severing his head from his spinal cord and, with it, his connection to life.

And that very day, King Ahasuerus gave the property of Haman, the enemy of the Jews, to Queen Esther. Mordechai presented himself to the king, for Esther had revealed how he was related to her. The king slipped off his ring, which he had taken back from Haman, and gave it to Mordechai; and Esther put Mordechai in charge of Haman's property.

P.'s mother fell in love with the theatre. She did not miss a single opening; she knew the seats and the smells of the Madách Theatre, the Katona, and People's Army Theatre, she noticed if a new woman was working at one of the coat checks, and everything interested her. Mainly the rehearsals, the great loves, the separations, the fights. And since she considered it her duty to know the lines of the plays, in the summer of '57 she started collecting the booklets of the Film Theatre Music. The first, which she kept in a paper folder with a green cover, was Lajos Nagy's one-act play *A New Guest Is Here*. In 1919, on the evening of the 1st of May in an artist colony on the edge of a city in the country, a few rabble-rousers send for Weisz, the shopkeeper, to bring them wine. The landowner István Petur threateningly shoots the bottle out of Weisz's hands. Just then a member of, and later a commander in, the Red Guard named Mihály appears. He is ready-ing the denunciation of the group, among them the painter Miklós Duhay, who in trying to show by dis-sociating himself from his indolent white friends that he never had any connection to political activities, painted the same way under the kingdom and the repub-lic as he does now under the Hungarian Soviet Repub-lic. At the end of the one-act play, the commander asks Duhay, 'Why are you afraid? You still think they're going to cut off your head? You . . . (*He looks around, his glance falls on the painting*) you'll keep painting. We have a need for the arts. Of course we're not nec-essarily after these kinds of paintings. But you can paint other things, if you'd like.' Crumbling before the commander, he answers, 'Yes . . . yes . . . (*He looks above the door*). But what will happen now? It's awful!' The commander: 'See! You're a real counter-revolutionary.' Duhay: 'Why do you say that, Comrade Commander?' The commander: 'Because you're afraid of us' (*He smiles with piercing irony*). Curtain.

On the back of the armchair by the window, arranged neatly on top of one another, lay a pilled flannel shirt that smelt of cigarettes and sweat, brown cloth pants hard to the touch, a damp pair of underwear that had yellowed around a slit and a pair of rubber socks which were almost always wet. P. could not avoid sitting in that chair. If he did not do it, it would have been an insult, a sly, painful insult, and, as a result, the indescribable disgust and the pangs of conscience remained. Though what was the source of his repulsion? The clothes soaked through with sweat or his father's penetrating, excessively close bodily presence?

And Esther spoke to the king again, falling at his feet, and asked him to avert the evil plotted by Haman the Agagite. And the king extended the golden sceptre to Esther, and Esther arose and stood before the king.

When the remaining portion of the group was on its way home, it happened in Znajm and Brün that when the old woman went into the city together with P.'s mother, every so often, a woman stopped her on the street and asked where she had found her child. The old woman confessed that she had not lost her.

Since all this began to repeat itself, she stopped taking P.'s mother with her, she left her back where the group was resting for the night.

The old woman for ever had sour breath, as though she'd been turning over a piece of cheese under her tongue for who knows how long. While P. bent over the book, or was writing in the blue spiral note-book, he constantly felt that breath on the back of his neck, enclosing him, the book, and the notebook in a single sour cocoon.

And Esther said: 'If I have seen kindness in your eyes, Your Majesty, and if the proposal seems right, let dispatches be written undoing the Haman son of Hammedatha the Agagite's plans. For how can I bear to see the disaster which will befall my people, and how can I bear to see the destruction of my kindred?'

The first girls to knit at P.'s grandmother's house worked in shifts at the state knitting factory. The old woman always referred to them as girls, though they were not much younger than she. They came over after work for one or two hours; wearing nylon work clothes and slippers they stood by the machine, clusters of varicose veins visible between their clothes and socks. And holding the bone-coloured handle for hours on end, they pulled the machine back and forth on the track. How to operate the machine was guarded as a secret of the trade. Each of them promised to teach the old woman, but they didn't mean it, since they feared for their places. And she, when she could, watched them from the door to see what they were doing and why, but could not figure it out. Until, finally, one night it came to her in bed. The next day, she went over to the machine and right away made herself a sweatshirt; she picked a pattern for the front from the machine's sample books.

On the evening of 23 October 1956, *Intrigue and Love* was playing at the National Theatre. When Miller, the court musician, was being dragged off by the bailiffs in accordance with the prince minister's order, and his daughter, Luise, was writing the fateful letter to Court Marshal von Kalb, it seemed as though shooting could be heard from outside. Ambulances raced down the Ring Road, many people had reason to believe that they were not carrying the sick but the secret police. Luise's terrible words were still ringing in her ear: 'They say that women are fragile and weak—don't believe any of that, Father! Perhaps we may be frightened by a spider, but we do not shrink away from dark death. You should know, Father, that your daughter is happy now.' Arriving at Lujza Blaha Square, P.'s mother did not dare go all the way down Rákóczi Street. It was ten o'clock at night. She headed down to Dohány Street, armed men opposite her. Turning right in front of the synagogue she started to run to get home sooner. The guard was not yet standing at the gate. The door was open, and when she went into the entryway, it turned out the old woman was not home. P.'s grandfather was sitting next to the table in just his underwear, it was almost impossible to get it out of him that the old woman had gone out in the direction of the National Theatre; it seemed like they had missed each other. At this, P.'s mother became very angry, she would have asked most kindly whether he would let her go back out while he sat there in his underwear; instead, she sprinted back down to the street and waited anxiously by the gate entrance to catch a glimpse of her mother. Some time before midnight, she saw her coming from the direction of Deák Square. She looked surprisingly calm.

And King Ahasuerus said to Queen Esther and Mordechai, 'I have given Haman's property to Esther, and he has been hung from a tree. Write in the king's name as you see fit and seal it with the king's signet. For an edict written in the king's name and sealed with the king's signet cannot be revoked.'

Every so often, a greyish brown city butterfly snuck in through the window and, for the entire night, could not find its way out. Just as with the flies, P. caught butterflies but rarely tortured them; spreading out their wings, he preferred to look at them, he could hardly get enough of the sight of their monster-like little masks. It was also a surprise to find a rich fur above the abdomen similar to the plumage of a bird. And there above the wings was the head, a strong line between the eyes and underneath it an enormous proboscis for the size of its head. P. imagined how scary a butterfly would look, if by some miracle it were to grow to human size. But for now, the situation was reversed. He knew that his fingers were much more powerful than this little creature, and that he could do anything to it.

There were signs by which one could have deduced that P.'s father, months or only weeks before —it was difficult to know when—had cheated on P.'s mother. Of course it wasn't certain that P. understood these signs correctly. He could imagine the situation, anyhow, and tried to picture the sort of woman complicit in his father's affair. Someone taller than his mother, and blonde. He thought of one of his father's colleagues from work. He already knew enough to know that this sort of thing happened. And there were also signs that his mother had cheated on his father years before, at the very least, there were mentions of a certain a 'Trabant man', whom she went to see after work. One could come to this conclusion from the words that rang out amid their arguments. To P., every word was important.

And the king's scribes were summoned at that time, on the twenty-third day of the third month, that is, the month of Sivan, and letters were written, at Mordechai's dictation, to the Jews and to the satraps, the governors and the officials of the one hundred and twenty-seven provinces from India to Ethiopia: to every province in its own script and to every people in its own language, and to the Jews in their own script and language. He had them written in the name of King Ahasuerus and sealed with the king's signet.

After 30 October 1956, the residents of the house organized a twenty-four-hour guarding of the gate, with changes every two hours. They also divided up among themselves who would go out for bread and lard. Strangers were not allowed in. After twelve years, everyone was crouching again in the shelter. News had come that they had written up the names of the Jews in the nearby houses, and that there were other lists in circulation, too. There was a certain likelihood to this, without a doubt, for there were always lists. Here, anyhow, it didn't occur to anyone to write down names. The children played cards until they were bored, and then played some more. After 4 November, someone lost his patience in the neighbouring house and fired at a tank from the window. The tank very casually rotated its turret and, with grenades and machine guns, shot up the entire street. For days, they cleaned up the glass and rubble. Everyone already had experience doing this.

And the movements repeated themselves from day to day. P.'s grandfather set out his shaving mirror on the kitchen table, took out his Moscow electric razor from his case, plugged it in, and, as the blade touched his face, the little bee-like buzz of the razor became an electric grinding sound.

For a day the hot wind arriving from deep in Africa dried out Haman's body; for a day he hung from the heights of the narrowest tower in the royal palace. Mordechai, after stepping out of the king's court, stumbled across the city in a daze from the heat among the yellow walls. With his mouth open, he breathed in the hot, dusty air with increasing difficulty, his tongue dried out and swollen. He watched as the couriers galloped from the palace in herds of fast royal horses and, advancing past the centre of the market square, disappeared in the direction of the gates. He wanted to follow them but it would have been like entering a maze. The small alley-like streets, the carpenter's, the saddler's, the smith's, on which at other times one could hardly walk, what with all the people looking in shop windows and servants shouting; but now there was hardly a shop open on any of them, as though they were ensnaring him in a trap; and they led him back to the same corner where Hatach had found him two days before. Shushan was a dead city, the great distance trembled yellow behind it. And the next day, the terrible massacre had its start. It was hard to know precisely who killed whom and why, not even whether the situation was indeed serious or not. From the far reaches of the city, news arrived, almost by the hour, of lynchings and clashes; but by the time anyone could arrive to do something against the untempered emotions, the unrestrained feelings, they were met with quiet streets and locked-up houses.

P. would have stopped reading there with pleasure, to say nothing about the writing. Even the sight of the blue spiral notebook repulsed him. But he was too far along in the story of Mordechai and Queen Esther to have left it then, to have asked his grandmother one more time—and it was not only his curiosity that wouldn't have allowed this; soon he began to take an interest again in what might happen next, not simply because of the barely perceptible, nevertheless quite real, threat that his grandmother's strictness presented. What kind of celebration could have come out of all this revenge? Haman's hatred—directed at a small, despised people—revealed Mordechai's true face, but not at the moment when Haman flew into a rage against him, but when he turned his maniacal hatred against himself, as Mordechai exited the king's palace with the golden crown on his head, wearing the crimson-and-white royal garb and the red silk cloak. Was this then the great triumph? P. felt his grandmother's fear for the first time. She was the one trapped in Shushan's alley-like streets, and turning his head halfway to the old woman, he had the vague feeling that whichever way she turned, she would never find her way out of the labyrinth of the empty, peopleless, dead city.

P. and his grandfather crossed a park on the way home. A path laid out with concrete slabs divided the wide, grassy area in two. On the side of the path, old women sat on benches. They sunned themselves and fed pigeons from a bag. They scattered a handful of seeds or crumbs and the birds, fluttering their wings, hurried over. The pigeons remained wild and the old women invited this wildness.

And the letter, which was sealed with the king's signet, permitted the Jews in every city to assemble and fight for their lives; if any people or province attacked them, they could destroy, massacre and exterminate its armed forces, together with women and children, and plunder their possessions.

P.'s grandfather was somehow always old. Before the ambulance came for him and placed him in a wheelchair, he waited a pitiful half-day entirely helplessly in a worn-out, brown armchair. His feet hung down from underneath his bathrobe. His ankles were thinner than P.'s wrists. There was nowhere else to look. Everything had the smell of vinegar.

In the middle of the park, behind the benches, rose a fountain. Gazing at the old women was a statue of a bearded old man, a stone tray above his head, the muscles in his arms and legs flexed, his feet hidden in sandals, and standing in the middle of the tray was a beautiful girl, her flowing stone dress gathered in the usual folds, her stone hair up in a simple bun. She also balanced a tray on her head, smaller than the old man's, and water from one tray was flowing into the other. Behind the curtain of water the old man seemed to be smiling.

The time came and went, and with increasing frequency P. and his father paid tribute to his favourite pastime: argument. Real passion, and the passion for contradiction, flared up in both of them, into which just as much feeling was added—hurt, love, anger, the bitterness of 'either him or me'. The most important question, from which all else stemmed, and into which all else flowed, was the old dilemma of whether experience determines knowledge. They understood the question both as a philosophical abstraction and something entirely concrete. Namely, in their situation the father was experience, and the object of the argument went something like whether P., that is, knowledge, could reach different conclusions than those which experience had given him, and if this was true, did it then prove what a hypocrite he was, how disrespectful. He didn't practise what he preached. Because, of course, the argument never reached the point of whether experience was responsible for supporting and teaching knowledge. If, for example, experience asked, What do you want for dinner?, knowledge did not respond, You shouldn't want to determine me, or say, Hot dog or scrambled eggs, but remained silent, faithful to his ways. Of course, because he knew that a hot dog would still end up on his plate and he could still choose to add mustard or horseradish; he could even take a slice of bread. And if he took one, which naturally he did not need to thank his father for, what would he say, that freedom does not exist? To say nothing of the fact that knowledge would become experience. But experience, think of itself what it may, was still violence and power.

And in every province and in every city, when the king's command and decree arrived, there was gladness and joy among the Jews, a feast and a holiday. And many of the peoples of the land professed to be Jews, for the fear of the Jews had fallen upon them.

For a long time, P. kept the shower water going. He sat in the tub, listened to the deep thrum of the gas flame, sometimes he ran his hands over his stomach and his chest, he took pleasure in the way the water trickled down his face, his neck, his shoulders, all the way down to his groin while memories, remains of thoughts, passed before him. When he looked up he saw that above the sink the mirror was covered in steam, and every so often a drop of water ran down it.

During conversation, P.'s grandfather fell asleep more and more often. If they were not speaking to him, he simply turned off; sitting in a backless chair, he stared ahead with watery eyes, rested his arm on the back of the armchair, soon his head lolled to the side, his eyes closed, his chin dropped and you could see his tongue, in his empty, toothless mouth, which looked as though it were covered in a thin layer of mould.

And on the thirteenth day of the twelfth month— that is, the month of Adar—the very day on which Haman had expected to get them in their power, the opposite happened, and the Jews got their enemies in their power.

On Sundays, P.'s father could never stay very long in bed. He woke up at dawn, went out to the kitchen, turned on the radio, ate something and started preparing the meal. They broadcast a programme on the radio for village business owners. P.'s father clattered the pots and pans in the kitchen cabinet, brought out onions and potatoes in a basket from the pantry, cleaned carrots, sliced up meat and boiled water. He splattered the soup stock on his tank-top. He moved slowly between the kitchen furniture covered in red wallpaper patterns, but his forever exhausted, sanguine face still puffed up like a slow runner's, then receded.

To him these hours represented complete calm. For a while now, he had been far too tired for conversation and paying attention, only sometimes, at really important moments, could he gather himself, but when he did, he radiated poise and confidence. By the time P.'s mother woke up, he was ready with almost everything. P.'s mother put the last touches on the meal. After she tasted the (half-ready) food, because of the quantity of salt and other spices, an altercation between the two of them could not be avoided. P.'s father, offended, marched back to the room. In the wake of their games, they both became increasingly bitter and they became better suited for each other.

Almost everything can be scary in a house. As doors open or close and people stare at one another, or the stairway landings with broken tiles, as a light suddenly goes on or off, the sounds coming from the attic, the bannisters running the length of the courtyard balcony and the distance to the ground, when you lean over, the sun over the roof and the night, the cool ever present in the cellar, the dark, the conversations overheard in the light shaft, the light shaft, the narrow open forgotten windows.

And throughout the provinces of King Ahasuerus, the Jews gathered in their cities to attack those who sought their hurt; and no one could withstand them. And all the officials of the provinces—the satraps, the governors, and the king's stewards—showed defer-ence to the Jews, because the fear of Mordechai had fallen upon them.

On the way home from buying thread, P. and his grandfather sometimes stopped by the tracks that led away from the Ferencváros Train Station. Together they counted how many cars long the trains were, tried to guess what they might be carrying and where they were headed, the cattle transport with barred windows.

P.'s mother was always scared that one day the phone would ring or she would even be there, and she would need to look at that familiar, old body, knowing that these were the last breaths, the last strokes, as though breaking down, losing the rhythm, he were trying to come in to shore, but his body had already sunk, it was only she who did not want this to be the end.

The doctor was impossible to get hold of. The older sister very kindly and readily said that she of course understood P.'s mother's worries, but believe her, as much as she'd like to, there was nothing she could do to help, the doctor didn't come in until the afternoon; it was possible that he was with a patient, in any case, he did not say where she could reach him. The ambulatory service, on the other hand, could not send a car without a doctor's call. This too needed to be understood, since they couldn't just run around the city. The attendant of course did not doubt that P.'s mother had better things to do than joke about such things, such as the fact that her father was lying there with his blood pressure of two hundred and twenty-two, perspiring, white as a ghost, and if the same thing had happened on the street, they would have been willing to go to him there, but not, however, to the apartment.

And Mordechai was now powerful in the royal palace, and his fame was spreading through all the provinces. And the Jews struck at their enemies with the sword, slaying and destroying; they wreaked their will upon their enemies.

Before the High Holidays, P.'s grandfather went out to the kosher butcher to buy chicken and fish. He baked the chicken and made paprikás with the fish. At such times, one could not talk to him. He was on edge, even rude. If someone was standing in the wrong place, which happened quite easily, since P.'s grandfather knew which was the right place, or if someone did not pass him a plate quickly enough or simply did not want to leave the gas burning, they could count on receiving a few unpleasant words. And while he was descaling fish, it was best just not to go into the kitchen at all. From outside, you could hear the clanging of utensils and the clattering of pans. When P.'s grandfather then came in—it was not clear why—standing for a moment next to the table covered in the floral-pattered oilcloth, he looked as though he wanted to smack P., but he only wiped his face. His palm was covered in a cold mucus.

P.'s grandmother often dreamt of her father. She listened to his advice, she never made important decisions without him; it wasn't as if she thought the dead could predict the future, but after their death, slowly, calmly, beyond the unexplainable anger, their spirits filled with wisdom and painful love. The dead to her were just like the living. In death, P.'s great-grandfather watched her movements, he watched what would happen, who remembered him, and if she died, the old woman would do the same thing.

Nearing the end of the book, reading and writing became an oppressive, almost unbearable suffering to P. As though all that he read, like a terrible vision, had been born of his imagination, and now there he stood among the horrible, faceless figures, shouting to them, but no voice would come out of his throat, starting towards them, but his legs would not move. And in the fortress Shushan, the Jews killed a total of five hundred men, Parshandatha, Dalphon, Aspatha, Poratha, Adalia, Aridatha, Parmashta, Arisai, Ariai and Vaizatha, the ten sons of Hammedatha among them, but they did not lay their hands on the spoil.

No one admitted, or no one was willing to admit, that these were P.'s grandfather's last hours at home. They asked him whether he was comfortable where he was, whether he wanted anything to drink, whether he didn't want to move perhaps to the armchair, whether they should draw the drapes. P.'s mother, meanwhile, kept calling the ambulance and the medical centre. P. sat next to the table covered with the floral-pattered oilcloth; from there he looked into the room while he fiddled with scissors, pens and pins. The last hours filled with an impossible waiting. Then, when the elevator gave off a clicking sound in the middle of the afternoon, you could hear as the doors opened then closed, and one moment later they rang up, everything happened too fast: the paramedics lifted P.'s grandfather into a red fold-up wheelchair, put back on his slippers, which had slipped from his feet, adjusted his bathrobe and carted him out of the apartment. On the way out, P.'s mother squeezed her father's arm, she said, Relax, everything will be OK now, and she tried to hold back her tears.

And the daily hospital visits began. On the bus in the afternoons, there was almost always a free seat. From the window, the rainwater trickled down in narrow rivulets; outside, the street radiated the day's rainy light. Even the memory of the late-September warmth had passed; the city now awoke to clouded-over, tired

131

mornings; damp body odours hung in the cars, every-thing slowed down, the passengers stared fixedly out the windows beside them or, inside the bus, a pole, a handle, an empty point in the sky held their gaze while the bus, jerking, creaking, went from one light to the next.

And this terrible vision—as though it said, If you want to see yourself, see yourself first in blood, forsaken—painted the walls of Shushan red. On the fourteenth day of the month of Adar, the bodies of three hundred men lay in the market square. And the Jews got together on that day and killed seventy-five thousand of their enemies, but they did not lay their hands on the spoil.

A row of chestnut trees led the way to the hospital. The wind carried the sand from a nearby construction site onto the pavement, leaving patches of mud behind. Only rarely did anyone appear on the street, first with a hung head and hurried steps, and the headlights of a car only sometimes lit up the intersection. It took a little under ten minutes to get from the bus to the hospital's little iron gate, where the attendant at the door was no longer stopping visitors by the second day. It was nice to be alone for a bit under the chestnut trees, continuing past the alternating patterned fences, free of thought, and only at the last second, cutting across to the side of the hospital. For P. there was no pain, none of the expected deep feeling in the face of death; he found only the autumn, the dull lights and the rain to be stifling and exhausting, as though he were not the one here and he had read in a book: 'A row of chestnut trees led the way to the hospital.'

For the High Holidays, the family always went together to the temple. They needed to leave early since P.'s grandmother was always anxious that someone might be in their usual seats and she would need to argue. People were hardly gathering in the square in front of the temple by the time the family entered the iron gate. Inside, under the stairs, everyone gave one another kisses, wishing others well, and the women went up to their section. P. no longer had his grandfather take him by the arm, and they walked unhurriedly beside the middle row of benches, where they usually sat. The lamps before the covenant were already lit. The attendant brought out prayer books from the back and put them on the stand extending before the bema. While the benches filled up, you saw the same faces that you saw each year, the same people in the same suits greeted one another the same way, they chatted, even when the organ sounded, but from the colour of their hair, the thickening backs of the heads, you could tell that they were getting older. And then the year came when P.'s grandfather was no longer sitting in his usual place. P. drew closer on the bench to his father; he placed his palm over his son's hand, and they stayed as a pair.

And the fourteenth day of the month of Adar was made a day of merrymaking and feasting, and as a holiday and an occasion for sending gifts to one another, sweet pastries, and making costumes and masks.

Still today, Leopold Blumenfeld was the last rabbi in the town where P.'s family came from. After his death, a story about him went around town. When Leopold Blumenfeld awoke before the gates of heaven, he knocked to be let in. From inside, the angel at the gate asked who was there. And he answered, 'It's the last rabbi, I ask you, please, let me in.' Just then it seemed as though the sound of laughter could be heard behind the gate. And the angel at the gate said, 'The thing is, right now all the spots in heaven are filled, there's a terrible crowd, we're not taking any more.' And Leopold Blumenfeld shouted, 'But I left so many down there, and so many still haven't even been born!' And the angel at the gate said, 'What kind of rabbi are you? You didn't know that the heavens are filling up with just one name?' Then, laughing, he added, 'And don't think that you're the last.'

P.'s grandfather gathered up all sorts of possessions from the tops of garbage cans and brought them up to the apartment. Boxes, string, saying, These will be good to pack; but a sweatshirt appeared from time to time, a strap or an alarm clock, too, and on one occasion, he came home with a short linen coat with little checks, which he took to the laundry that week, and from that moment on, the jacket practically could not be taken off him, sometimes even on cooler summer days he wore it in the street.

Several days before his grandfather took a turn for the worse and needed to be taken to the hospital, P. had something to do close to his grandparents' apartment. It did not occur to him to go up and see them, at this point he rarely did such things, he ran up to see them for half an hour twice, at most three times a month. When he was finished and came out of an office, near the temple, he noticed his grandfather in the passageway of a house downtown. He could have continued on his way, his grandfather certainly hadn't seen him, since he hardly sensed what was two or three metres in front of him. He was wearing the checked coat brought in from the garbage, blue underwear hung out from under his belt and reached his waist above a threadbare sweatshirt. P. went over to him, asked him where he was going and naturally promised that he would visit them in a few days time. As they said goodbye, P.'s face came in contact with his grandfather's. He should have been prepared for it, but he was still surprised how wet his grandfather's skin had felt on his own—the faces of the elderly are always wet.

And Mordechai recorded these events and sent dispatches to all the Jews throughout the provinces of King Ahasuerus, near and far, instructing them to observe the fourteenth and fifteenth days of Adar, every year. For on these days, the Jews enjoyed relief from their enemies, and the day's grief and mourning were transformed to that of festive joy.

And P.'s mother called the doctor each morning from her workplace. No, he said, her father's blood count had shown no signs of improvement. I think regular dialysis will be necessary. He's still lucky that his heart is in such good condition. I ask that you trust me, Miss, your father is in good hands, he is not experiencing any pain, we are doing everything that we can.

In the last few years, the family watched over each step of the deterioration of his body, the lack of appetite, the spells of dizziness, the greying of his skin. There, in the face changed from ageing was still the one they recognized, the familiar movements, the hoarse laughter and words—when P. walked with his grandfather they never hurried; they said, We don't hurry, no need, my colleague, we have time.

P.'s father changed in those days. He became meek with restraint and emanated an entirely different strength than before. In his robust figure there was a kind of frailty, despite which he could still be relied on. He knew for a fact that his father-in-law had weeks

to live at best. He had been through the many pro-
longed months of his own father's death, who in 1955
was so devastated by lung cancer that almost every
memory had died with him; he passed on to his son
only his severity and moral statements inflexible to
contradiction.

And the Jews undertook and irrevocably obligated
themselves and their descendants, and all who might
join them, to observe these two days in the manner prescribed and at the proper time each year. These days
are recalled and observed in every generation: by
every family, every province and every city. And these
days of Purim shall never cease among the Jews, and
the memory of them shall never perish among their
descendants.

P.'s grandfather's arm and hand were the colour of
a ripe plum. All the veins on his arm were cracked,
there was no space where they could slide in the needle.
Meanwhile, he did not know what he was saying. On
the opposite side of the hospital room, he saw a large
pile of potatoes and needed to brush off the many ants
from the blanket. His nose had grown, his ears, his
tongue stuck to the roof of his mouth, and he thought
of how he had been fired from his work in '68. By
morning, his pyjamas were always covered in blood.
If he was awake, he was insufferably grumpy, especially with the old woman. He kept repeating that a
wife's place is beside her husband.

But she could not bear to spend more than twenty minutes by his bed. There were five people in the six-bedded hospital ward. Those who could still get up took care of their business in a pail placed beneath a seat with a hole, which the nurses took out three times a day. The smell of excrement and urine were never completely aired out of the ward. Meanwhile, outside in the October autumn, summer returned for one or two days. The chestnut trees in the yard opened up their leafless branches, and the sun shone warmly on the faces of the patients. But in the hospital ward, only problems came of this. One time they had left windows open, one time they had left them closed, when they were tucked in they were hot, when they were untucked they were cold. They slept again like babies.

And Esther sent a letter to the Jews in all the provinces of the realm of Ahasuerus with an ordinance of equity and peace. And Esther's ordinance validating the observances of Purim was recorded in a scroll.

The white cabinet standing beside the bed collected more and more things of fruit juice. P.'s grandfather could no longer be made to drink, he could not take down fluids. But there were still moments of hope. He made a fuss about putting things in order on his shelf and had someone take his blanket home, since he was convinced that someone wanted to steal it. When they brought it home, however, he started to miss it, saying, the cold only comes from the walls at night, it would be good to stick between the wall and his bed. In the garden of the hospital, the old woman, in tears, complained, You have no idea what I needed to put up with, only I know how much he nagged.

To look up one more time at the blue of the sky and say, The sky is blue, to look out one more time at the trees in the lawn and say, It is autumn.

And one needed to listen to the exasperated shouts of his last morphine dreams. When P. turned and said, Go to sleep, he felt at once an endless pity and something else, that this moment was taking place unapproachably far away. When he went out through the door, he felt no pain, only a lightened emptiness. He fled, from the smell of excrement in the ward, down the dark and narrow corridor, past the blank, bitter glances.

Then back on the same street. Many people must have travelled here, sunken into themselves, without thoughts, with lowered heads. Under the moth-eaten chestnut trees, puddles had appeared, the rainwater gleamed blackly between the strata of concrete; one needed to pay attention to avoid everything else.

All of Mordechai's might and powerful acts, and a full account of the greatness to which the king advanced him, are recorded in the Annals of the Kings of Media and Persia. Because Mordechai was ranked next to King Ahasuerus and was highly regarded by the Jews and popular with the multitude of his brethren; he sought the good of his people and interceded for the welfare of all his kindred.

P.'s grandfather passed away with anger. The old woman had the apartment cleared, all of the junk that had accumulated over the years she threw out, she had the bed swapped out, the arm chairs, the kitchen cabinet, and cried a good deal.

The arrangements for the burial quickly needed to be made. They sent announcements to relatives, looked for a rabbi, wrote down for him on a sheet of paper the Hebrew name of the deceased, jotted down beside a few dates the more important events of his life, that is to say, they put together for the burial speech that he was always a loving son to his parents, that he was the only one of his family to have survived the war and that he had found true comfort in death. They also added for the rabbi's sake whom he should mention by name among the mourners during the speech.

P. recited the Mourner's Kaddish. He practised it for two days so that standing by the grave he would be able to say it, davening, as is custom. There in his pocket was piece of paper with the text phonetically transcribed in Hungarian; he thought that he would take it out if he needed it, but he didn't dare. He needed to read the prayer from a paper, the rabbi's fingers ran across each line, pointing to where they were. Then towards the end, as one might expect, P. faltered, then continued, but incorrectly. The rabbi corrected each word, and this bothered him greatly. Who grants peace in Heaven delivers us peace, he read, stuttering. Then came those offering condolences, and he allowed them to shake his hand, to squeeze his shoulder, to embrace him. Later everyone finally filtered out along the gravelly path of the cemetery and, for a few moments, he remained alone with the covered flowers, before the earthen mound of the grave—

Lazarus

TRANSLATED BY OTTILIE MULZET

The translator would like to acknowledge the kind support of the Translators' House in Balatonfüred, Hungary, where this translation was partially completed.

He steps from one colour onto another. The lowering son
an arching blade. On a shadow-camel beneath the
        curving arch
blindly he trudges round and round,

as if sand and stone could yet again fall,
the mirror-desert break apart and the dead,
setting off, could start towards Damascus,

To barter and trade the colours, but the arching sword
cannot descend, round and round he trudges on the
        shadow-camel —
green, red, yellow, blue.

Und da sie nichts von seinem Schicksal wußten
so logen sei ein anderes zusammen

'School had yet to begin. Still, they woke up early that day and, as they sat in the larger room, Péter began to tell his son a fairy tale about a fisherman and a water sprite. Péter sensed that the story was captivating his son much more than usual, and he would have liked to make the tale more elaborate, adding new characters, casting the fisherman into a storm and other perils, to make the story last longer, but he could not— he had to go to the hospital. His father had been taken there by ambulance the previous day, and the night before, an operation had been performed.'

That is how this book should begin. But it cannot, because you have forbidden me to write it, and in defiance of your prohibition I am writing about you, about those weeks during which, deprived of your voice, you suffered your last agonies. And now it is my turn to torment you, holding you fast in this silence. I shall build a sepulchre above your grave, made of words— that material completely alien to you in those last weeks—making it impossible that, apart from this book, which shall henceforth be your body and your home, there would be anything else between us; and

147

all the while, I perhaps shall be secretly awaiting that moment where, in a real house, you will open the door for me and be unable to comprehend my surprise. As if your body were consumed by a sudden flame. Without even time for us to scream. A great storm of fire, as if dreaming; we watched the flames, we watched your body as it burnt, and when we awoke, you were nowhere to be found.

'The fisherman took out the dress made of fish scales. The fairy looked at it, turned it over, then she suddenly wrapped herself in it, leapt into the water and swam away. The fisherman, who had only a harpoon, flung it after her. The water flared silver, and the fisherman realized he had mortally wounded the water sprite.' That is how the tale of the fisherman ends. I do not however want to write about the flaring of the water, but of the fire. About fire, about that man whom I knew—that man whom I could give any name at all, your name or someone else's—for the fire has separated you both: he is burnt up, nothing remains of him, while you are in this book, forever entangled with me—you will have to listen to me now, have to put up with my inanities. For the body belongs to no one. There is no way to tell one from the next, and even if there were certain distinguishing signs—a brown cicatrix on the leg, a long scarred gash running from the stomach to the abdomen—couldn't we imagine the same blemish, the same scar on another body? All that you were is nothing now. You live on as nothing, just as I myself am nothing, for I am writing now, although the words do not belong to me. I am writing a body, a burning book. I will let it burn anew, let the words perish with it—but not without a trace, for burning always leaves a mark.

You and I were always people without a language for each other, if in differing ways. For didn't our words usually mean something different from what we were thinking, and even more so from what we were feeling; that is, from what we should have been feeling and thinking, for each of our movements and acts were proof of something completely different than our words, forever corroding the other's self-esteem? Injurious words which we then tried, impossibly, to rectify. You were distrustful, sweeping yourself into permanent misunderstandings and solitude's endless pain, all the while childishly believing that one life can be vindicated by another, and in nothing else. But you never tried to break your truth into words. You thought that if I, for example—in a sneaky and treacherous manner—could divert you for a single moment from your conviction that words are not for conversation, your weakness would be a immediate target for others, at least those with whom you lived. And was this not a manifestation of your own profound self-contempt, fed by your own inferiority complex, chiefly with regard to me, in whom you could see at once your likeness and antithesis; were you not making yourself untouchable, outside my reach with that self-degradation of yours as you cut off every disclosure in advance, asking what did I want 'from a simple peasant' like you? And really, what did I want? I believed for too long that there are healing sentences, and even more strongly that even if they did exist, they could not be pronounced by us; all the same, though, their absence is a failure. It is only now, through this book, that I can speak to you as I have always wished. Not for you to reply, but so that between us there will be neither questions nor answers, which only I can pronounce now; let there be nothing, only the fire; let it burn everything, let it burn up the story that was painful to all; then let the fire itself smoulder out, so that all that remains will be the bare earth, empty flagstone.

When that man—let the first initial of his name be identical to yours; I shall call him M.—awoke briefly from the sleeping pill- and analgesics-induced stupor in his hospital bed, when it was already obvious what was to follow, Péter was turning the name of Lazarus around in his mind, until the name itself was threadbare like a tangle of knotted rope; he twisted it around ever more bitterly and impatiently, wanting a miracle to occur as it did in Bethany in the almshouse, although he must have known that his father would not have been grateful for such a miracle. M. had long since lost his desire for life, and if he had only been able to continue as a piece of human wreckage, deprived even of the possibility of casting life away, it would have seemed an undeserved punishment. Péter, then, wanted the miracle only for himself, so that they could make up for what they had missed, as his father's lack of language forced him into a bashfulness turning into coarseness or even worse, indifference.

Still, it was those two months which had been granted to them—the two months that his father spent in his filthy, sweat-sodden bed-grave—and if by some stroke of luck he might have been able to get up again, a possibility that Péter believed in so strongly until the last week that he could not bring himself to picture the opposite—everything would still have continued in the same way between them, or would have been even worse, for M.'s state after serious illness, the perforated intestine, the stench of excrement and the uncontrollable workings of a muddled consciousness would have embarrassed both of them.

These two months, however, were like a response to everything: their lapses, their faults, perhaps even the necessary derailments of those narratives whose beginnings stretched back to previous generations; a response both feral and grotesque, the jeering, meaningless outcome of their lapses, their errors, their destitution: and hence not even fate, only a feral grotesque mockery, just as, in a matter of two days, their entire previous existence was irresistibly transformed into a single gelatinous substance comprised of machines, tubes, infusion stands, drainages, liquids streaming in and out, bandages, pus, the body composed of half-dead masses of flesh; that substance moulded and uniformly modulated by the white shadows of the nurses, into which M. began to dissolve even well before the actual onset of death. But is it not a betrayal to regard something as an answer when its arrival was welcomed by no one, but experienced as only a blow—and when only caution, clear-sighted judgement or sound instinct could have offered protection? No, there was no meaning to what happened; it was not an answer to anything; it was not even inevitable. As Péter stood by the bed, and—exhausted from the despairing insistence on a miraculous recovery —he would place his hand on his father's arm or forehead, nothing betrayed more his desperation than those moments when he interrupted his own silence, unable to bear it any longer, with a few comments such as 'it's raining' or 'there's a bit of sunshine'.

But what did M. himself experience during this period? Only you could tell me that. But even if you told me, I would hardly understand, I wouldn't even want to understand, because you would never use a word like 'experience'. Your language would be a completely different, made of feverish thought—grimier, more gelatinous and perhaps more direct than words, always with a trace of a hero's stridency. In this language, everything would strive to be heard at once, yet nothing would be audible except for your lungs' spasmodic gurglings and the contracting windpipe, as when you tried to cough, or as when the nurses drained the perpetual liquid discharge through the tube placed in your larynx.

At first, Péter had the impression, through a few movements of his father's hands or a smile, that his father perhaps noticed and even sanctioned their being together, but these gestures soon vanished into incommensurable suffering, which in the last days were something no human existence could ever deserve. Dread was the first to disappear from his father's eyes. When he had been taken to the hospital and was awaiting the first life-saving operation, he had looked at Péter with frightened eyes pleading for help: something Péter had never seen before. His father still could not really believe that what was happening was real: that he would not be able to awaken, that death could come like this—he had known for a long time, however, that death could only come like this, before its time, with inchoate dread. Something wears out, spasms set in, the process of termination starts. And it was not then, but after the second operation, when the 'half-measures' of the first had to be corrected, when Péter no longer saw fear in his father but, rather, an indifferent, apathetic attentiveness, and perhaps much less trust: M. must have felt sensed these natural processes were no longer severable from what we call 'I'— what was happening to his body, within his body, every procedure—was identical to himself; he was now the plaything of nature, of its desire or its relinquishment: of that single material, the pulpy mass animated only by the asystalic beating of the heart, the breaths extracted by the respirator's machinations—of the life-force itself, the desire of separation and disassociation.

Now, however, you are no longer your body, not even the memory of your body. I cannot say what happened to you, and I do not wish to offend your muteness, brought on by the incision in your windpipe; the unperturbed silence of the last two months, interrupted only once or twice by a rattling attempt at speech, an irritated licking of the lips and tongue-clicking which at once descended into an unintelligible murmur: in itself only the sorrowful conclusion of a process that had nonetheless lasted an entire life. And, exactly as before, it is your muteness, the petulant wounded refusal of conversation, that plunged me—always wanting explanations and stories to make the impene-trable bitterness explicable—into a state of absolute despair, compelling me once again to speak, although this time without any hope of response, all the while wishing to preserve the perfect silence of your muteness. Only speech can silence your death.

As I write, there is a photograph in front of me. It is a picture of Péter and M. At the time, M. was thirty-three years old—the age I am now. The picture was taken in the courtyard of M.'s parents' home; visible in the background is a row of bushes, and behind that, a dilapidated unplastered wall; beyond the fence in the distance one senses obscurely, or, rather, suspects, that part of the city—poor, formerly inhabited by Bulgarians, carved up by dirt paths—where M.'s story began. This house was always frightening to Péter. Within the confines of its chill mildewed walls, in the narrow room with a door opening onto the veranda, lay his grandmother, whose face he was, later in life, unable to remember. The interior was perhaps not dissimilar to others of its kind as often described in memoirs: an abundance of rugs laid out on parquet floors, tables, divans and sometimes even carpets covering the walls. In this house as well, it could not have been any different, for Péter's grandmother in her old age, when proper hand-woven carpets were no longer attainable, unceasingly produced embroideries, wall coverings, pillow cases, one after the other, and gave them away. Péter, though, could not remember any of this—not the carpets, not the wall hangings, not the furniture, not the scenes depicted on the white lace curtains; he was even less capable of imagining how all of the carpets would be wrapped up in mothball-scented paper when the rooms were being cleaned before the autumn High Holidays. If he tried to recall his grandmother, he could only see in his mind's eye a shapeless, exhaling body, lying on an improbably high bed—or, rather, he only sensed it, and he felt the body of his grandmother to be a perpetual threat; that, like an over-filled balloon, it would burst and inundate the room with a viscous brown liquid, with the dense and ill-smelling moisture of her distended organs.

In the foreground of the photograph can be seen a father and a son, posed for the shot, although comfortably so: M. is squatting down, his head turned slightly to one side; he smiles proudly into the camera, all the while embracing Péter's stomach with his wide palm; Péter, his elbows positioned on his father's arms, is resting within the proffered sanctuary of the adult frame, leaning with his entire body into his father's thighs, so that his shoulder is directly underneath his father's chin, concealing exactly half of his father's body. As this pose is repeated in other photographs taken at about the same time, always with the front door of the house or a tree-stump forming the backdrop, not only the person behind the lens but M. himself must have been pleased at being photographed with his two-year-old son. The latter, however, never—in any of these pictures—looks at the person behind the lens, but only at his father. He watches from below and from the side, in wonderment, as someone for whom this closeness is welcome but rare. He ignores the camera; or, rather, he himself behaves like a camera, wishing to gaze directly into his father's eyes, to see his face in all of its detail; but however much he strains to turn around, drawing back his left shoulder in the attempt, the chin and one side of his father's mouth are all that the parent reveals of himself.

In M.'s left hand—the one not clasped around Péter's belly but resting on his left knee—there is something loosely grasped between the fingers; in this picture as in all the others. Most of the time, it is a half-smoked cigarette, but in the photograph I have in front of me at this moment, instead of the usual cigarette, there are a few stalks of a lily-of-the-valley. The lilies always grew in the garden a few steps from the silently opening gate. Their scent was the single gift of this house. The innermost parts of the garden showed the work of someone who knew that they had neither strength nor inclination for its upkeep; every plant that might have demanded attention, devotion or exertion had been eradicated, with the exception of the lilies-of-the-valley, so that in the garden behind the house, there were already many arid patches overgrown with thicket, resembling an abandoned graveyard. From time to time, Péter sought out these places, using a tall tree branch for his walking stick. Later on, in his memory, the entire house and garden likewise became overgrown with the thick shrubbery: the walls of the house and the creeping ivy entirely interwoven with the dry branches, at summer's end mottled with spots of colour like congealed blood, down the length of the stone pillars to the black-and-white flagstones, not a single one of which remained intact.

No doubt the lilies had been picked by Péter for his father. Or perhaps for his mother, who, with her usual anxiety that something wasn't taking place between father and son that should have been, might have said to Péter, 'Give them to your papa.' M. is holding the stems of the flowers between his index and middle fingers in front of his son's belly, as if it were a cigarette, as if he were about to flick away the long grey stem of ash that had grown there.

I try to find within myself the feelings that might have arisen within Péter during this nesting pose, in which from the nape of his neck to his heels, with nearly every limb he could sense his father's body, and the two bodies were so close to each other, much closer than they were ever to be later on. It was as if something had shifted, shifted from this feeling of childhood security and peace, but not in me—in that child whose

entire upper body fit into his father's palm and who is
no more, just as you are no more; as I gaze at the picture, I can feel that touch only dimly, but not touching
him and not touching me, only floating somewhere
between the two of us in the voided air; and when I
turn my head away to begin to write, even this dim
apprehension quickly passes away. For now, your
death has extinguished in me all that remained distant
from you. Still, it was probably around the time of this
photograph that a sense of bodily aversion was first
awakened in Péter, an aversion that only became more
painful as the years wore on; and in fact only in those
last two months before his death did everything that
had repulsed him in his father begin to fade. That realization, with its consciousness of failure, came late,
much too late, and not to him but to me: that in the
midst of their perpetual battles, the stakes of which
were nothing less than hope, freedom and, above all,
the human possibility of love, not only did there form
in Péter a kind of acceptance of his father's bottomless
despair and spleen—traits covered over in this picture
by his smile—yet over time he came to feel a secretive
concord; even if incapable of sounding his father's
despair to the very depths, and even if his rebellion
never ceased, he came to feel a certain agreement with
the inevitability of the final conclusions. For they differed from each other so drastically, differences that

were so perilous to each, that if they had been able to examine their behaviour in the years to come, they would have had to assume that M. would crush Péter; for his bitterness and silence, poised so evidently within his manhood, gave him a force that his son was never able to match. Because of that, when his father's strength began to wane and his health, his appetite, his harshness were not what they used to be—for although M. never spoke of memories, nor, for that matter, of anything connected to the past, when arguing (for M., there was no discussion, only argument), he became even more shrill, even rude—when his self-satisfaction and tenacity lost their aura of absolute certainty and his ire less frequently burst into flame, the realization, embarrassing as it was, of how fundamentally little they truly differed from each other struck them both with even more unexpected force.

The house that can be seen in the background of the photograph—in which M. is exactly the same age as I am now—no longer stands. When M.'s mother died, it was sold—Péter did not attend the funeral, yet could nonetheless recall the sale of the house—and the new owner demolished the building to make way for a new one. I would therefore like to locate his father in this house—non-existent and, in Péter's memories, barely perceptible in its invisibility; not so much to look for reasons, the reason why, for example, he became convinced that his feelings, as soon as he would show them, would be used against him, but because I would prefer to dislodge the history of those silences and oblivions—that is all I can do now. I cannot put that narrative back in place—for which we both, you with your silences, I with my compulsive need for speech, were equally late; creatures hermetically sealed off from the possibility of understanding—any more than the new house, itself soon demolished as well, could reveal a trace of the former floor plan; Péter's visit there, years later and of course not in the company of his father, was entirely in vain.

Péter first learnt something about his grandmother in adolescence; exclusively from the—no doubt justifiably—malicious observations of his mother, some of which were uttered within his father's earshot. What he could put together across the years from these observations was that the one-sided enumeration of accusations left his grandmother without any hope of defence, and that M. never once defended his dead mother. The chief accusation was that Péter's grandmother did not contribute to the raising of her own son, leaving that task to various servants and neighbours, at the same time sanctioning in her devotion everything the child did. This phenomenon could also be formulated in a different way, and, I believe, in a sense possibly closer to the truth: that M's parents, both for different reasons, projected their most precious dreams and aspirations onto their son, perhaps even envisaging him directly as the liberator of the family, although it was soon to emerge that he had been born in an age ill-suited to such aims, when, to put it mildly, the chances for liberty were null; later on, it also emerged that M. was not up to the task. But M.'s parents —again, for different reasons—could not take this into consideration, because if they had done so, they would have been forced to realize that there was no point in surviving the laws now threatening their very existence. M., the product of a second marriage—it is characteristic that Péter discovered this only years later, that just like himself, M. was born not of a first but a second union—came into the world at a time when the prohibitions already in existence against him were greatly multiplied, bringing still-newer decrees into force. First he was excluded, strangely enough for a child, from entering into intimate relations with a woman of another race, never to bring her home, never to take her in wedlock. Later, though, such decrees came into being that had a more direct effect upon a child's life, regulating, for example, when he could and couldn't go outside, mandating the wearing of an emblem clearly visible above his heart, sewn onto all pieces of clothing, for the Master of the Law was solicitous and loving; and finally, one fine day, there came the decision that M. and his mother would move into the cellar of a benevolent neighbour, where they dared neither to weep nor to make even the slightest noise, for if the servants of the law were to come upon them, they—and these very neighbours—would be slaughtered on the spot.

When her son was born, M.'s mother was no longer young. She knew that if she lost him, she would have no one left. At the same time, she was aware that she had only him, and that was not enough. She was employed as a bookkeeper for a commercial enterprise; judging from her name, the family had long since assimilated and she herself no doubt carried within herself all pettiness, insecurities and arrogance of the Jewish petty bourgeoisie of Pest in the 1920s, crippling herself with her envy of those whom she perceived as having more successfully escaped their own fate than she had. This was reflected in the malignant yet most likely justified observation of Péter's mother: that after the war, her mother-in-law, all party affiliations aside, fervently lamented the 'good old days' of the time of her son's circumcision, when sorbet had been ordered from Hauer's. But didn't her compulsive adherence—causing justified aversion in others, yet at the same time understandable—not only to the past, but to what one of the finest confectioners in Pest embodied, the assurance that one could be the master of one's own fate, conceal a hopelessness, even more inadmissible than bereavement and ostracism, regarding all that was to come in her son's life? That defiance—with its obstinate refusal of the hope of liberation—that M. most likely instinctively cultivated within himself from early childhood, coupled with his experiences at school, was not a form of self-validation; instead of launching his vindicatory conquest, it drove him to the draymen's stables and the Bulgarian gardeners' flower beds, and must have deprived his mother of the last shreds of joy in life. Certainly she could not admit to herself her son's ignoble betrayal. As compensation, she demanded one thing: to keep the traitor continually by her side, to chain him jealously to herself, so that he would never belong to anyone else; there he could do his expiation and penance, and she would ultimately receive from life the trifling recompense that was her just reward.

The figure of M.'s father is more enigmatic. A legend persists—one that later Péter himself readily told and may even be true—that his family had come to Hungary from Galicia some time towards the end of the nineteenth century, from a certain region where — according to another legend—bandits, pious Hasidim, perverse nobles, and untamed Hutzuls arriving from the Carpathians felt themselves at home; a region where, not long after his family purportedly set off on their southwards migration, a certain chief lieutenant, Kiekeritz by name, who had just executed a prisoner-of-war in a forest, was himself overtaken by death on the tumbledown steps of a third-rate Jewish guesthouse in a derelict town; the bullet, however, ultimately came to rest in the skull of Second Lieutenant Carl Joseph von Trotta, who after the shot took one more faltering step, then fell to the ground, knocking over two overflowing buckets, while from below, the Ukrainian peasants cried out in chorus, 'Hail to thee, Lord Jesus!'

M.'s grandparents upheld their faith, although it would be difficult today to determine exactly what that meant, and how religious they really were. It might have been simpler for Péter to visualize his great-grandfather in terms of Kafka's depiction of Rabbi Löwy: defiant, high-strung, the ever-faithful servant of truth, restless; but the reality was that he was incapable of visualizing him, just as Kafka was incapable of visualizing Löwy; still, there he was before Kafka's eyes: what he writes about him seems more befitting of Moses or any other patriarch than of a living human being. I myself am not capable of seeing M.'s grandfather as a living human being, but merely as a legend existing before history or, more accurately, before the writing of this book; a legend which I could embellish as fancifully as I wish and, in doing so, I would not exactly be consigning him to oblivion, as M. did, almost completely forgetting about him—but, rather, I would be asserting that he never even lived, that he came into being as a fairy tale devised by someone a long, long time ago, telling the story over and over again, until even the story-teller forgot what tale he was relating, and the story in this book could be given only one title: the Closed Gate.

M.'s grandparents never could have been real to him, at least once he reached adulthood. Once, when Péter asked M. for his grandfather's name, M. had to stop and think about it, and even though he eventually came up with something, his hesitancy was all too obvious. Greater than his uncertainty, however, was his incomprehension of why it would even occur to Péter to ask such a thing. Indissolubly linked to the memory of M.'s grandparents' house was the recollection of certain 'Jewish' foods, which M. himself strove to prepare in the least 'Jewish' way possible; yet these visits could not have been too great in number, given the short amount of time remaining to them. And in any case, as Péter was to discover—this time not from his mother, but from another relative's equally malicious yet in all likelihood equally objectively verifiable observations—M.'s mother was on equally bad terms with both her in-laws until their deaths.

And indeed, didn't everything beyond these sensory impressions belong to the realm of legend, didn't

M.'s memory function more effectively when the place of recollection was not his heart or mind, but his stomach? Not names or stories but, rather, tastes and scents, which are completely different and can be discerned even from recipes that diverge from the original. Why would anyone reach for what is hidden? Why try to find what has vanished? I have a need for stories, nonetheless, just as Péter in his childhood made up all sorts of narratives about his father, his mother and himself, which, as M.'s meticulous detective work always decisively proved, were lies. Because doesn't everything that wants to be a narrative become one— wasn't it a story that led to the creation of this world, or, to put it even more precisely: we can never have mastery over objects, inasmuch as we can only create something by telling a story? In the meantime, I only want to talk to you, about your body, about the impressions of those two final months when, deprived of your voice, you suffered your final agonies, about your body, which always repelled me and, as far as I was concerned, was the only real obstacle to the mute path of our coexistence. But your body is for me a narrative; who knows, perhaps the only one which I am able to tell; the only one which I am forced to tell. So that this book will not only be your grave but, at the same time, the place of your birth; a body which I shall give to you in place of another; a body which you shall inevitably detest. You shall be born and shall die; you will live and at the same time not live, in this same book.

In M.'s family, silence was the amniotic fluid of life—perceptible, tangible to all, the medium of the beginning and the end: emanating in all directions, mainly from the impenetrable solitude of the men in the family. And that is how I picture them: as bodies standing next to each other in dreadful suffocation, each absorbing the solitude of the other, consuming it, digesting it and consuming it anew, until they all become as one material, now truly having been become each other's kin; all the while not desiring anything but freedom and independence; something that is indigestible by both resemblance and instinctive repulsion; something that resists solitude.

When M. was lying in his hospital bed, and the sight of his wife and son occasioned resentment rather than joy—for he no longer belonged to them, and with their dull-witted mechanical exhortations to hang on, to pull himself together, they did not want to see this— there at once awakened in him a sense of capitulation to the mute and final material of solitude, and to the grim intoxication of an unlikely liberation; that in the last moments he had successfully escaped from the suffocating proximity of those bodies, for he did not have to die among those with whom he had lived but, rather, among his new set of acquaintances, the young

nurses of whom he knew nothing, apart from the pleasure of their touch—and who likewise knew nothing
of him, although perhaps instinctively they suspected
everything.

And yet the stifling and mute proximity of these
bodies still created stories—silenced stories, which in
the succession of generations rendered the muteness
evermore impenetrable, until every trace of the original was completely eradicated. M.'s father had had
three siblings. One brother and two sisters. Péter had
heard different things about them, all seemingly
incredible, though it seemed likely that one of the sisters and the brother—who had already started his own
family—had never obtained Hungarian citizenship, or,
more accurately, had never foreseen the necessity of
doing so. Thus they remained, in accordance with the
family's place of origin, citizens of Poland, 'Galician
Jews'. As such, when in July 1941, the Cabinet issued a
decree for all Polish citizens residing in Hungary—that
is, as Poland no longer existed, those with no citizenship, 'the stateless' and their kin—to be rounded up, the
two siblings and the brother's family were among the
first to be placed in a cattle car and sent back to where
they had come from, or where they were supposed to
have come from; forced to journey to a mythical land,
expelled from any story that could conceivably be told,
and only permitted to take with themselves, to this land

existing nowhere on earth, one small suitcase of personal possessions. The gendarmes came for them at night. The next day it rained from morning to night, at first drizzling, bursting into a shower of tiny drops, then relenting slightly. Everything was grey, and from morning to evening the family ran back and forth to Páva utca—where the gendarmerie had ordered all stateless persons to assemble—bringing what they could: shoes, coats, bread. It did not occur to them to bring their winter boots; this would later on figure as a particular item in the list of omissions. In the meantime, M.'s older cousin—who had changed his surname to a Hungarian one while it was still possible and played forward on a village football team in Transdanubia, thus also acquiring Hungarian citizenship— tried to save his parents from deportation at the last minute, or failing that, at least to go with them. To this end, he used what connections he had, but the management of the football club gave him to understand— more precisely, permitted him to suspect—that he would be better off dropping his interest in the subject; his parents were beyond help now and he would only be putting himself in danger.

According to a different, no less legendary, version, everything that occurred was the result of a mistake. M.'s great-grandmother—for we need now briefly to retreat even further back in time, if indeed it is still time and not something more like a fairy tale,

like the one about the water sprite and the fisherman—
M.'s great-grandmother, after the death of her first husband, left with four little children, married a Galician
Jew, who also soon passed away; the family then
moved back to Hungary. M.'s grandfather nonetheless
became convinced that he had been born not in
Budapest but in Poland; this was the information he
dictated in every office; it figured on all of his documents. And if this mistake—in place of the creation of
the defiant, high-strung, truth-loving, restless, in short,
the fairy-tale patriarch—made him, if not a living real
person, at least one more suited for a real story, the
result of his obstinate misapprehension was also the
attribution of Polish citizenship to everyone in the
family. One of the sisters, thanks to her husband, was
at a later date able to acquire Hungarian papers. She
could not have known that ten years later, this would
mean the difference between life and death. M.'s father
perhaps did know when, at the end of the 1930s, he
submitted an application for naturalization, though
without informing his parents or his siblings. At that
time, there was practically no hope of a Jew obtaining
Hungarian citizenship, so perhaps he too was able to
use certain connections to get it; in all likelihood, that
decision was not meant to determine whether everyone
in the family, or only him, could have a chance at survival, but, rather, if he could rescue himself from the
collective fate of the others. His younger sister, his

younger brother and sister-in-law, together with their son on the threshold of manhood, were transported with the other 'quislings'—that is, collaborators—to the town of Kolomea in Galicia. Quisling: that was the word, the name of one former prime minister of Norway, written on one of the labour-camp postcards sent back to the family in Hungary, or at least so the story went. Once, M.'s uncle wrote that they were living with a family in Kolomea, that his sister often sang to the family's little boy but that in doing so often began to weep. And at one time the boy asked her, 'Why are you crying, are you a quisling too?'

Péter never saw this postcard; it was lost. I've seen many like it, though, written with a mechanical pencil, the writing worn down to the point of illegibility, and the paper it is written upon also turned grey. I really cannot say if a little boy would perhaps ask such a question in 1941.

On another such postal card, M.'s uncle related how they were invited to the house of the chief rabbi of Kolomea for the autumn High Holidays. It must have been at the rabbi's that they heard the old story, itself a legend as well, of why the name of Yahweh was inscribed in Hebrew letters on the cross at the top of the tower of the small chapel not far from the market square. Many, many years ago, when the Catholics of the town decided to build the chapel, the builders and the members of the congregation saw with fear that with each passing day, the newly completed church was sinking a little further into the ground. The priest and the bishop of Kolomea were at a loss as to what to do. At last, someone suggested that they talk to Rabbi Chaim, who had recently arrived in Galicia from Czernowitz, and was well known for his piety. The bishop went to see Rabbi Chaim, and the rabbi said to him, 'Even I cannot help you, Bishop. In a case like this, only the Almighty Himself can do so. Inscribe his name at the top of the cross, and if He sees that you have praised Him on high, perhaps He will be merciful.' Thus it was done, and from that day onwards, the church sank into the ground no more. And this is how the chapel in Kolomea became the only Christian house of worship upon which the name of the Almighty is inscribed in Hebrew letters. M.'s uncle and the rabbi must have laughed together at this story but no doubt fallen despondent very soon after, for those times had long since passed. Before the Russian army occupied Lemberg, most of those living in the vicinity had fled to Kolomea, and from there across the Romanian border into Czernowitz. There were many as well— chiefly Zionists—who, hearing of the imminent Russian invasion, opted instead for those regions of Poland now occupied by Germany. The worst off were the ones who remained behind—awaiting first the arrival of the Russians, then the Germans—in Galicia. M.'s uncle wrote that they had taken part in a great feast at the rabbi's house in Kolomea. Perhaps they dined on maize with baked potatoes.

This story, which no one in the family was capable of telling without inconsistencies and gaping holes, was heard for the first time by both Péter and M. together. Before that, M. only knew that his aunt and uncle had been 'taken away' and that they 'didn't come back'. He never knew anything about the postal cards sent from the labour camp. Not even about the very last one, dated December 1941, which contained only this sentence: 'It is midnight, we are being rounded up, and I do not know what is to be our fate.'

These words were written by M.'s uncle, but is the significance of this statement not really the following: 'I know what our fate is to be, and you knew it too when you left us alone in Páva utca'? What followed could not have been deduced from anything: they were sent there, they were murdered—for that is still fate. And is what we call fate ever anything but a mass of blunders and deceptions, vain intentions orchestrated and re-orchestrated, which in order to enhance our capacity for endurance, ever increasing the embellishments, we view as a coherent path? M.'s uncle did not write this, but the silence that followed his statement— the silence that we must reach—expresses something

akin to your muteness. How many times did you
admonish me to beware of the dangers, not only of
blind faith but of all hope as well, and how intolerable
to me was the despairing simplicity of the oft-repeated
phrase 'you keep walking, walking, and then you fall
down'? I should relate the story of M.'s family in your
language, a language in which there is neither hope nor
hopelessness, no exaggeration, only an exacting self-
hatred that takes everything into account. Although
you were not extreme even in that, because—despite
your attempts to conceal it—you too were sentimental.
If there was no fear in you and no self-love whatsoever,
there remained a definite residue of self-pity.

In that house in whose courtyard Péter's mother—
for who else could have it been—photographed M.
with his son, as he clutched the stems of the lilies in his
fingers, no word was ever spoken about those who
were sent away, or even about the significance of the
decision, after that event, of M.'s father to have himself, along with his new wife and child, baptized in the
Lutheran faith. Why should anything have been said?
After the perils and unpredictability of the preliminary
stages, the final denouement was too clear. And, as far
as Péter had been able to judge, it was precisely the
vivid consciousness of this result that made the gaze of
everyone around him—primarily the men and particularly his father—so impatiently sharp. As if they had

all been the sum total of a calculation, the deductions and incidental errors of which they were unable to discern; indeed, any such effort on their part would have been wasted, because the accuracy of the final sum resulted not from deduction, but from the certainty that nothing in their lives could have been otherwise, and that however much Péter might protest, he too would repeat it.

The circumstances surrounding the deaths of the deportees were long concealed from the family. Late in 1942, the sister who had remained in Hungary met with a driver who had been in Kolomea. He said that before the prisoners were shot, they were forced to dig their own graves, and that after the soldiers had covered the ditches with earth, the ground was still moving. Most of the deportees from Hungary had been sent to Kamenetz-Podolsk; the Russian army had retreated from there only a few weeks earlier. At the end of August, an SS division, accompanied by a Hungarian military engineering unit, surrounded the camp and ordered the prisoners to set off on a forced march. After walking some fifteen kilometres, they came to an area devastated by bombs. There, the prisoners were ordered to undress, and after that they were gunned down. That is what the driver might have seen.

M.'s uncle, however, had not sent the cards from Kamenetz-Podolsk but from Kolomea, and in the winter of 1941, they were indisputably still alive. So what had actually occurred? As late as a year after, people in that district were still being rounded up. I once found in an archive the report of the police commander who, in September 1942, directed the transfer of the Jews from eastern Galicia. Oberkommandant Wassermann reported to his superiors on 14 September that in the first days of that month—thanks to the meticulous preparation of the operation as well as the smooth cooperation of the police division and other forces—the transfer to Kolomea of Jews from the surrounding towns of Skole, Stryi and Hodorov had been successfully completed without the least case of resistance. Here, on 7 September, all persons were ordered to present themselves for registration at the assembly point of the Reichsarbeitsamt. A total of 5,300 people were registered, in addition to the 600 who were led out by Wassermann's men from the sealed ghetto. The loading of the rail wagons was completed that same evening, each being crammed with a total of 200 persons. It is therefore easy to calculate that 24 wagons in all were required, as slightly more than 1,000 individuals were also transferred to the capacity of the security forces. Here, let us allow Oberkommandant Wassermann to continue: 'By day, the heat was immense, greatly affecting the entire operation, and severely hindering the progress of the consignment. After the proscribed nailing shut and sealing of the wagons, the transport set off towards Belzec at 9 p.m. In the growing darkness, several Jews were able to force themselves through the ventilation shafts after removing the barbed wire and tried to escape. Part of this number was gunned down by the soldiers accompanying the transport; the others were executed by the station guards and other police forces. The consignment arrived in Belzec without noteworthy incident, although taking into account the length of the train and the darkness, the guard proved to be ineffective. On 7 September, some 300 Jews—old, in poor health, unfit for transport—were executed. In conformance with the transport order, dated 4 September, automatic rifles were used for the executions, pistols being employed only in exceptional cases.' In the days to follow, more Jews were rounded up—altogether 8,205 of them —from the wider region surrounding Kolomea, including Kuty, Kosov, Horodyenka, Zaplatov and Snyatyn. In the course of the operation, due to 'usual causes', 400 persons were killed by automatic rifle. 'Given the great heat and the exhaustion of the Jews, the overloading of the ten wagons filled in Kolomea, as well as the ten wagons from Horodyenka, was so catastrophic as very nearly to greatly endanger the success of the transport.' Despite this, the train did eventually arrive in Belzec, although after the onset of darkness, the Jews still attempted to break out of the wagons at every station where the train briefly halted; thanks to the speedy arrival of reinforcements, however, such attempts were either successfully thwarted or the fugitives shot. At this point, Wassermann also notes that 'due to the effects of the heat, the Jews in every wagon had removed all of their clothing.' In the meantime, the locomotive which had been attached to the transport in Kolomea broke down in Stanislau, its repairs taking half an hour. The addition of another transport in Lemberg increased the number of captives by 1,000. Here, the locomotive was also replaced, but the second engine was so old that 'the transport could proceed along its route only with continual interruptions. Those Jews whose strength had not yet been completely exhausted took advantage of the slow jolting of the train to force themselves through the holes they had broken in the wagons' sides, for because in jumping from the train they only had to fear light injuries. In vain I alerted the engine driver to increase speed; this was impossible, and the frequent halts on the open tracks became more and more unpleasant. Ever greater panic spread among the Jews due to the great heat. Upon emptying the train, we found 200 corpses in the wagons. The transport arrived in Belzec at 18 hours, 45 minutes, and I handed the consignment over to the camp commander at 19 hours, 30 minutes. Because of the special circumstances, it is impossible to ascertain the precise number of Jews who disappeared during the transport. It can, however, be assumed that 113 of them were shot down or otherwise rendered harmless while attempting to escape. No special incidents occurred during the operation. The cooperation between the police units deployed and the security forces went smoothly.'

The story of how the Jews were rounded up in Kolomea, in the course of which at least half of his own family was murdered, was never known to M. The older relatives buried within themselves what little knowledge they had of these events. Yet this story, as well as everything else that perceptibly began with it— for who could say, as with fossilized sediment, when it had originated?—had left the family convinced of the impossibility of change, embittering every hope in advance; in Péter's view, this was transmitted by M. If they happened to be watching an international football match on the television together and M. started mumbling, after the first goal scored against the Hungarians, something about 'it's good if they get it', the word 'they' was especially painful for Péter, hoping 'they' would only lose by five. If it would only be five. And most vexing of all was that M. was almost always right. If the defence wasn't strong enough to ward off five goals, it could at least manage to keep it down to three from the weakest opposing team. Péter felt ashamed of his father's judgements. He might have been twelve or thirteen when a choking desire first arose in him to live his life differently from his father's. One day, after a quarrel, he left home resolving never to return. But no sooner had he stepped outside than he began to realize —after the first paroxysm of self-pity—that to leave a place for ever, to leave it behind oneself for all eternity, was not so simple. Within half an hour, he was already back home. M., with the derisiveness of someone for whom any inclination to buoyancy or joy had been long since withered dry by solitude, told Péter upon his return, in calm matter-of-fact tones, that if he thought he wasn't going to ruin his life, as M. had—if we can even speak of ruin, when nothing has to be ruined and it comes about of its own accord—he was mistaken. He would end up just as miserable as M. himself, surrounded by the same bleak desolation, and it was obvious even now that Péter was much more irresolute and dishonest than his father. M., it appeared, had not the least suspicion of his powers. And yet Péter too was capable of retaliation, in the midst of their evermore-frequent battles; he knew what he was doing, and it pained him, but he couldn't restrain himself, and it was not until a considerable length of time had elapsed—much too long—before he felt regret for what he had done. He loathed his father in those moments, but he was at his mercy; it only occurred to him much later that his father was just as defenceless as he himself.

M.'s extreme bitterness, however, did not entirely dampen his aptitude for understanding. He often surprised Péter with the openness he could display towards others. In contrast to his mother, whose interest was most often sparked by the stories of those less fortunate and more impoverished—her words of commiseration always more dramatic than necessary, bearing the unspoken acknowledgement that things could have turned out much worse for her own family— M. was capable of manifesting real attention, which however did not imply that he was able to hear the story to its completion. If Péter, after Sunday dinner, with the soup tureen and platters still on the table and the ticking of the wall clock ever louder, began to relate something, M. most often curtly interrupted that he had no time for these details, even when he had nothing else to do just then. If—at the emphatic request of his mother—Peter did not immediately rise from the table, M. quickly subsided into impatience, his eyes narrowing more and more, his heavy eyelids with their lashes that at other times rose forcefully upwards to give his gaze the moroseness of a school custodian, now sinking down lower and lower, and before his head completely snapped downwards, Péter's mother would demand to know, in a voice even more wounding and wounded, if it really wasn't time for M. to have a nap.

At first, Péter thought the reason for his father's behaviour was his perpetual fatigue. Later on, though, he realized that the attention necessary for conversation was entirely missing in him. And this lack did not stem from an inherent weakness—for if there was a decision to be made, or the pros and cons of a dilemma needed to be weighed, his father was the one to be counted on—but rather from his unswerving denial that anything outside of what one did or did not do could be relevant. The realm of feelings, in particular, had no significance, nor did what one could say about oneself. If anyone in his presence began flirting with such deceptions, his response was unvarying: 'All right, just another tale.'

This is why, if at any point earlier he might have accidentally overheard the story of what happened to his uncle and the others, M. had certainly forgotten it immediately. The reason for his silence was in fact completely different from that of the rest of the family. If they did not speak about their lives, it was because it would have meant touching upon things that were too painful; M., on the other hand, firmly believed that 'what's past is past', never thinking for a moment that there could be anything beyond the immediate concerns of daily life that justified the wasteful expenditure of words. This, however, did not turn him into a man without a past. The components of any sequence of events could, within days, undergo a radical transformation, losing all original coherence: M. was able, without any difficulty, to reassemble and embellish his own versions, not infrequently placing words in the mouths of others that they had never said. He presented his own variations with such persuasion, so captivated by the strength of his own narrative that any attempt to cast doubt on it, or even hint at the possibility of another version, was labelled a falsehood, an outrage, revealing the other family members' secretly nourished contempt for him. The phrase always shouted by his father when an argument broke out—'Don't lie!'—rang for a long time in Péter's ears; he always stressed the last word admonishingly, thundering out his son's name with the same force and menace. M.'s stories, without exception, confirmed how 'base' everyone around him was—along with 'dishonest', this was his favourite adjective for others, in particular for Péter's mother, although he hardly could have been fully aware of the weight of these words—and he eagerly awaited the next opportunity to bare his fangs. In spite of all this, he was not disloyal, at times trusting in people with a childlike naivety; he was capable of forgiving insults; after more than one of Péter's unjust or hurtful retorts, which only a child can inflict upon a parent, he generally behaved as if nothing had happened.

As I write this, tormenting you with my words, I know full well that I can no longer coerce you as I wish, and that you will not hear me out to the end; just as M. never listened to Péter's stories, you would interrupt me, saying I'm lying, I'll tell you how it really was—that's what you would say. You are right—it wasn't like that. I knew Péter, and I knew M., but everything that I remember about them, which isn't much at all, is in the past now, dead; it perished long ago in that fire that burnt unceasingly in the depths of their days. But where there is fire, there must be shadows as well. And it is these shadows I would like to depict, the shadows of the days, their forms as shifting and mercurial as the clouds in the sky, and just as elusive. This is simply one variation of the story of Péter and M., one variation that I am now relating to you, so you can place your own unnoticed beside it, or you can help me to place something there from your own story: you work on this book too, you work on this grave where we shall be enclosed together.

Where, though, would your story begin? Perhaps at the end? Perhaps when M., for several weeks confined to the hospital bed, having lost all sense of time, one evening happened to glance up—the pacifying effect of all the tranquilizers and painkillers having suddenly subsided, at least enough to allow him a faint notion of where he was and of his earlier life, unimaginably distant and yet within arm's reach. He would have liked to move his hand but couldn't. It seemed to him that perhaps he had been tied to the bedpost again, but he didn't feel the gauze bands on his wrists. He could open his eyes only slightly, squinting with difficulty. None of the objects in the room could be made out, nor could he perceive the space around him, only sensing that everything was white or silver-coloured, mute and clean. He tried to pull up his leg: he could sense that his leg still moved; most likely the sheet, soaked in pus and sweat, had been rolled up, but he could not feel it. Is this where your story should begin? Would you even tell a story at all? Or would you only swear? Would you curse me, the ambulance drivers, the doctors, all the governments, the talking heads on the idiot box, the neighbours, all of those bitches who can't even pick up the phone and if they do, they say they'll put you through only to disconnect you immediately; you would curse your relatives, who knew only how to cheat and swindle, the gilded youth who got their diplomas with our money and now dictate to us who is right and who is wrong; you would curse all of these people who, without blinking an eye, contradict what they said yesterday; and you would curse yourself for having been such an idiot. The stream of profanities would pour fourth perhaps even more relentlessly than it did in your life; your curses would come down like rain in a heavy storm.

M. was also possessed of a particularly beautiful, if rarely seen, smile: quiet, content, approving, it could give rise to a rare happiness in the person to whom it was addressed. Péter had no positive memories of having enjoyed it in his childhood, but he did believe himself to be acquainted with the persistent and awkward joy that followed only in its wake. These warm impressions, the minute signs of recognition however rare they might have been, still gave sufficient opportunity for there to emerge between father and son, as much was absolutely necessary, not only leniency, but even a kind of secret alliance, yet one in which clemency played no part. Perhaps M. never even noticed that for him the notion of fatherhood comprised almost exclusively an obdurate, harsh superiority coupled with a series of moral pronouncements that brooked no contradiction. Lurking in all this was the continual suspicion of attack, M.'s own barbed aloofness being the chief obstacle to any potentially shared moments of masculine intimacy, based on mute comprehension and without gesture, with his son. From the omnipotence of his superiority, from the shadows of its shattered fragments, he judged all Péter did. And in doing so, he preserved the memory of his own father. In his might—the oppressive proximity of its powerful and expansive corporeality weighing heavily upon Péter—there was contained a greater, far more ruthless power, before which Péter had no defence, as M. himself was no more than the unwitting servant of its commands. How often did Péter hear the words 'My father would have skinned me alive for that!', after which he could imagine how his grandfather, whom he knew only from photographs, would pull out his belt and begin savagely flogging his son, in whose place Péter inevitably pictured himself. And only later did he realize that this sentence meant something even more appalling than what M.'s words inadvertently revealed; for if Péter broke something, which occurred often enough, his father did not immediately begin to scold him, saying 'I'll skin you alive!'; his response had, rather, an embittered and disappointed tone in which there was no menace. And yet it was true that at times he was capable of holding back from Péter that strength that he himself hardly knew, and to which his entire nature was subjugated. In these moments, M. was capable of rendering perceptible tribute to their affinity: Was this not proof that in this alliance, unknown to both of them, M. was the weaker one, who would have gladly taken his son's side against himself, had not the child's ruthlessness—sensing that strength to be vanquished slowly seeping into his own frail body—made this impossible?

For the time being, however, I do not intend to explore their interdependence—for it was only in the last moments of his father's life that Péter pushed all of his other experiences into the background—but, rather, that compulsion which swept M. into a bitterness without remedy, into a life—if not intentionally then at least unconsciously—grown odious; or perhaps his only refuge was to escape into such a life, assuming a role perhaps made ready by previous generations, providing him with a sizeable arsenal of means. For Péter's upbringing was composed of nothing more than the meticulous transmission of this storehouse of mechanisms: initiating him into the mystery of how to make use of his injuries—that ultimate residue of every human relation—in the defence of a relative tranquillity, as well as of the indefatigably repeated prophecy that the less Péter would be inclined to admit the futility of his attempts to break free, the more igno-miniously they would fail.

All of this manifested itself in the most insignifi-cant details. If, for example, Péter entered the room carrying a tray full of drinking glasses balanced unsteadily on his hand, M. never cautioned him to 'hold on tight' or 'make sure it doesn't fall' but instead predicted 'you're going to drop it', after which Péter would strain all the more to ensure that what his father expected would not happen. There were moments when Péter felt so choked with rage and so powerless that he was himself terrified of how much anger bridled within himself against his father.

Yet are we really capable of such transports of rage when the possibility no longer exists within us? The course of events did, after all, vindicate M.'s stance, and it would have been impossible to decide if he himself had unconsciously formed them as he did in order to justify his woundedness and solitude—or if in reality all those whom fate had thrown in his path were truly so depraved, or at the very least indifferent through selfishness and calculation. M. was already seriously ill when he received the news that a relative who now lived abroad—with whom he was on bad terms—was coming to Hungary for a visit. It is impossible to say whether his negative experiences with this relative were based upon a true event, an unconscious transmutation of those events, or simply an outright fabrication. M. in any case decided, as always, that he would drive to the airport to pick up his relative, although he hardly dared make a firm promise in advance, not knowing if on the given day he would feel up to making the drive.

On the appointed day, he naturally set off for the airport at Ferihegy. The rain coursed in rapid streams down the windscreen, the wipers clicking rhythmically. M. arrived at the airport ten minutes before the flight's scheduled arrival time. He waited for an hour, amid his aches and pains, then returned home. The rain had, in the meantime, subsided somewhat, but the sensation persisted of being wrapped in a sodden, warm towel. Later, it emerged that the flight had taken off earlier than planned and that the relative, not daring to hope that M. in his weakened state would come to meet him

at the airport, had got into a taxi a quarter of an hour
before M. arrived at Ferihegy, continued to his accom-
modation in the city and only telephoned M. on the following day. Péter, in this case, was actually much less
inclined to forgive than his father. It was this irreme-
diable bitterness which compelled M.—and after a
while Péter—to devise injuries, to which the response
was a necessarily impartial if long since battle-weary
self-preservation that held the family together. And
this same force held together M. and Péter's mother,
whose emotive world-view so profoundly differed
from her husband's, so as essentially to render the
dilemmas of their relation insoluble; her demeanour in
relation to the wider world, the never-failing consciousness of loss, was well suited to M. Péter's mother
was otherwise better able, than M. with his oppressive
insistence, to protect her son from his inarticulate
desire to burst free, to be different; so as to save him
from disappointment later in life, she would pester him
with sincere anxiety in her voice, asking what would
become of him, would he be able to bear it if he were
never to rise above mediocrity. Removing the slightest
traces of risk in her life, choosing only the greatest
sureties in her work, her husband; indeed, not even
choosing but, rather, accepting and occupying the first
nook offered by life; and if possible, even to love this
with the sense of a debt that can never be repaid—that
was the true experience of Péter's mother, with the

instincts of a survivor who has lost all security: inclined to lock herself up within an impenetrable enclosure, one into which she sought to draw her son as well. This was why, after some time, Péter began to feel a sense of profound gratitude to M.: his renunciation—more tragic and not without struggle, but attuned to the wisdom of the necessity of ultimate defeat—protected him from his mother's hopelessness, saturated with anxious solicitude and thus even more despairing than his father's. Indeed, M. prodded his son to have the necessary courage to face the slings and arrows of defeat, accompanying his first struggles in the face of inequity and injustice with no small amount of pride. The earliest victims of these battles were the female teachers of Péter's grade school.

M.'s grandparents passed away not long after the death of two of their children and grandchild. They lived in a side-street near Szazádos út, in what was known as the 'Artists' Colony'. M.'s grandfather was a house-painter who, in the course of years, was taken into the guild leadership. He must have worked skilfully and reliably with his assistants, because István Bárczy himself, then the mayor of Budapest, entrusted him with the refurbishing of his villa. When the painting was complete, István Bárczy surveyed the results and was satisfied. He paid for the work, and then asked M.'s grandfather if there was anything in which he could be of assistance. He, with the impudence of a father of four, yet doubtless with a befitting modesty as well, burst out: indeed there was—a bigger home. And, as just at that very time the Artists' Colony was under construction, Bárczy legitimately regarding it as one of his principle achievements, in this moment two masters of their respective trades stood face to face. Not long afterwards, M.'s grandfather and his family were able to move into a flat in Szörény utca.

In the garden of the house stood a pear tree, which grew along with the children of the family. In the springtime, it was like a sprig of myrtle. From the neighbours' courtyard to the left a peach tree, and from the courtyard to the right an apple tree stood facing the pear tree, whose shadow marked the dividing line in the family chronicles: everything that came before the pear tree was legend; everything that followed grew with the pear tree into the world, perhaps even emerged from it. M.'s grandmother set up as a seamstress in the flat. She sewed undergarments and shirts for the artists; Stróbl and Czigány came to her to have their measurements taken. Due to their age and state of health, M.'s grandparents were at first granted an exception from the consequences of their status as Polish citizens. However, the grandmother—at approximately the same time as a train made up of cattle-cars rolled out from a non-existent train station in a non-existent country, with her children and grandchild on board—came down with influenza, the fever so over-taxing her heart that within three days she was dead. The grandfather then sold the residence in the Artists' Colony, relinquishing with it the pear tree, and moved in with his sole remaining daughter. He lived with her for three years. One day, after the Germans had occupied Hungary, he went out to buy a newspaper and never came back. He somehow had found himself in the middle of a raid—the gendarmes were hunting down Jews—and as it emerged weeks later, he and the others were taken to Rökk Szilárd utca, and from there to a furriers' workshop on the island of Csepel. His son-in-law, who was also a forced labourer and also disappeared, once caught a glimpse of him at the Király Baths, where the forced labourers were taken once a week to wash. M.'s grandfather's emaciated, arched nose stood out sharply from his desiccated bony face; his sparse grey beard had grown, his hair had turned completely white. He did not look like a patriarch. His gaze hung, void of expression, in the air. And thus, with his ravaged face, he withdrew from the family history, not even leaving his name to M., just as he himself had never known the circumstances of his own birth. There remained, in place of him, an obstinately repeated mistake, although it perhaps was merely an attempt to tell a story to the end, its hair-thin strands interwoven with the pear-tree standing in the courtyard of the house in Szörény utca—like a sprig of myrtle in the springtime— the dense forests of Gorgana and the gorge-like channels of the Prut River, above which, in a strait, the Kolomiya bridge suddenly appears, standing on three high supporting pillars.

If someone today travels to that region by train, and leaves Kolomiya going in the same direction as did that transport laden with naked prisoners sixty years ago, there is nothing to remind one of what happened; and yet the landscape somehow makes everything imaginable. Proceeding beneath the dense masses of the Gorgana, where there is no trace of human labour, steeply rising on the edge of the forest, one's gaze is drawn to a particular cemetery with its nearly unmarked graves; they look more like molehills. This is the cemetery for a nearby women's psychiatric hospital. And after a moment, in the depths of the chasm, tiny human figures really do appear, strolling among the buildings, all of them clearly delineated against the landscape, all of them alone. M.'s grandfather wanted to make the roots of the pear tree given to him by István Bárczy extend all the way to here, to the Prut valley, to the precipices of the Gorgana forest, of which he had perhaps childhood memories, never knowing that soon there would only be ditches here, unmarked graves.

And before that gaze devoid of expression, hanging in the air, images and scenes drift away. Of the family's four siblings, two were to survive the war. And with that begins the era in which M. too is visible—increasingly only him. After the Germans occupied Hungary, a neighbour hid the child, along with his mother, in their cellar. Everyone who lived in their street was no doubt aware of this, including old Bozai—later the district council leader for the fascist Arrow Cross—who, in happier times, had driven the Rákospalota tram and whose wife, perhaps from a sense of shared effort, used to dangle a small bottle of milk towards M. over the fence every day. M.'s father returned home from the labour camp in the middle of 1945. So the three of them were there, to be sure, but the son born from the first marriage—whom M. looked up to, as a little boy looks up to his almost grown elder brother—wasn't there, the grandparents weren't there and all of those who had been murdered due to a mistake in a story and the silence of M.'s father weren't there either. The family moved back into the house, in the courtyard of which, twenty-five years later, Péter would be photographed next to M., his body touching his father's in as many places as possible. A few battered steps led up to the glassed-in veranda, itself leading to a narrow hallway opening into two narrow rooms; the movement of stepping from the veranda into the house would even later call forth, in Péter at least, a sense of confinement, of bodily fear, of captivity. On the veranda was a large table, where Péter often liked to sit after lunch. One day, a dove happened to stray into the enclosed porch. Its body and the flapping of its wings were too large for this space. Everyone inside knew that, with their flustered gesticulations, they were more likely to frighten the bird half to death, disrupting its sense of orientation. The dove's beak and head beat repeatedly against the glass panes. Instead of trying adroitly to propel the bird towards the door, or letting it to find the way out on it own, they chased the dove from corner to corner, brandishing a broom and striking it, screaming to get out already. The dove flew about in confusion, until it finally managed to emerge into the open and, straight as an arrow, shot across the air in the direction of the nearby streams. Behind the glass door, all of the objects were suffused with decrepitude's heavy, musty smell: the apple-green chiffonier, the wrought-iron floor lamp with its broad lampshade, the smudged walls, the dark-brown waxed parquet floors that creaked loudly with every step. When M.'s mother died, the younger generation took practically nothing with them from this house. Although M. never collected mementos of any kind—he had no sense for such things—Péter nonetheless marvelled in later years at how little desire he had to take with him any object from the house that bore his parents' touch. So that when the house was emptied, only the practical interests of Péter's mother prevailed: the sole objects to be taken away were that floor lamp with its broad lampshade, a small wooden chest with a lock and key, a coffee service and a book bound in faded blue linen.

Still, it emerged slowly over the years, that while M. hardly ever spoke about his parents—and what he did know about them grew ever more hazy—he still measured his own life against what theirs had been. One or two years before his death, he began to repeat—and this at a time when his frequent trump card in arguments was the reminder to calm down, you won't have to put up with me for much longer—that he really had little reason for dissatisfaction: he had already outlived his father, and wouldn't last longer than his mother had anyway. It was as if he had placed himself in a common grave with them, and not with Péter's mother, even though he had never bothered much with the actual graves of his parents. His own mother had been cremated and her ashes placed, in a public cemetery, inside a two-metre-high columbarium that resembled an efficiently reduced concrete housing estate, and he visited his father's grave once every ten years at the very most. He said he couldn't pay visits to ashes.

Will I visit your grave? Is there anything there? If there is, it must be, I believe, something utterly different from what is engraved upon the headstone: may the deceased be tied to the bonds of eternal life. Rather this: *totus homo fit excrementum*. As all else in self-loathing, you hurried this up, making it happen while you were still alive.

After M.'s father returned home from forced labour, he tried to pick up and continue his life where he had left off, as if there were something left to continue, as if there had only been a pause in things, as if a chord had been struck and the sound died away—he strove to keep going as if all the people missing around him had simply never been. When the firm re-opened, he went back to his trade as a printer. By then he no longer wore bowler hats, or the stiff collars delivered by messenger boys that, in his trade, had been practically a mandatory dress code before the war. And much else had vanished as well. The Roman Embankment, where the printers' trade-union recreation area and boathouse once stood, had disappeared. On weekends, you could once pitch a tent there, or rent a canoe to row across the Danube. In springtime, M.'s father used to accompany his sisters to the Embankment, they were the centre of its society. All of this slipped away, like the memory of an imagined life that never was, which with a sudden single blow, was transformed into a lie, and the waters of the Danube—which had hardly borne the corpses away; at it's bottom the intact bullets still lay—were transformed into the waters of oblivion. The time of the long summer rains had come.

M.'s father was the only zincographer in the printing plant. At one time, xylographs or metal engravings were used in the preparation of zinc plates. The image to be reproduced was transferred onto a perpendicular wooden scale board or drawn directly onto it, after which the engraver would cut away the wood from the outlines of the drawing, so that only the image to be printed stood out in relief from the smooth wooden plane. The excess ink was wiped away from the wooden surface, then additional colours were added to the plate by the inker. A similar procedure was employed in the preparation of metal engravings. Later on, woodcuts were used less frequently, and after Max Thalbot discovered the principles of the autotype in 1852, the nuances of tone in the images were rendered using coarse cloth, then reproduced onto the metal plates through an extraordinarily fine mesh screen. Following the invention of photography, images were transferred through similar means onto clean, light-sensitive plates; after minor corrections; these plates were used to prepare stereotypes suitable for use in printing.

Two years before his death, M.'s father wrote a manual for printing apprentices concerning all of these techniques: a beautifully written, technically expert text, nearly aglow with the knowledge of printers' tools, objects, colours and, most of all, vision. Still, I tend to read this book, *The Technology of Stereotype Preparation*, as if M.'s father also had secretly inscribed within it, in the year 1953—that year so full of hope and yet devoid of promise—all that he knew of memory and oblivion. Before he begins his discussion of photography, the reproduction of images and the processing of printers' stereotypes, he first instructs the reader, in the introductory chapter, in the art of retouching photographs and drawings, only to return later to the question of 'repairability'. 'It can happen,' —the account of M.'s father begins—'that an illustration, title or body of a text from an old print or book may be needed for reproduction.' What exactly is the meaning of those words: 'can happen'? What else could have happened with him; it was, after all, his trade. And why does he mention only old books and printed matter—and not photographs, although, as it later emerges, page by page, he views the retouching of photographs as his true task? I believe that the sentence needs to be read in reverse order, where—much like the result of that complex procedure through which an image appears on the metal plate—one question stands out more and more: Can a face be reproduced, can it be amended?

Meticulously, through carefully articulated stages, the text leads the reader to the development of this question. 'At such times,' M.'s father continues, still speaking of old books and printed matter, 'it is suitable to first prepare an enlarged paper copy of the image, which can be retouched using Chinese ink. After retouching, the image should be placed in a solution of Farmer's reducing bath. The copy is then bleached, while the drawing rendered in ink remains clear.' But will the image obtained in this way really be identical with the original? In the course of the enlargement, the reproduction, the bleaching, does a transformation not take place, one that compels us to speak of two distinct images? The book does not touch upon this subject here, or even in later chapters. M.'s father merely speaks of what he knows: the properties and the various uses of implements and tinctures, the mutual effects of adjoining colour fields, while only the verbs at the beginning of the sentences, 'it can happen', 'it may occur' allude to something altogether different, casting doubt upon the entire operation, upon the possibility of reproduction and preservation. In the book's subsequent passages, the copy is viewed only as a variation of the original, yet M.'s father remains silent on the question of how far one can really go in fixing or modifying an image, what the solutions and tinctures really allow us to do, and above all the precise location of that boundary beyond which a picture can no longer be regarded as merely a variation of the original— although that question might well have been the true impetus behind his book: it was certainly M.'s in the course of his fabulations, and mine as well, as I write about them for you: 'At times, it happens that a stereotype needs to be prepared from an original that is not suitable for re-copying, an original that cannot be amended or retouched in any way. In such cases, an enlarged copy-print should be prepared, bleaching areas of dark shadows with a diluting bath and a medium-sized brush; a piece of dampened buckskin or cotton wadding should, however, be kept constantly at hand, in order to swab the solution away from the copy if necessary. Afterwards, the copy should be mounted on a frame, as this facilitates the repairing of the image.'

What is this original that we are not permitted to repair? Clearly, an image that is unduly valuable even in the state that it happens to be in. A repair, in such a case, would merely ruin it, rendering it worthless as a keepsake, even if—since it cannot be re-photographed —there is no way to preserve it. Nonetheless, M.'s father is intrigued by the question of retouching the image, of fixing it, or at the very least he seems to want to persuade us of this, for surely he wants to go on living, to preserve everything so that the picture in his hand at the end of all these procedures contains no disquieting elements: 'Any troubling details in the picture can be covered up with a carefully mixed combination of grey and white inks. Excellent results can be obtained with an air-pistol. Admittedly, this is a demanding process. The individual sections should be excised from a celluloid sheet with a sharp knife, and fastened with drawing pegs; the parts of the image requiring adjustment should be airbrushed with the necessary transitions. If the background is too vacant, we should prepare a stencil overlapping the main subject of the picture. This is well suited for subtle transitions, such as the highlighting of cloud details. This technique demands much in the way of dexterity, patience and draftsmanship.' Indeed, M.'s father—much more than either of us—rightly suspected that oblivion, and by that I mean true oblivion, leaving not a single trace in its wake, is murderous and hopelessly difficult work. Look at the tools he employs: pistols, knives, blades. As if we were watching an operation which suddenly turns out to be an execution, and the executioner's goal turns out to be the creation of a new body, a new face. But before a face begins to loom up from the text, troubling cloud details swim before us, which need to be subdued. Why does the book present the reader with this example, and why only this one, before it begins to discuss the question of retouching portraits? Does not the author intend to convey us a message about the transience of all things, the impossibility of preservation, the prohibition of memory? For the book was given to M.—and through him to us—with the inscription 'Knowledge is power!' In its author's handwriting, I can recognize traces of his son's. Exactly what kind of power is it that instructs in the art of amending and preserving clouds, the celestial formations changing moment by moment, which only the very last glance before death can stiffen into a fixed image? How many times in my childhood did I gaze at the clouds—and how many times did Péter as well— recognizing all kinds of figures and faces in them! Is M.'s father not conveying a message to us: Don't follow me, don't remember me; for to remember is to amend, and then you shall no longer be my progeny but, rather, the sons of death? Is the hidden commandment not directed at us: 'Thou shalt not amend or retouch the image?'

If that is true, then it was M., and not I, who truly understood the sentences written in this book and who followed its pronouncements for his entire life. That compulsion to write, of which, as you can see, I am the prisoner, perhaps wants death, complete metamorphosis, disappearance, both yours and mine, because there is no survival: only the clouds that easily become smooth after a storm, as a face never can—a face always looks as if it has been carved with a sharp knife, bearing every trace left upon it. 'When retouching portraits, we must proceed with even greater care,' M.'s father writes—perhaps now addressing only me—'so that the details of the face, the eyes' exact shading, the character of the portrait and its likeness may remain.' So it's not even about identity any more but only likeness, character. Perhaps we too are merely variations of one another, our faces irreparable, obliterated, just as Péter is a variation of his father and what remains, the lethal hoax of technical expertise, overlappings, shiftings. 'The plastic transitions of waves of hair, drapery and folds of clothing can be effectively resolved with the aid of the airbrush gun. If the theme of the picture allows, a lightly emulsified positive image can be prepared from the negative. Then, after drying, if the images are placed on top of each other, shifting one of them slightly within the bounds of good taste, a bas-relief effect can be created.'

M. heeded the message, although even he could not screen out those troubling details with the aid of carefully mixed inks—as most likely, the master of zincography could not do himself. I see his illness—his body inundated from within by excrement, being poisoned by his own faecal matter—more and more as the inevitable consequence of that mental agony which for long years dragged on outside of M.'s body—not in him and not in the zincographer, who had unwittingly become the accomplice in the murder of his own siblings and nephew, but somewhere between the two bodies in the emptiness of time. During those two months that M. spent in the hospital, and for a time afterwards, it seemed as if his illness had suddenly filled this void, as if his strength had been exhausted, and he were incapable of further escape—due to the prohibition against memory, he himself could not even know from what—as if the illness with no hope of recovery had been his own response to a life in which he had long ceased to find any joy, although perhaps he had never even been capable of joy: he no longer wished to put off that decision which could only be made against him. Still, I feel now that his illness did not, could not replenish that emptiness which hung suspended in the air, left behind by the fragments of stories and borne away before that gaze devoid of expression, borne away and disintegrating, dispersed into the many doubt-riddled variations, themselves perhaps as much of an inextricable mesh of fabulation and silence as the legend of the family's origin. Like a cloud, the story of an illness falls away. I will relate it for a time, but it shall pass with me: it never was, it never shall be.

Until now, though, only you and not I have been able to follow him, only you can follow the zincographer's path, for M. did walk to the end of that road down which his father had unintentionally led him; although it was as if his father had been swept away by the usual collusion of carelessness and misfortune, and everything that could occurred between them, just as everything that could occur with your body, did occur.

Now, however, you have no words. I cannot do anything else, I must stand in your place and in theirs: I must make a copy of my own portrait and put it there in place of theirs, although I know that a face can never be copied, any more so than a cloud. I must live their lives anew, as best as I can, even though writing does not repair anything: I must live your death anew, although this too is surely impossible. I don't want to fix anything and I can't, because I don't know what happened, so I must confabulate: I invent you and them, as I try to grapple with that which cannot be grappled. For where is that body, that human form, that doll-like figure covered with a white bed sheet, with which I would grapple once again—whose shoulder I would once more squeeze in a sunlit hospital room?

There is nothing else, simply the time between us turned to emptiness. And yet I yearn for a body, I want to relate your body. How many times did I see you on Sunday mornings, freshly showered with hair still wet, coming unclothed into the room, your scent pleasing, with that heavy, slowly wavering gait—which always made it doubtful whether your skinny legs could bear the mass of your upper body—as you went across to the wardrobe to get yourself a pair of trousers. Or perhaps I didn't see this, perhaps only Péter did? M. always tried, with a painstaking effort that had hardly altered over the decades, continuing even up to those final months, to render that body—depleted as it was, displaying more and more creases that could never be ironed out, ungainly, increasingly malodorous—smooth and scented, although even years earlier it had already seemed unspeakably weary from any movement not directed at the nearest objects within reach. Péter could not recall a time when the slightest physical exertion did not produce in his father a slow rhythmical puffing and blowing. M.'s face would become swollen, as if on each side of his mouth he were hiding a plum between his teeth, and his face really did turn a shade of purple; then leisurely, in the rhythm of slackening effort, he would exhale so that his face, like a tiny sack, would once more fill up with air. Over the years, more and more thread-like red veins appeared on his skin, spreading upwards from the lymph nodes, slowly growing more dark and engorged. And yet M. never spared himself. None would have willingly competed with him in effort, hauling heavy cases, carrying boxes and cartons, doing his accounts late into the night, and if daring or courage was required, he never failed to meet the challenge.

Péter, as he was often in the shop with M., witnessed all of this; and he knew, without the two of them needing to discuss the matter, just how difficult his father's work really was; he also knew he was doing it for the sake of the family and most of all for his son.

During their arguments, M. often voiced the complaint, in tones of self-loathing and thinly veiled accusation, that he was little more than a beast of burden, 'no good for anything else', making Péter see, more or less, how he viewed things: he had done everything for his son, wrecking himself prematurely so that Péter's existence could be the easy cakewalk that it was, leaving him free to study what he wanted, to have no worries about having to earn a livelihood, in fact not having to worry about anything at all. M. did not expect gratitude in return—he knew how ungrateful children were—but he would at least have liked to see an attempt to make them closer, a sign of understanding; instead of which Péter always hid from him, escaping into his room, his books, his crazy friends, his grandiose ideas.

From the beginning, however, Péter had followed his father's complex and obligatory programme of workaholism, self-vindication and self-annihilation only irresolutely. Although for M., work was no sacrifice—nor was it for Péter—but above all a goal in itself, thus excluding the possibility that it could be placed into a chain of succession, resulting in a meaningful assertion or designation. M. simply crammed his life full of work to ensure that there would be as little time as possible to reflect on how the whole of that life was merely the result of a series of mistakes and character flaws petrifying into omissions: a succession of mistakes and errors that resulted in the deaths of half of the family, deaths for which no one could be held directly responsible. M. had settled the matter once and for all—happiness was not for him. And indeed, who ever said that we were put on this earth to be happy? His one aspiration was to liquidate the remnants of his freedom—even the possibility of reflecting on another way of life, or even the desire for it—to be 'a slave to his job', tenaciously working himself to death.

And yet it was true that he sacrificed himself for his son. The realization came late, yet it did come: he had committed almost every imaginable crime against himself, and it was surely not his mistake that Péter learnt nothing from his example beyond his ability to transform despondent self-hatred into a fondness for asceticism.

In addition to his work at the printing trade, M.'s father quickly found a new occupation for himself. He purchased paints and canvas, bargained at the flea market for a discarded easel, with sketchbook and pencil, he took all these items up to the attic. The arch of the window below the rooftop was too tiny for the sunlight to penetrate into the entire space, and he knew very well that painting can only be done in natural light. Because of this, he placed his easel right in front of the window, all of his painting implements well within reach. On Saturday and Sunday mornings—because only on those days did he have time to paint—he arose early, and stealing out of his room, crossed the glassed-in veranda, climbed the steps at the back of the house, and waited for the sun to fill his empty canvas with golden light. At first he attempted larger paintings; then he continually reduced the canvas size until at last he produced the tiniest of pictures, hardly larger than the palm of a hand. As the canvases grew smaller and smaller, he must have realized that certain details would irretrievably be lost. At the same time, he had to treat space differently, because forms contained in the background of a tiny painting are often vague with surprising mutations. That tiny blotch of colour which, before, resembled a human being could, with the addition of one careless dot, be transformed into a bird-like creature, particularly if, in the imperfect lighting conditions in the attic, the arms stiffened next to the body, as if wings.

M. liked the new fragrances wafting through the house, the turpentine and oil-paint scent that hovered in the air around his father at the weekends and penetrated into certain items of his clothing. He never could see the pictures, though: he wasn't allowed to go up to the attic, and he never thought that what was going on up there was relevant to him. And what was M.'s father painting up there? Whatever he saw from the window?

But what could he see from there? Clouds, only clouds, grey or white, fleecy, oleaginous, thick windswept veils. Yet is it common knowledge that clouds always mould themselves into curious forms, each one is different, endlessly changing—nothing at all like the moon where King David lives. There are clouds like large tables, clouds like plates stacked with dumplings, and there are clouds where two people embrace. And beyond that, of course there are the clouds about which we may not speak. Because they look too much like someone.

One day, M.'s father abruptly left off painting. After Sunday dinner, he bundled everything up. He wrapped the blank remaining canvases in newspaper, poured all of the paints together into a tin box, bundled up the easel, and—M. never knew precisely when—removed everything from the house. He discontinued his habit of going up to the garret on weekends. The scent of turpentine slowly evaporated from the house, the painters' smock and trousers disappeared; only a few blotches of paint remained on the outer staircase, but they were washed away within a year or two by the rain and the snow. The pictures never turned up, and no one ever spoke about them.

There is a section in *The Technology of Stereotype Preparation* that seems to have been written particularly for you and for me. In this chapter, M.'s father discusses the creation of half-tone images, the process through which printing colours that appear as unified wholes are in fact obtained through placing tiny dots, imperceptible to the human eye, next to each other. The value of these dots often displays considerable divergence, as dark and light tones each bring forth a different kind of optical illusion. In the case of lighter shades, the colours do not blend together, the minute dots of yellow, red, blue and black remaining separate. Dark tones, however—if I understand well—fuse into one another: black, for example, is created from the combination of the three primary colours. M.'s father likens the functioning of this optical effect to the rapid spinning of a circular saw; as it rotates, the individual teeth are no longer visible to the human eye. Thus the seeming unity of the isolated dots of colour is dependent upon the proportions; the apparent unity of events that occur in our lives, in turn, depends upon the speed of their occurrence. All these matters, however, can only be perceived from the outside: the dots of colour, just like the teeth of the saw-blade, do not move in relation to one another. The question then is not whether we ourselves are located outside or inside; that is, are we able to fit together the incidents that occur in our lives, and is there a viewpoint from which our doubled existence could merge together as one alloy, but, rather, this: what can be deduced from the difference between the picture as it is seen and the placement of the coloured dots? Is not everything that we think about ourselves and each other a deception; that I see my story as a part of the narrative of your body? Was not M.'s father, with his simile of the saw-blade, trying to convey this message: Don't follow me, don't remember, don't believe that one day follows the next, that your tale began with mine, that Péter and M. can be seen as two figures of a single story, for everything, including this, is an illusion, the illusion of time quickly passing?

And if that can't be jolted back into place, can't be adjusted—since time itself, the power-saw's spinning blade, is what dislocates—every event is minute compared to the infinity of time, and no eye can distinguish these tiny points. That perhaps is why M.'s father ended up painting upon tiny canvases the size of his own hand, ultimately abandoning painting altogether. I suspect that more accurately, he never wanted to paint pictures at all, merely to scrutinize the clouds, and perhaps then he wondered whether it would be possible to create a painting in which the colours and forms would change as ceaselessly as the heavens. When he realized that such a picture already existed—the attic window itself—this discovery calmed him. We never can, it seems, extricate ourselves fully from the realm of legend.

Once, M. told Péter how, after the war, the other children often bullied him, turning his life sour with humiliating pranks in which they could rely upon the teachers' silent complicity. M. seemed to feel he had it coming to him as the one Jewish student in the class. For a time, he withstood the underhanded cruelties of his schoolmates; then, fed up, he challenged their ringleader to a fight next to the embankment. The faces and clothes of the two combatants were thick with mud. Though M. never spoke in much detail about the bullying, he described how he kicked the boy so hard in the shin that he was left hobbling for a week afterwards, how he smashed in his nose until it began to bleed, and how he threatened him with more of the same if he was not left in peace. When M. told this story, he had already been seriously ill for half a year. It was evident that the retelling of the fight brought him no small satisfaction; in his mind's eye he was once again dealing out the blows and kicks on the embankment. Through this incident, he said, he had learnt for a lifetime that this was the only way he could protect himself.

As M.'s father's attempt at painting was coming to an end in silent fiasco, he sought a new occupation for his spare time, one demanding much more effort: he revived the printing works' choir. In the years leading up to the war, before such activity was forbidden, the

choir regularly gave concerts in the trade-union cul-
tural hall, the Gutenberg House. Supposedly, even the
poet Attila József himself once performed with them.
Voices strong and pure, singing in harmonious part-
song, these thirty or forty men both young and old
sang workers' songs and adaptations of folk ballads.
There were, at the time, a few other such workers'
choirs in Budapest. Among the factory workers, most
of the singers were members of the Social Democratic
Party. During the public discussions that always followed the concerts, the names of the leaders of early
1919—Garami, Kunfi, Landler, Böhm, Szende, Juhász-
Nagy—were most often invoked, along with the poets.
Was it right for the Lander faction to have held nego-
tiations with Béla Kún and his followers, when did
Károlyi, Jászi and Garami learn of this, and would
things have been different if Garami and the others had
been allowed back from their Vienna exile, and if
Bethlen had held talks with them? Yet when M.'s father
revived the chorus, not only Garami and Bethlen but
even the Social Democratic Party itself had long since
disappeared, and the print works had become nationalized. The singers brought out the old sheet music
and once again gave performances on Saturdays in
the Gutenberg House, but the audience had grown
apathetic, more timid, more suspicious. The faces
had changed. M.'s father didn't sing himself: he was

interested in organizing things, preparing the scores, the librettos, booking the concert halls, negotiating with the secretary of the Communist Party cell, encouraging the more reluctant singers. Whenever the subject of the chorus, or more precisely the 'choral society' as M.'s mother logically termed it, came up in the room in the little house behind the paint-smeared front door, a repressed unease filled the air, the name of the secretary and another man were mentioned, and M. could be certain that his mother would again, that evening, scold him with the usual phrases: for always leaving the house, especially to spend time with those filthy Bulgarians instead of studying at home—he obviously wanted to be everyone's fool, just like his father.

And there is a moment, in the middle of screaming the most terrible things, when one suddenly hears the sentences as if they were coming from somewhere else altogether, and one is filled with wonder at this hatred towards one's own child—for whom 'I would lay down my life', as slowly but surely one does—where in one's limbs does that barely restrainable passion come from, where that gratifying frenzy, like a squalling cat that would lacerate, tear apart that body originating from its very own, rending the thin fibres just beneath the surface of the skin, the brittle ribcage, the intricate structure of the hips so easily destroyed, that tiny being incapable of resistance, which at other times is so pleasing to touch and to hold?

Towards the end of his book, M.'s father presents a brief series of chemical formulae. At least for some of them, it is difficult to decide whether they are recipes for concocting deadly poisons or really for rendering metal plates light-sensitive. Egg yolk, bitumen powder, cyanide and other unheard-of substances—potassium carbonate, Prussian red alkali, methylaminophenol sulphate, acetic acid, cadmium iodide and methyl violet —are mixed with alcohol, water, methylated spirits or glue. These recipes are like a mordant postscript that the author appended to his book not only so that those who had read this far would lose his trace but also so that they would become eternally lost beings themselves. For memory itself is a toxin, afflicting the organism slowly at first, then assaulting the optic nerves and rendering its victim blind, incapable of realizing that it is no longer the world around oneself that one sees but rather a world that has passed, or perhaps never even was; the memory-pictures are displaced and transformed, with grievous consequences, as one no longer knows where one is, the self is lost, falling ceaselessly into oblivion.

As Péter was later to think back on it, the best moments spent with his father were when he sat next to him in the car. They didn't speak if they didn't feel like it, just sat next to each other and watched the road. M. drove with perfect mastery, precisely assessing the distance between themselves and the other cars as he overtook them with the most audacious manoeuvres. While driving, he radiated a sense of tranquil, serene responsibility, and this tranquillity at times loosened Péter's tongue when they drove somewhere together. Watching the road, the telegraph posts gliding by, the headlights of the oncoming cars, he said much to M. which otherwise would have remained unsaid; not because he was seeking his advice but because it was good to travel like this, to feel again and again the complicity of that manly, serious aura re-established between them practically every time that they shut the car doors and M. revved up the motor. If Péter's mother was with them in the car, every trace of this shared aura disappeared. During M.'s more adventurous manoeuvres, Péter's body strained backwards and he clutched at the small leather strap above the window, as if he were treading on the brakes with the entire weight of his body while his mother screeched out the name of Jesus, and, after the car had swerved back into its own lane at the last possible moment, M. would say, in tones of equanimity, with a completely new tone in his voice, one blasé and impudent, 'What's the matter, kids, I'm at the helm here, not you.'

M.'s father died in 1955. Two or three years before that date, in exchange for giving up his directorship of the choir, he was appointed manager of the printing plant. The works were still outfitted with the old machinery once ordered from Vienna, the colossal and dully gleaming cast-steel components that could be moved by knobbed metal levers and made to slide along lubricated tracks. At that time, photo-mechanical procedures were not yet employed in the reproduction of printed texts. The composed letter-forms were placed into a leaden bed, and once the composition of the page was completed and checked over, a cylinder was used to cover the plates with lead-based inks. Everywhere, the heavy smell of ink accompanied the printers.

Half-tone negatives, prepared using an apparatus that registered the blue, yellow and red films in a single exposure, were employed in the creation of polychromatic stereotypes of enormous oil paintings, smaller vignettes, landscapes or group portraits. The mechanism could also be used for snapshots, as the filtered negatives, one for each primary colour, gave a perfect single negative, even when photographing a living theme. In the middle of the apparatus was a filmic prism, so that the image was projected not only onto the plate facing the lens but also onto two laterally positioned light-sensitive plates. From these three negatives, two displayed the image in reverse, which in the course of creating the final film positive formed into a unified image. Colour filters were placed in front of the plate holders: opposite the lens was the green filter, through which the red stereotype was created; on the left the violet filter, which produced the yellow plate, and on the right the orange filter, which produced the blue plate. The matt glass ended up where the opposite plate stood; the sharpness of the image was determined by the setting of the lens aperture.

When M.'s father was appointed manager of the print works, he had to join the Communist Party. Yet he was not, most likely, trusted by the higher-ups, because after a while a young party activist, who had hardly even had time to warm his seat at the plant, was appointed as his deputy. He was, from the very beginning, on bad terms with this activist. In the late summer of 1955, M.'s father was unexpectedly sent to the printers' trade-union summer residence on Lake Balaton. For two weeks, alone. He suspected that something was up, and that was why they wanted him gone. Three days later, he was brought back to Budapest in an ambulance. He was suffering from a high fever, the diagnosis was acute pneumonia. Antibiotics had no effect. The two weeks of obligatory summer holiday had not even passed when he was already buried. M., who was seventeen years old at the time, was convinced for the rest of his life that his father had been deliberately subjected to negligent treatment, even suspecting a surreptitious poisoning. The burial, with a

Protestant service, took place in one of Budapest's public cemeteries. Twenty years later, M.'s mother also having long since passed away, a letter arrived from the cemetery director, in which the responsible party informed M. that the allotment where his father lay resting was to be liquidated at the end of the next month. And so the remains of M.'s father were cremated in their turn, and placed in the urn next to his wife's ashes, near the back wall of the cemetery.

'The radio's on.' This was always the comment of Péter and his mother when M., the better to amuse himself, began to sing while driving. His store of old Budapest cafe ballads was inexhaustible. He kept his eyes to the rain-glistening road, reflecting the headlights of the oncoming traffic, all the while singing in tune ever louder in his deep voice, moving his head with the rhythm of the song, tapping on the steering wheel, as the impetus of the music propelled him towards ever more reckless tactics in overtaking the car in front. 'Laugh all you want, oh girls of Debrecen, if you see my Budapest sweetheart, you'll all be a-cryin'.' 'Every leaf whispers here as if speaking of tearful eyes, of love lost and lamented.'

'Rain everywhere conceals the most, and renders the days not only grey but homogenous,' Péter was later to read in one book. 'From morning to night, one can perform identical activities—playing chess, reading, engaging in lively debate; the sun, however, in sharp contrast, casts shadows upon the hours, and does not favour those immersed in reverie.' Yes, thought Péter to himself, it was as if his entire childhood he had been awaiting something—he had no idea what—yet he was certain that whatever it was, it never did arrive; the minute circumstances of his childhood dissolving weightlessly in the interminable, monotonous intervals of the years.

When the telephone rang and, picking up the receiver, Péter heard the opening bars of a well-known children's song, he had a presentiment of what was to follow. He knew that M. was very unwell but did not believe it to be so serious. Two days before, M. had gone to the hospital on his own accord accompanied by Péter's mother. He had brought the results of his heart and lung examinations, which most likely alarmed the attending physician and, after his stomach was palpated, M. was sent for an X-ray. On his way there, he passed an open sick ward. In the narrow darkened room, an elderly man in pyjamas could be seen crouching on the side of a bed. His nose protruded sharply from his desiccated bony face, his ears stood out like lampshades, scrawny hairless shins dangled from his pyjama legs, propping himself up on both sides with his hands, as if he were asleep with his eyes open. M. decided he would not remain here. He went back to the doctor, telling him that he did not want any further examinations and taking responsibility for this decision. The doctor wrote him a prescription for castor oil and let him go home. With Péter's mother supporting him under the elbow, they slowly made their way back, and as they turned into the street where they lived, M. suddenly found himself in terrible pain. Even the next day, Péter was still hoping that it would somehow all pass of its own accord, deducing from every tiny signal the theory that his father would soon be completely healed. He was in the car when the call reached him; his mother said that M. might die. Péter replied ungraciously, warning her not to exaggerate, but he promised to call a doctor friend of his. That was on Tuesday morning. M., thanks to the interventions of Péter's friend, was admitted on Wednesday to the university clinic, where after the first examination, preparations were immediately put into effect for the operation necessary to save M.'s life. Péter's hopefulness and incredulity, which were nothing beyond a manifest compulsory indifference towards M.'s body, even towards its inner disintegration, the final or seemingly final repudiation of the vanquished yet never defeated double, contributed to the week-long delay in the treatment of the disease.

I am telling you the story of a father and a son, and in their story there are many other stories, which you should be telling and not I, purging them of that disillusionment, that betrayal, because I feel I am betraying you now: speech betrays us both. I am writing about you in spite of your emphatic request that I not do so. I write because I have a need of writing, so that afterwards I can lapse into silence: I can observe your prohibition. If only you were speaking instead of me! You have no traits now, the contours of the air do not trace your features, and if they by some chance could, your gaze would be as void of expression as that of the old man seen for the last time amid the deportees in front of the Király Baths. And if you were suddenly to open up the door, if you were standing here in front of me, would I be able to bear your presence? You are nothing, you exist as nothingness. You are here with me in this book, mute, indulgent, as only the dead— and not the living—know how to be. Let me speak now, let me betray you—grant me the time.

Six months after M.'s first short-lived marriage ended, he found himself alone again with his mother in the house, in the courtyard of which, with a row of shrubs in the background, that photograph would be taken of him later on, clasping his son across the stomach with his arm and the enormous palm of his hand, Péter's shoulder directly underneath his father's chin, only able to move his head in the captivity of the adult body—six months after M.'s divorce from his first wife, in the hopes of creating a happier union, a distant relative introduced him to Péter's mother, then twenty-two years old. During their first meetings, M. did not do much to create feelings of sympathy in his future wife, about whom he most likely could not say whether he liked her or not. If, on a Saturday night, he took her to the casino on Margit Island, M. sat with his back half-turned to the table, gaping at the orchestra and the ballad singer for the entire night, singing the numbers along with her, moving his shoulders and swaying his head in time to the music. 'Have you been to the Fishermen's Bastion, when the sun begins to set? And Parliament's shadow hides the evening's kiss? Have you seen the night-time darkness in the arcade's depths? If you haven't seen all this, you haven't seen Pest.' Péter's mother attempted nothing; she let the moment to take offence slip by. After the couple had been joined in legal union in the Second Matrimonial Hall of the Budapest City Magistrate, and then underneath the chuppah, they were granted the smaller room in the woodbine-covered house.

Péter's knowledge of what followed was acquired exclusively from the stories of his mother. At the time of the wedding, M. was working for a collectivized farm outside of Budapest, returning home late at night. The garden door could not be locked shut with its key, but hung aslant on its hinges. Anyone coming there could push their way in. After Péter's mother forced down the handle of the door onto the veranda, she would cry into the air 'Good evening, Mama!', to which no reply ever came. Her nose was struck by the odour of frying mixed with a heavy musty scent. Next to the veranda door was a water spout, from which the water dripped in a slow, uniform rhythm. Péter's mother had to be careful as she calculated the shortest possible route to the room placed at the disposal of the young couple, not to bump into the water tap. She had to take seven or eight steps until she reached her own door. Her gait was quick; still, she knew she had to be restrained and not hurry too much. After she had closed the door behind herself and put down her bag, she sat down, still in her coat, in the chair covered with yellow polyester, next to the tile stove.

While his mother narrated, Péter tried to picture the second room off of the veranda, where his grandmother lived. He imagined that it would be dark even in the morning—it had to be, as an imposing wall cast its shadow onto it from the opposite end of the narrow courtyard. If his grandmother had wanted to read a book, she certainly must have sat by the window, under the wrought-iron floor lamp with the large shade, and she almost certainly held the book tilted in front of herself, compensating for her weak eyesight. For as long as Péter's mother resided in this house, she lived every moment there as a stranger, always fearful. Her mother-in-law over the years never ceased hoping that through her intrigues, unpleasantness and lies, she might deplete the endurance of her daughter-in-law and thus regain her son. The very next day after the marriage, an impure and fatal struggle commenced between the two women.

M.'s mother accused her daughter-in-law of being filthy and slothful, of decking herself out in all sorts of cheap gimcrackery, of wearing blouses with necklines so low that her breasts were practically falling out, of doing nothing for her husband—never cleaning for him, never cooking for him, and God forbid she should ever wear herself out with a bit of housework. It was obvious that she'd been taught nothing at home but to go whoring, *that* she certainly knew how to do. M.'s mother hurled everything at her, everything that a sick old lady condemned to solitude could throw at her despoiler. Once she invited M.'s first wife into the house. An altercation ensued; the two women screamed terrible things at each other, then began to weep. M. left the house, slamming the veranda door behind himself.

On another occasion, a woman with blonde hair turned up at the woodbine-covered house. She opened the garden gate, walked in-between the lilies towards the house and knocked on the glass. Péter's mother opened the door and asked the woman what she had come for. The blonde woman said it was all the same to her whether she spoke to Péter's mother or to her husband; the main point was that she was an economist, a colleague of M.'s at the collective farm, and that she was now expecting M.'s child. She, however, did not want to keep the baby—she had come to demand that M. pay for the curettage. She was also putting her own health on the line. When M. got home, he admitted to having slept with the blonde economist, although it really couldn't properly be called sleeping together, as he had just had one shag on the office desk; in addition, she was the one who had wanted it, not he. Besides, M. was not the only one. The director of livestock breeding and the payroll accountant had all taken their turns, and more than once. So it was far from certain that he was the actual father. On the other hand, the paternity of the child could not be determined with certainty until after its birth, an event that no one wished to see. M. accompanied the blonde economist to a doctor who performed abortions, slipped five thousand forints into the pocket of his white coat and the subject was never again broached in the house.

There was silence.

Péter heard this story while M. lay in a deep, drug-induced sleep. If the attending nurse left open the valve of the stomach probe, the tea bottled up in his stomach began to drip out of his nose, pus-wounds formed on his heels, and the tube placed in this throat breathed for him in regular, easy rhythms. Why was his mother telling him all this? And why did she tell him about all the other betrayals? About all the women she already knew about, whose photographs M. himself had shown her, saying, 'So you want to know?—here, have a look, look, goddammit, I was with her, see, I fucked her, I screwed her, I banged her, and it was good, do you hear me, it was good!' If Péter's mother had been silent for thirty years, why couldn't she keep her silence now? On the way out of the sick ward, she once said to Péter: Believe me, it was not easy living with your father. It wasn't, Péter thought, that is true. But he's still alive, don't you see, he's still alive!

To tell stories, still more stories. A collection of indebtedness, of disgrace. To watch the fire as it consumes your body. And slowly in the blaze, writing is itself devoured. I watch the flames—that day shall always be with me, in vain has everything shifted—in the midst of the blaze, glasses clink, someone sits down at a table, leaving no place-setting unused. Knives, forks, spoons rise up, wobbling from the oilcloth cover slashed with ivy-green stripes—shop receipts, labels, official notifications and letters were always slipped beneath it—and the fire incinerates the table, inscribing the stories into oblivion, from which nothing readable remains.

L et this be a place of rest in this book. I will tell you a story of farewell. A wise old sage, when he began to feel that the time of his death was drawing near, summoned one of his disciples, whom he had often previously chided for his inattentiveness. As the disciple entered the room, the wise man asked him to sit down next to the low writing table. The disciple sat down and signalled to the old man that he was ready. The sage then said to him—As I speak these words to you, write them down, as my hand is far too weary to entrust them to paper.—Then he said, 'One day, we shall all have to resign ourselves to silence, when words no longer shall have need of us.' The wise old sage then closed his eyes and dozed off. From this silence, the inattentive disciple first wrote down the Book of Night, and later, the Book of Days. When he had finished the second book, he took a fresh sheet of paper, and using the handwriting of his master—for his script was by then indistinguishable from that of the sage—he inscribed a single sentence: 'The coming of the dawn is not a farewell, yet every farewell has within the dazzling audacity of the dawn.' After which, he cast both volumes into the fire, left his master's house— where he was never to return—and a year later took one of the women from the neighbouring village as his wife. For a time, they lived together in great poverty, and when they were both no longer young, two children were born to them.

W hat happened in that house where M.'s father
watched the clouds from the attic, and which
in Péter's memory remained full of dark, frightening
places, where it seemed as if his grandmother had gathered all of the darkness into her ailing self, as if the
house were nothing more than that diseased body
threatening to burst like an over-filled balloon and
inundate everything with a viscous brown liquid, with
the dense and ill-smelling moisture of her distended
organs—what happened in that house? One Sunday
morning, M.'s mother began to shriek curses at her
daughter-in-law from behind a closed door, calling her
a village milkmaid and a slovenly wench, at which
point M. grabbed a slipper from beneath the bed and
threw it at the door's glass panel. From that point on,
Péter's mother knew that her husband loved her. Even
so, she could not have been too certain of his love. Two
years after M. accompanied the blonde economist to
the doctor, slipping five thousand forints discreetly into
his coat pocket, he found himself once again standing
in front of the same white smock, and with the now
familiar gesture slipping the five thousand forints into
its pocket—but this time it was not so he could rid himself of the economist or another such acquaintance but,
rather, so that Péter's mother could terminate her own
pregnancy. Once again, there were altercations in the
house, blows were exchanged; much weeping, endless
grievances and far more besides filled the air, to be

sure, which Péter never heard, or which he forgot. After Péter's parents were finally able to move away from his grandmother's house, M.'s mother rented the vacant room to a young married couple so as not to be alone, not to be afraid in the evenings.

Péter's maternal grandparents supplied the money for the new flat. The five-storey building stood in the square right beside the Király Baths, and on the fourth floor, at the end of a long open gallery, M.'s name was written on the door. Upon entering the flat, on the other side of the narrow vestibule, you found yourself in a cramped kitchen, more accurately a kitchenette; the door next to it led to the bathroom, and at the end of the narrow, linoleum-floored hallway was the living room, in which two cupboards, a Murphy bed, a railed cot, a coffee table and one armchair completely occupied all of the usable space. Péter was sitting in this armchair when M. came over to him and told him that four days previously, his grandmother had died. Péter didn't know what he was supposed to feel and was relieved when he realized that nothing was expected of him. Not long after that, the cast-iron floor lamp with its large shade, the small chest that closed with a lock and key, the coffee service and the book with the pale-blue linen cover appeared in the new flat. 'Altogether, there were a dozen buildings of three storeys in the town: the one in which we lived, the two military barracks and a few governmental offices. Later, the headquarters of the army high command, also of three storeys, were completed; the building also had a lift that ran on electricity'—this was the opening passage of the book. 'The sky was light blue, a pale summer blue. Not a single white cloud drifted past'—was how it ended.

The window of the new flat faced onto an acacia tree and the back of a Catholic church. Every Sunday morning, two bells in the yellow tower opposite would suddenly peal out, their reverberations flowing into the room, rolling across the bed, between the armchair and the cabinets, colliding against everything, mixing up the colours of the linoleum in the vestibule, green-grey, green-grey, causing the entire flat to resound, and for Péter—who sat in the armchair deep within the tolling of the bell, or lay on his parents' bed—it was as if he were shielded within a hand and, as the chimes subsided, he fell asleep. The sight of the church itself, however, remained alien to him. He never crossed its threshold, yet if the tall, carved wooden doors facing onto Fő utca were open, he would always sneak a glance inside. From the windows of the flat, the foliage of the acacia tree was visible. He often wondered what it would be like to jump, if he climbed onto the window sill and leapt off, but the acts of jumping and falling were somehow always absent from his imagination; it was death that interested him, what it would be like to be dead, to lie there on the ground, his body pulverized below the green of the acacia and the pale-blue sky. From time to time it happened, someone from one of the nearby buildings did actually throw himself from the window. Once, Péter saw a group of people standing around a body covered with a black plastic sheet; blood covered the pavement. He stood behind their backs and watched for a while, then, on the way home, imagined what would happen if the next time the black plastic sheet would be in front of his own building and he would realize that the body underneath was his mother's. In the end, he thought, jumping could be easy.

Like a leaf drifting downwards, a stone plummeting to the ground, a sheet of paper gliding through the air, a ball tumbling down. To look, look and see how beautifully they drift, they plummet, they glide, they tumble; how beautifully the bodies fall. And to look in the meantime at the bicycles' track-marks on the gravel paths of the park, to look at the church's yellow tower. To look and to know there is nothing which is not beautiful.

At that time, M. no longer worked at the collective farm. For a time, he was employed in the Artificial Insemination Laboratory, a kind of animal gene bank, in Zugló. Sperm was collected from carefully selected bulls, then diluted and refrigerated in ampoules and stored in insulated containers; quantities of the sperm culture were then delivered to both of the two main Budapest rail stations. Selection of the bulls was preceded by a long period of observation. Each of them serviced about two dozen cows on the experimental farm, and the growing calves were examined on a regular basis for two years while the bulls who had fathered them rested. The bulls were selected for industrial breeding only if the species-specific properties of their calves demonstrated clear improvement. The morning postal train dispatched the bull sperm that was the carrier of these qualities to every region of the country, so that the local inseminators—the 'bulls in boots', as the lab workers called them—could receive their doses to impregnate rutting cows throughout their districts. Not long after Péter's birth, M. left the profession of animal breeding for good. He did not do so willingly; his father-in-law decided everything for him when he said that it was inconceivable that M., himself already a father, would have to spend two to three days a week in the countryside, away from home. To make a long story short, he spoke to a former colleague who arranged for a position for M., starting the next week, at the State Vegetable Cooperative. He'd be working behind the counter at first, but M. would be enrolled in a shop manager's training course as soon as possible. And so M. became a state retailer by profession. In those memory-pictures preserved from the first years of Péter's life, and which Péter, with forced hopefulness, turned over in his mind again and again in the hospital's first-floor waiting room, the figure of M. is hardly visible; although it's true that Péter could have crossed his path only at certain moments—M.'s activities commpressed into automatically repeating phrases and movements, like the words and gestures of his coming home in the evening; and yet Péter should have been able to summon up more traces remaining from those years. When M. got home from work, there came with him into the flat—perceptible even under the powerful stench of nicotine—a strange, foreign scent that hung in the air all night, around the armchair on whose back M. draped his plaid flannel shirt, trousers and socks. A similar smell also emanated from M.'s artificial-leather briefcase, which Péter was never allowed to open, although there were times when he secretly did so. It was the scent, chilly and slack, of potatoes and sacks of onions heaped up in dark cellars, touched with the vapour of decay; and on M.'s clothes, mainly on the downy flannel of his shirt, it was mingled with the reek of cigarettes and sweat to create that compound whose presence—at once cosy and repulsive—was transformed, as Péter passed into manhood, into a cogent knowledge of what it meant to create something through the sweat of one's brow—what it meant to work.

In spite of the flat's minuscule dimensions, the various scents and odours hardly mixed with one another. The kitchen with its scent of food, the bathroom with the clothes drying on the rack, urine and excrement spattered in the toilet, and the hallway with the smell of coats and shoes, the dusty exhalations of the furniture and the carpets in the main room—all these smells demarcated invisible islands whose borders could be traversed only by the three human bodies, leaving their traces wherever they went: M.'s with its suffocating bitterness, Péter's childishly sour-sweet, his mother's sweeter exhalations. From time to time, Péter's mother opened the window and the front door, the resulting draught sweeping away all of the smells. If she did so at noon, the kitchen was flooded with gleaming sunlight. For an instant, Péter was blinded by it and, stepping out into the corridor, delighted in the translucent colours of the wire-laced yellow glass under the staircase gallery's banister. Yet when he leant closer to the glass to examine how the wire threads ran through it, he was suddenly terrified by the depths below. It became his habit to let various small objects fall: he slipped them through the crack at the bottom of the yellow glass panels, down into the courtyard of the adjoining house, so that he could observe how long it took for them to hit the ground, hear them crack and watch them split apart. This activity never failed to make the German shepherd, left tethered in the neighbours' courtyard, frantic.

While I relate the story of M. and Péter to you, I see them clearly in my mind's eye but I do not hear their voices. Voices have disappeared from my memories, and they—the ones I am now recalling to memory —have grown deaf and mute, just as you and I are deaf and mute to each another. A voice cannot be brought back. I can't teach them to speak through touch; I can't conquer the shame in them, can't give them what was given to me in those final two months of your dying, when my very hand could sense of the odour of your body's disintegration and I could place my palm upon your forehead. I can't say if you knew or if you felt— as I did—that we had stepped across a border previously unknown to us. I don't know if you felt anything at all. But when I stepped out of the hospital room for the last time, closing the glass door behind me, or, for that matter, a few hours later when the telephone shrilled and I knew what I was about to hear, my hand could no longer remember all those touches. While your body grew cold and was being taken away somewhere else, my hand also grew mute. My hand has fallen silent, I told myself. And the air between us also fell silent.

The side of the park facing the church was lined with trees and bushes. Under the bushes, you could often find sparrows, their wings or claws broken as if someone had carelessly taken aim at them with a sling-shot; thin streaks of dried blood were visible on their feathers. An old lady living nearby took care of the wounded sparrows; every day she came to the park and took them home in a covered basket.

On the other side of the park, a grassy embank-ment rose upwards to the Király Baths. The cupola of this low-lying green building bore a recumbent half-moon at its top. If it rained, the cupola gleamed dully and water collected at the foot of the walls. A football, rolling downwards, always had to be retrieved from the water with a long stick. The building always excited Péter's imagination: Who was sitting beneath the cupola, were the Turks themselves still inside, did the shawms still wail and the slave girls dance, were the pasha's servants still serving up poisoned drinks? Péter had to stretch himself out along the ledge to look inside the window of the baths. Clinging to it, he pressed his face against the glass. All he saw, however, was the reflection of his own eyes. He stared at the image of his eyes in the glass; seeping up towards him came the smell of sulphurous water.

In this park, he often played with one boy in par-ticular. He know that the boy was adopted, which meant that his parents were not his parents; no matter how much they loved him, they still were not his real parents. Péter didn't understand why the boy's parents, who weren't his real parents, didn't say this to their son. During that time, doubts began to arise in him as to whether he too was really his parents' son—for if that boy didn't know his own story, he thought, it was conceivable that Péter himself didn't know his own story—perhaps he never would. His doubts were reinforced by M.'s threats. Namely, that M. often told him about a children's market in Debrecen: you could leave bad children there and buy new, better ones in their place. There's even a song about this market: 'To Debrecen I must up and go / Come back with a new brat in tow.' If Péter misbehaved or irritated his parents, all M. had to do was to say it was time to set off for Debrecen to the children's market. Péter's mother laughed at this but her laughter always sounded as if something in her had caved in, had broken down. She laughed, yet remained sombre.

In those years, at the beginning of the seventies, there was increasingly talk of money in the family. M. was already a store manager; he had completed the course at the Marxist–Leninist evening school and had bought his first car, a sand-beige Lada, which he referred to as the 'horse-cart' or the 'little wagon' with languorous affection in his voice. The 'little wagon', bearing the license plate of UL 94-31, was stored in the garage of the Foreign Ministry, behind the park. M. would step into the garage and greet the elderly attendant who sat in a glass cubicle to the right of the retractable garage door. Inside, the boys who washed the cars ran back and forth in their high rubber boots, scrubbing-brushes in their hands. Water continually trickled from the hoses snaking along the ground. Here and there, small lakes collected, and the echoing space between the concrete columns resounded with commands and masculine humour. The ministerial chauffeurs—in their black Volgas with government plates beginning with the letter A—usually did not interact with the garage workers beyond a simple greeting. They entered, sat down in their boat-like sedans, rummaged for a while in the glove compartment, started up the engine, beckoned to the glass cubicle and drove out through the retracted garage door. M. too always spent more time inside the garage if the attendant came out of his cubicle; he always enjoyed chatting with him. In the meantime, Péter would wander around the Lada, running his hand along its side, tracing the chrome circles of its headlight rims several times with his index and middle fingers, knowing that sooner or later one of the youths who washed the cars would start talking to him, saying how old are you, buddy, started with the ladies yet?

Ever faster, the days spun round. M.'s thirty-sixth or thirty-seventh year had hardly passed, yet the signs of early aging were already manifest. His hair looked as if it were sprinkled with poppy seeds, his movements were slowed, his paunch slackening. In his obsession with work, however, he was still the same old M. Although his employees succeeded occasionally in stealing larger or smaller sums from the till—once almost resulting in persecution—his business, as emerged from the yearly December inventories, showed ever greater profits. The administration recognized his achievements, but was never fond of him. Péter's mother was right when she said that he really felt happy only somewhere out in the middle of a cabbage patch.

M. rose at dawn even on Sundays. As he sat up in bed, the mattress springs squeaked, waking up Péter's mother, who muttered something to M. about how even if one could fall asleep, there was still no peace and quiet, or else commenting: when you get up, it's like cannons thundering. She would then turn over to the other side and try to go back to sleep. M. put on his slippers, pulled on his bathrobe and shuffled out into the kitchen. After a moment, the murmur of the radio could be heard; the village farming programme was on. M. clattered loudly among the pots and saucepans, taking onions and potatoes from the string bag, peeling the carrots, slicing the meat, boiling the water. Gravy went splattering across his undershirt. He moved with difficulty among the kitchen cabinets covered with red-patterned wallpaper, his thickly veined face puffing and collapsing like a bellows. Péter liked to sit with his father at these times, watching what he was doing. If M. felt that he was about to break wind, he would turn gaily to Péter, saying, 'Here, take this!' When Péter's mother awoke, M. had everything almost ready. M. left the final stages of cooking to his wife. After tasting the half-completed dish, sharp words concerning the amount of salt and other seasonings never failed to be exchanged between them. M. would then withdraw, injured, to the other room. After these chamber theatrics, both of them grew ever more bitter; both of them ever more perfectly matched to the other.

There is a chapter in the manual written by M.'s father that would seem to speak of both of them. It is the only section in *The Technology of Stereotype Preparation* where, perhaps, there is love mixed in with the practical advice of the father. The chapter that speaks of the difficulty of faithfully rendering the tints and shades of the original colours draws our attention to one phenomenon: that the lack, or even the excess, of a given tone can in no way be judged uniformly. If one colour appears to jump out of the image, it is inappropriate to try to mute it; instead, it is better to strengthen the complementary colours or the black tones. If, for example, a colour doesn't have the desired effect, the plate should be etched to heighten the clarity of the surrounding colours. Different colours behave differently, however. 'If a certain shade of colour is too dark green, the blue and yellow plates should be made brighter; if the green tint is too bright, the intensity of the red plate should be strengthened. If, however, we perceive that there is an insufficient quantity of red in a given shade, we should not try to reinforce it but, rather, subdue the blue and yellow. Should the opposite be true, that is, an overly bright tint is perceptible, we should follow the opposite procedure. The error is always related to the formation of the intensity of a given hue. Errors in colour formation should be thoroughly studied—whoever has done so will understand the proper task of colour lithography. Even in the very first etching process of the colour plates, it is necessary to see, to perceive which colours should be left unaltered, which should be reduced and which strengthened. If in the course of this process, a miscalculation occurs, one is compelled to rectify the damage later, yet this is possible only to a limited extent.'

Every Sunday morning, M. took himself into the bathroom, filled the tub, lay down inside it, propped up a book and a manicure kit next to him on top of the spin-dryer, and dozed off. Water slid up and down along his stomach, waves were created from the rhythm of breathing. After one hour, Péter's mother went in and washed his hair. Following the second rinse, M. pulled the plug from the drain, water gurgling as it swirled downwards, and next to the now opened door, squatting, M. rinsed himself off with the shower-head. Holding the nozzle in front of himself, M. splashed water on his face, his eyes closed, and into his mouth. Then he dried himself off with the towel, blow-dried his hair and shaved. A whistling drone came from the cylindrical dryer. When M. was ready, his hair meticulously combed back, he stepped naked into the main room, his stomach sagging against his loins. Péter was always amazed that such skinny legs as his father's could support such an enormous body. He watched as these legs, swaying, carried the body, like a boat, to the armchair. Short of breath, M. would lean down, pull out an undershirt, then his briefs, smoothing the shirt and below it the underwear's elastic band; then he would sit down to slip his feet into the legs of his sweat-suit. This always transpired at five minutes to twelve. Always with exactly the same movements. At noon, the family sat down to lunch.

It could have been on a Sunday as well when the furniture from the flat set off and travelled across the city. On the creaking, groaning platform of a canvas-sided truck, the two cupboards, the folding day-bed, the coffee table and the armchair swayed rhythmically, leaving behind the Király Baths, the Turks, the pebbles scarred with the skid-marks of bicycles; and as the truck continued along its route, the odour of sweat and nicotine sailed with them along the banks of the Danube, the smell of coats and shoes, the dusty exhalations of the furniture and the carpets, the cellar-dank scent of the artificial-leather briefcase. And everything continued exactly as it had before. The quarrels, the evenings submerged in fatigue, the Sunday dinners. The family sat down, the radio was on. We shall now hear from our correspondent in Bonn, our correspondent in Moscow, our correspondent in Beijing. The Druzhba Pipeline, the increase in productivity, the fall in the trade deficit. The expectations of scattered rain showers, the cloudy skies, the temperatures, the long-term average. After a few minutes, Péter's mother asking: Tell me, is it really necessary to have the radio blaring like that? And M. answering her: No, nothing is necessary. And Péter's mother getting up and, with enraged satisfaction, turning the radio off.

Pictures, pictures. To shift them onto one another, to embody the muteness and, all the while, to amend nothing, for nothing can ever be amended. Clouds, grey or white, fleecy—oleaginous, thick windswept veils.

In the new flat, between the front door and the intercom receiver, hung a picture of small dimensions, hand-painted on Egyptian papyrus. In the foreground stood a person with the head of a dog, although it was impossible to tell if it really was a dog's head or only a mask. Its long thin arm stretched out towards a figure swathed in gauze and canvas from head to toe, who looked, bundled up in such a way, like a corn-husk doll with no limbs. Above the doll hovered a bird with a human head. Perhaps because Péter recognized his own features in those of the bird's—and really, in the contour of the eyes, of the forehead, if you took one step backwards and squinted, there really was some-thing of his own likeness—he felt for a long time an irresistible urge to lift and take up the wings of this strange creature, which hung next to the scrawny body as if weighted down or broken by the vacant look in the dog's gaze. In the corner of the painting, above the dog-headed creature, various figures, including eyes and birds, were depicted in two vertical lines. Péter gazed often at this picture, which the family had received as a gift from a relative just returned from holiday in Egypt, and he never could decide if he should be afraid of the human-headed bird, or if he should see in it—and perhaps the dog-headed man too—a kindred being, a companion. In any event, he secretly attempted many times to depict the bird with the human head, never copying the painting directly but always from memory, and though he could never draw the wings properly, the face that appeared on the paper more and more resembled his own. As he drew, he felt that the dog's gaze was hanging in the air above him, as if it were examining where he was placing the lines, what he was erasing.

The picture of the man with the dog's head and the bird with the human head illustrates us now. You have died, and not only has the world remained unaltered— because only children are alarmed by the knowledge that the world would be the same, even if we hadn't been born into it; even during our own lives, everything is as if we had never been born—but you have passed away from me as well, from my own time, as if you had never existed in any other way than you do now. A few days after your burial, I read these lines in a poem:

Is there anything which, if touched by fire,
is at once not consumed?
Rain, O sweet rain upon the earth—
Coarse silk, crushed into pieces
by dawn seeping from the stones
the granite masses of thought, slashed
by the dorsal fin with one single faultless arch
and the fear, then everything made smooth,
no scars, no creases remain—

Yes, the surface disfigured by fear is being made smooth, with no creases and no scars: and there is no hand which could lead us to the sea. We have gone astray, we are lost.

The days, the weeks, the years passed with such uniformity, as if with each awakening time had to be reinvented, the days and the months newly discovered, the Mondays, the Tuesdays, the Wednesdays, the Januaries, the Februaries, the Marches; so that the uniform streets traversing the city, as much as the uniform movements, uniform facial expressions and uniform words could differ from one another, for they hardly differed from their own selves. At times, a desire arose within Péter to watch the others' movements, to listen to their words, as if they were specks of dust whirling in the sunlight before him, for at that time, this was what interested him the most: the sight of the whirling dust-specks, the air full of tiny movements when, with a sudden gust of breath or the wave of a hand, they swirled upwards, then, returned to their slow, languid drift. Instead, though, he felt that someone was observing him, watching him tidy up in his room, as he drew or wrote beside the bed, as he slammed the door behind himself after an argument, as he wept. Not infrequently, someone actually would be watching him from a first-floor window of the building across the way: an elderly lady, the grandmother of one of the girls in his class at school; yet Péter knew that even if these prying eyes were hateful to him, they need not be feared—far more terrifying were those eyes that he had glimpsed many years ago, in the window of the Király Baths.

Every Sunday afternoon, M. sat in the kitchen with the bound ledgers, writing out stock inventories or price lists. His tall, spiky letters seemed as if balanced on an uneven arrangement of rocks, sometimes wedged painfully into a crevice, or else unexpectedly expansive, stepping out towards the centre of the graph-lined paper; and the hand that led them seemed as if it continually had to break free from its own spasmodic inability to write. Aligned below one another on the page were the names of the vegetables, the fruits, the conserves: pepper, potato, tomato, onion, apple, cabbage, red beet, cucumber, grape. Next to each fruit or vegetable were numbers. The first figure referred to the inventory, the second to the price per kilogram, the third to its wholesale value. M. performed all of the multiplications in his head; he could calculate quickly and accurately. Péter liked to watch as one of these columns of numbers, arrived at through sheer mental calculation, descended from the heights like the pillar of an invisible building towards the bottom of the page, where it would come to rest on the plinth of the sum total. As M. leant over the columns, assembling them from clumsily scrawled, spasmodic figurings, his ball-point pen travelling upwards again across the steps of formation of each individual column, his hairless chest all the while visible through the wide neckline of his undershirt, it was evident to Péter that his father's connection to these numbers was serious and passionate; it never would have occurred to him to disturb him with questions.

For a time, Péter went to work in his father's shop for one month every summer. He enjoyed carrying the crates and boxes with the other shop assistants. He could yank down the tailgate strap, leap onto the truck bed and throw the sacks of potatoes onto the others' backs; if a consignment had to be picked up, he could sit next to the driver in the front of the truck and listen as he shouted random comments through the open window at the pedestrians. All day, he scampered around half-naked, his skin burnt dark brown, pricked by the sweat and grime. M. made Péter work as hard as any of his other shop assistants, all the while ensuring that he never lifted anything too heavy for his strength. If Péter grew obstinate, which occurred often, M. never hesitated with the reprimands; he only had to strike him once, though. Péter especially enjoyed the arrival of a consignment of watermelons; the workers would form a human chain between the trailer and the vendors' stalls, catching the watermelons and throwing them to the next man in the chain, and when the pile of melons grew so high that it could no longer be enlarged from below, they sent Péter to climb to its top, and he was the one who, while reaching for the huge melons, had to make sure the vivid-green mountain did not start moving beneath his feet as he caught them one by one and released them onto the pile. The sun-freckled melons, ready to burst at any moment, rolled smoothly into their places. Péter felt that many eyes were trained upon him, and he imagined himself, like every other sunburnt shop assistant and driver, the king of the marketplace: the little gnome-like figure standing on the trailer bed whistled at every young woman who passed; while another, if he didn't have enough melons flying his way, aimed pebbles at stray dogs, giving out falsetto shrieks if he happened to hit the mark.

And so Péter became 'the boss's son'. Later on, M. let him work behind the counter as well, selling beer to the construction workers at the Csepel water park; he learnt how to open a beer bottle with his bare hands on a stone slab, how many packing crates could fit diagonally onto a loading pallet, and one other thing as well: what it means, in a country where nothing ever happens, when someone is taunted for being a Gypsy or a Jew. One day followed another like the stack of green melons piling up—the heap grew and grew, and at any moment it could begin to slip out from under one's feet. There was no goal to any of this, no straining of energy; there were no distorted features, only fatigue and work. Péter didn't understand it. He just knew it was good to sit next to his father in the car going home; good to hear the drone of the motor, to watch the traffic lights changing from red to green, to see the dividing lines painted along the road.

A fire brought these summers to an end. One morning at dawn, the spirits warehouse on the edge of the market burst into flames. The stores of alcohol blazed; you could hear the crash of the bottles as they exploded, white artificial fibres floated beautifully up through the air. The firefighters said that it all had to burn down. The corrugated-iron sheets shrivelled up in the blaze and turned white; white filaments clung to the sweaty skin underneath one's clothes. It was useless to try to remove them, even days later you felt as if you were being pricked by a thousand tiny needles.

And in the blaze of the fire, time began to pass; the autumn rains followed upon the summer. Water trickled down from the windows in thin streaks, became trapped in the cracks in the pavements; in the sunlight, the road sparkled with watery illumination. On the trams, people stared fixedly in front of themselves or, further inside the carriage, they stared at a hand-rail, a strap, focusing their gaze on a voided point somewhere in the air. And the overcoats grew damp and clammy, the skirts, the blouses, the papers in the briefcases grew damp and clammy, as did the smells, the staircases, the rooms, the pillows, the bodily odours; the thoughts were damp and clammy, the pictures on the walls, the voices, the earth itself. And in the ground, every face turned to muck, the wooden planks became drenched, the skin turned black. The day after your death, it also rained like that. The documents necessary for the funeral had to be obtained, a gravesite found. Water stood in patches on the oily rubber mats in the tram; the leather straps swayed in unison. I sat down; the stitches on the seat, the size of a hand, were like the stitching left after an operation. I closed my eyes, leant my head against the windows. I was grateful for the coolness.

Péter's parents differed from each other so much in their entire characters, and so much stood between them—unspoken yet palpable recriminations, indivisible suffering, their bitter, impossible attempts to escape both from their own selves and from each other—that it was a very long time until Péter understood what it was that kept them together. When, after lunch on Sundays, M. lay down to read and, after a minute or two, the book would collapse onto his chest as he drifted off to sleep, or on certain nights when Péter and his mother waited up for him until ten o'clock or even midnight not knowing where he was, nervously pacing to the window again and again, hoping against hope that M. had only had to wait for a shipment from the countryside and the truck had been stopped because of a punctured tyre or some other reason—at such times, Péter's mother would, with increasing frequency, begin to interrogate him, wanting to know what he thought of them, what he thought of his father. Then, sensing that the boy did not want to take sides in the struggle between the two of them—and attributing this to ruthless indifference rather than tact—she would begin a long, disjointed monologue about her girlhood aspirations, about everything she had to endure in her mother-in-law's house, all the while signalling unequivocally to her son that there were matters of which she could not, for the time being, speak. And these monologues always concluded with the same, unanswerable question: Still, your father is a fine man, isn't he?

Indeed, a fine man. Péter felt that in these moments he was stronger than his mother. And his mother told stories over and over. How, as a young girl, she was in love with this boy or that, how she would peer from behind the lowered blinds when he turned the corner next to the Basilica, what a wonderful crowd gathered to go skating on the artificial rink in the City Park, how they played tag and crack-the-whip on the ice, how much she always read and how she never missed a single premiere at the Vígszinház or the National Theatre. And she told the story of why, after finishing her secondary-school course in industrial food-processing, she let her parents talk her out of going to university— she had wanted to become a microbiologist—and then of how she ended up in the workplace where she was to spend the next forty years, how she came to know M., how she stood next to him in front of her parents who cautioned her against the marriage—saying that maybe this young man was handsome, serious and decent, and his being divorced wasn't a problem, but he was uncouth, unrefined, she wouldn't be happy with him—and she told stories and more stories, and again there she was in her mother-in-law's house, and again she accused her of letting the servants bring up her son, and again she wept and, while weeping, asked Péter if he would ever be able to forgive her for choosing such a father for him.

When this happened, Péter pretended not to understand what his mother was talking about. As the years went on, though, he penetrated evermore deeply into the dense forest of fantasies, fears, recriminations, complaints, the entire unknowable past of his parents and grandparents—while seeking, withdrawing ever more into himself, that narrow, perhaps even non-existent, path between sympathy and betrayal. Of course in this forest there were clearings where he felt good about things. There were stories he was happy to hear, stories that were always told in the same way, with the same words: how his mother waddled in spike-heeled pumps all the way down Bajcsy-Zsilinszky út to the civil marriage hall, how once on a boat trip in Poreč, M. ate two entire plates of freshly harvested mussels, and how he lost his gold wedding ring while he was serving up pickled cucumbers from a jar. Or was it that a wave had swept it off his father's finger as it tumbled above their heads at Poreč? There were stories which he had heard in too many variations, that contained too many wrenching details, and he could never piece together what had actually happened. For example, a few weeks after his parents' marriage, his mother had to go to work in dark glasses, so that no one would notice the bruise under her eye. According to M. this story was untrue, as opposed to the about his mother's friend, the one with the Trabant, or the one where his father-in-law came to their flat one day—he had the key to their front door—and stripped them down to their last hundred-forint note, kept in a metal box underneath the oven. Péter had to decide if all of these accusations —for each story was also, somehow, an accusation— was true or not. In any event, he became a traitor. Every time he sat down next to his mother at the kitchen table while M. slept, he betrayed his father; and yet at the same time he betrayed his mother too, for he was silent, he did not decide in her favour, he never chose among the stories and he never forgot any of them.

And now—in the same way—I am betraying you as well. I am telling you a story concerning certain events, which meticulous investigation could perhaps reveal to have been, every one of them, a lie. You, however, are no longer capable of investigating, and you cannot raise any objections. Even if you were able to do so, you could hardly say that a given event didn't happen like that, because how could anything that I am relating here bear any relationship to reality? For what we call reality went up in flames with your body, and perhaps nothing ever was real in our relations than that colossal, almost shapeless male body that made its way across the room every Sunday morning with its heavy, slow, wobbling gait. Thus the only possible objection arises, one that I have to make in your place: that things never fit as neatly together in reality as they do in my story; life is something more than a jigsaw puzzle. And still, I hope that by the time I reach the end, I will nonetheless be able to convey something of the truth, to bring some peace of mind to both of us, to ease the burden of life for me, and the burden of death for you.

Above the folding bed where M. slept hung the printed reproduction of a picture. It depicted a rocky seacoast: vortex-like waves pounded against colossal brown rocks, further from the shore casting up sprays of white foam, yet the surface of the sea itself was peaceful, the blue-grey shades without disturbance, swimming into one another like the colours of the autumn sky covered with thick, greasy clouds. The shoreline was barren; only one house was visible above the rocks, a tiny whitewashed hut, its roof seemingly thatched with branches; a thin path led to it from the shore. Below, near the bottom of the path, stood a woman. The breeze clutched at her dress as she waved a white handkerchief towards a boat that was at sail far out in the sea. Péter could never decide if the boat was approaching or drawing away from the shore. And if it was leaving, who was it taking away? If it was approaching, who was it bringing to shore? A father, a sibling, a lover? Would the one who had left ever return? The one who arrived: how long would he stay? Or perhaps the woman wasn't even beckoning to the ship with her white kerchief, but to M., asleep and snoring below the picture? If she was waving to him, than who was she? Had M., even if only in his dreams, ever trodden the winding path between the cliffs and, if so, what words had sounded up there in the tiny thatched hut? Péter felt that the sea, crashing untroubled against the rocks, could at any moment lash out onto the shore with full force, sweeping the woman away into its blue-grey depths, as it had swept the ring from M.'s finger. The next day, the ring was gobbled up by a fish and the fish in turn caught by a poor fisherman, who brought it home, found the ring in its stomach and gave it to his wife. She then sold it at the market and, with the money, bought a nicely fattened goose; she stuffed its gullet and roasted its liver. And in the house of the fisherman, there was great joy.

M. nearly always awoke in a sullen mood. How can you be so heartless, he would mutter as he lay on the bed, out of the darkness towards the lighted kitchen, like someone coming back to the surface of life from the depths. Péter remembered him waking with a start at the sound of a slamming door, or the rattling of a pot lid. If he was sullen, it was no use; in vain would Péter's mother murmur into his ear, Don't be so gloomy, would you like some coffee? In other respects as well, he was difficult to live with, because although at times he surprised his son or even his wife with the offerings of his affection, calling Péter 'my little chickee', just as Sergeant Csupati and his dog Kantor in the movies, or placing his enormous palm on the nape of Péter's mother's neck, caressing it—at which point she would murmur, Papa, your caress is like the bucking of a horse—there was always something, a comment, a glance that rebuffed, and M. would immediately snap back into his customary serviceable woundedness and fatigue, wanting nothing other than to be left alone. He turned up the volume on the TV higher; it was all the same to him what programme was being broadcast, he gaped into the screen with the same inexpressive gaze. And if someone stood in front of him, he grew indignant: How can you be so inconsiderate, was your father a glass-maker?

If anything at all could stir M. from his indifference, it was argument. As time wore on, he indulged

in this pastime with his son with ever-increasing frequency. A true passion flared in both of them, into
which so many emotions were mixed: the passion of
opposition, love, rage, the bitterness of 'either him or
me'. Most pressing, the single question from which all
the others ensued and into which everything else
flowed, was the old dilemma: whether or not existence
determines consciousness. A question that they grappled with both in its philosophical abstraction and in
its concrete application. In their opposing stances, M.
was existence, and the argument went like this: Could
Péter, that is to say consciousness, arrive at different
inferences than those that existence had determined for
him, could he wish for a different life and, assuming he
could, would that not be proof of his hypocrisy and
mendacity? He drank wine and preached water. The
debate, of course, couldn't extend to posing the question of the obligation of existence to sustain consciousness and have it educated. If, for example, existence
asked: 'What do you want for dinner?', consciousness
would not answer, 'Don't determine me!' and not even,
it's true, 'sausage' or 'scrambled eggs', but would, out
of good habit, remain silent. For obviously, consciousness knows that the sausage will all the same make
its way to the plate, it can even throw in a bit of
horseradish or mustard on the side, or a slice of bread.
And, if it takes a slice of bread, it, of course, doesn't
need to thank anyone, so how can it possibly claim that

there is no liberty? Not to mention that one day too, consciousness will become existence. However existence may wish to think of itself, it is brute force and power.

One time when Péter might have been fifteen or sixteen, the family travelled to Munich, having briefly visited Vienna and Prague. This was Péter's first trip to the West. They strolled through the Frauenplatz; they admired the flowers on the lamp posts, the cleanliness of everything, the shop windows. Yes, people really know how to live here, they said to each other. From Dienerstrasse, they turned into the Hofgraben. They read how the ducal palace, which the citizens of Munich termed the 'Altschloss', had been constructed during the reign of Ludwig Wittelsbach in 1255, acquiring its present form after many reconstructions. One noteworthy feature was the late-Gothic gate-tower and the balcony, built in a similar late-Gothic style. They looked at the tower and they looked at the balcony. So that is what late Gothic looked like. Péter's mother closed the guidebook and they headed towards Marienplatz, the old market square. On the corner in front of the main post office, a young man stopped them. He spoke Hungarian, and Péter was filled with disappointment, for he felt then for the first time what he was to experience very often later on: that foreign speech, foreign surroundings can be liberating. The young man introduced himself, and set about relating his story. He had arrived in Munich that morning on the early train, having come only to purchase something: a stereo, a coffee-maker, face cream, but before he had had a chance to buy anything, his wallet had been stolen, he had been robbed in broad daylight, and in his wallet was the ticket for the train journey home. He asked for money and he said how much. Twenty marks.

Was the story true or false? Péter, who at that time had been reading a lot of Dostoyevsky and had even brought one of his works, perhaps *The Brothers Karamazov*, with him to Munich, began to reason with himself: 'This man is either lying or he's telling the truth. Granting this, which supposition should we accept? Intellect alone cannot decide in this matter. However, inasmuch as a choice must be made, we must also scrutinize any potential forfeiture. Truth and goodness. And there are two things that must be avoided: error and penury. The wager of our decision is, therefore, nothing less than consciousness and salvation. Thus, however, there is no longer a real wager to be made. Where infinity is at stake, and the endless number of chances of losing are not opposed to the prospect of gain, there is no room for deliberation— everything must be staked.' It took only a moment to think all of this through, so that before M. could even reply to the young man, Péter had spoken: 'Give him the money.' M. looked at his son, and Péter could interpret his gaze as seeming to say: 'Consciousness, salvation, what kinds of words are these? The question of whether this individual is lying or not can be answered by one thing alone: experience. I've never read as many books as you have, and I never will. You've certainly never had any reason to poke your nose out of them before this. If you even had, though, you'd have realized that words like crime, salvation, conscience—even duty, sacred duty, all reek of the stench of infamy. This man is lying. But all right, let's bet on it! Let him be the unwitting judge in our dispute.' And M. pulled a twenty-mark note out of his wallet and handed it to the young man, who promised to return the money in Budapest. When the family returned home, however, it turned out that the telephone number given to them belonged to the branch of a savings bank and, as for the address given on Vaci utca, Péter's mother said, even while in Munich, that it was the site of an industrial building.

Péter knew that he had lost. All along Sendlingerstrasse, he explained why the fact that the young man was a fraud did not depreciate his father's action but, in fact, reinforced the justness of it. He fully realized that to swindle a compatriot while drawing upon the sympathy of a fellow Hungarian is particularly depraved. But goodness requires neither gratitude nor reciprocity. Suffering is cloaked in the mantle of love, yes, completely covered by it, so that one would never even suspect the pain caused by unending disappointment. This is what Péter said, or something like it. And then he added—like one who now truly felt himself to be in the saddle—that it fell to every new generation to discover faith anew, to seek to find the strength that could lead to that faith, without having to rely on the previous generation. M. looked around at the buildings on Sendlingerstrasse, at the church consecrated to Saint John of Nepomuk, and only later on in the hotel made the comment, as he was about to lie down for his after-lunch nap, that love is not a human attribute.

The following, however, are human attributes: envy, conceit, greed, resentment, mendacity, impatience, misery, umbrage. Eight in all; the greatest one being the last. The offended face is as if cast in bronze, forever concealing itself; it never sees itself in the mirror. The wounded face only gazes inwards, no one ever knows its pain; and were we to search for it, we would never even find it anywhere, as we can hardly hear the melody of a flute or a zither if the instrument itself is lifeless, if it gives forth no distinct sounds. And every wounded face is the same, the suffering of every wound is as one. When M. spoke of love, Péter, lying on the other side of the room, on another bed, closed his eyes; and it occurred to him that he could not picture his father's face to himself. Yet still he felt reassured, sensing that all the same, he was following in his footsteps.

As this book—this final resting place of yours—is being prepared, I, on the other hand, am disquieted. You, the one to whom I am now speaking—where have you been until now? For I cannot speak to you as if you were a living person; and certainly not to one who is no more. My gaze wanders through the empty air—you, who stepped out of the fire, have left the entire infinity of your absence here, which belongs to you and not to me, as this book belongs to you. Who can tell if I have not, in my travels, gone astray, if I can ever get to that place where, following your body, your words too shall burn? Can I share that place with you? No, no, the question is not where you are; the question is where am I. Every evening, when I leave off writing, is like an interrupted sigh, and every morning when I start anew, a painful intake of breath.

For Péter, from that day on, that day when M. spoke of love in the hotel room in Munich, time began to fly. He attended university, got married; two children were born. Every two or three years, M. became involved in an entirely new undertaking: he was appointed the manager of a wholesale business, leaving for work at six in the morning and arriving home at

seven in the evening; he would have his supper in the
kitchen while telling Péter's mother what idiot X or Y
wanted him to do, asked what was going on with
the children, cursed the politicians, and fell asleep
in front of the television during the evening film. Péter
and his family lunched at his parents' every Saturday.
M. always prepared the meal. He would go to the
market as early as Thursday, hoping mainly to please
his daughter-in-law. The lunches, however, always
went poorly. It began as soon as the young family
arrived. M. never came out into the front hall to greet
them, because he wanted to see the end of this or that
television movie; Péter's mother, who made no secret
of how much she suffered, then yelled to M. in the
other room that maybe he could be so kind as to come
out, the children are here. M. would then, rising from
his armchair with difficulty and leaving the TV on at a
deafening volume, come out to receive the obligatory
kisses. By the time the family actually sat down to eat,
there would have been ample reason for mutual
rebuke. The children quarrelled endlessly. While the
soup was being served, M. either annoyed Péter's wife
with idiotic statements intended to be jokes, or Péter
could not repress a comment that seemed to call into
question the entirety of his father's life. If, however,
neither of these things occurred, the meal did proceed
in relative tranquillity. Péter's mother made excuses

for the overdone meat, the inedible pastries. Péter knew, as did his father, that his mother only wanted their praise; thus she became the continual target of their banter. M., as he tried to chat with Péter's son, called him 'fairy-face' or 'lardass', exactly as he had called Péter twenty or twenty-five years previously.

Towards the end of the meal, M. would always dredge up whatever it was he had heard that morning on the news or the political talk-shows on television. He cursed the government, the new parties, all the opportunists stripping the country of half its wealth, and above all those who wanted to make him believe that his entire past life had been little more than a lie. At the beginning, Péter tried to reason with him from a balanced perspective; later on, however, as the years passed, he was compelled more and more to admit that M. was right. After they got up from the table, M. went to have a nap; at the end of the afternoon, he was delighted to be woken up again by his grandchildren. At the time, M. had already undergone more than one serious illness. His ankle was completely purple from the time he had served three years in the police force, and the network of varicose veins under the dry skin was being mixed to a deep-brown shade by the first signs of thrombosis. After that, there followed a lengthy stomach operation, and continual heart complaints. If the conversation turned to the topic of illness, Péter's mother tried to persuade M. that it really was time to lose some weight, to have the devitalized arteries cut away from his heart. M. did try to lose weight. He was, however, afraid of open-heart surgery, the procedure that, according to Péter's mother—as she began the enumeration of all her male acquaintances who had survived the operation—was no longer such a dangerously invasive procedure. M. was silent for a while, then said, Leave me in peace already—stop bugging me, you won't have to put up with me for long.

And he said other things as well: that this wasn't really a life any more. In his sixty-second year, after a long-delayed urinary-tract operation, he was given the sack. From that point on, he stayed at home. In the morning, he occupied himself somehow, did the shopping, went to the bank and the post office, twice a week brought groceries to his mother-in-law. By the afternoon, he was exhausted. He was almost completely glued to his armchair; for hours, he would flip through the television channels. In the first few weeks, he tried to find some kind of work. He called friends, acquaintances; everyone promised they would do their best—don't worry, something is bound to come up, we'd really look good if we can't find something for an old crackerjack like you. But they didn't find anything, there was nothing suitable for him. After one year, M. announced that he was going to start work as a parking attendant—to sit inside the attendant's gutted caravan, record in a notebook the licence numbers of the cars parked in the empty lot, chat with their owners (as much as was possible)—and even get money for it. Péter told him it was a bad idea to spend his evenings sitting in a caravan. If someone has a nice heated flat, why freeze outside on the street? Péter's wife said something else to the same effect. Words such as these, though, only reminded M. of his diminishing strength, his defeat. He said his greatest horror was of not being able to take care to himself, of being a burden to others, and if he felt himself to be approaching that state, he would be sure to fling himself over the staircase railing in time.

Summer passed, the autumn holidays came. As always, the family went to the synagogue. They had to leave early, because Péter's grandmother always fretted about the possibility of someone else sitting in their usual seat and a dispute breaking out. People had hardly even begun to gather in the square in front of the temple when the family entered the iron gate. Inside, beneath the staircase, everyone wished each other the best, made their embraces and kisses, and the women went up to the gallery. Péter and M. slowly strolled, side by side, between the two rows of pews and sat down where Péter's grandfather, decades ago, had chosen a place for himself. The lamps were already burning before the Holy Ark. An attendant brought the prayer books from the back and placed them at the foot of the railing, in front of the Torah stand. As the pews filled, the same faces became visible, identical from year to year, the same people in the same clothes greeting one another in the same way, chatting among themselves even when the organ began to play; yet from the colour of their hair, the thickening of the napes of their necks, it was clear that they were ageing. M. put his palm upon his son's hand. They sat down and listened to the rabbi's homily.

The rabbi told the story of the two goats. On the Day of Atonement, the high priest, who wore the white robes of the dead, the linen tunic, the linen breeches girded with a linen sash, and the linen turban, led two healthy goats, a ram and a bull, to the entrance of the Holy of Holies; he slew the bull in atonement for himself and for his house and gave up the ram as a burnt offering. Then he took the two goats and cast lots upon them before the abode of the Lord. In this manner, one of the goats was dedicated to the Everlasting, the other to Azazel. He took the goat to be consecrated to the Everlasting, preparing it as a offering for transgressions. He stepped into the Holy of Holies; Adonai did not appear in a cloud and did not smite him to the earth, and the high priest took the brazier filled with burning embers from the altar, scattered aromatic incense upon it and drew back the veil. The cloud of smoke from the censer concealed the mercy seat, which was upon the Ark. And the high priest slew the goat allotted to the

Everlasting, took the blood of the goat along with that of the bull and sprinkled it towards the east, onto the mercy seat, then seven times in front of it. Stepping out from behind the veil, he sprinkled the blood of the bull and the goat seven times with his finger onto the horns of the altar as well. When the purification of the sanctuary, the tabernacle and the altar had been completed, he brought forth the live goat. He laid both his hands upon the head of the goat and confessed upon it all the iniquities of his people, he laid upon it all of their transgressions and sent Azazel's goat away by the hand of a fit man into the wilderness. And the goat bore with him all of the people's iniquities, outwards into the barren lands. Then the high priest and his attendant put off their linen garments and bathed their bodies in water; the high priest prepared the burnt offering and fumigated the fat of the offering for transgressions.

Péter and M. had already heard the story of the two he-goats; they knew that the high priest could only enter the tabernacle on the Day of Atonement, and that he purified the altar with blood; yet the breath of faith, permeated with a dread that burst out from the story as from behind the half-drawn veil, was so distant and mute to them that they would have been incapable of re-assembling the story's fragments. In the meantime, the rabbi had begun to explain the meaning of the high priest's deeds; what he had to say, however, no longer bore any importance. Péter was wondering what had happened to Azazel's goat as, after wandering through the shouting, the blows, the whistles of the people, it reached the gates of the city and ran out onto the barren plain. Did Azazel come to the rescue of his goat? Was it rescued, or could it have been rescued, by the Eternal, or had it been cast, like a stone from a slingshot, by the city stretching out into the desert? Péter imagined that Azazel's goat would have wandered aimlessly for days. It would have rejoiced to find even a few blades of grass in the parched land. Then it became emaciated, its coat reduced by dust and grind to a greasy pulp; the tiny scraps of rock whirling up from the ground wounding its legs. At night, the goat crept behind a bush or into a recess in the ground. Had any human being ever glimpsed the creature, he would never have dared to approach, never to raise a hand against it. It was enclosed in silence, and behind that silence lay another silence, one yet more profound. When, on the dawn of the sixth or seventh day, a lion sprang upon the goat, it didn't even try to defend itself, didn't try to flee; the lion, though, practically showed it the route to escape. Those who, later on, came out through the city gates would say, Look, there are the bones of Azazel's goat.

That is what Péter thought, and now I am telling the story: I am following you, you who have died. As if I were following Azazel's goat beyond the city gates; yet I cannot recognize your footprint, I cannot discern any traces, for you have no footprints, you make no sound with the slipping of a stone, an object falling to the ground. Last night in my dream, I saw you again, walking through the door, but I told myself that it wasn't you. Just as the story, M.'s story, cannot be yours, and even less so mine. What you are now is something that never existed, it doesn't exist even now and only shall exist while this book is being written, this book from which we are both slowly disappearing. I don't even believe now that I can speak to you, that you can hear me. We no longer belong to each other. Our wanderings, without a doubt, are calculated and arranged. Driven by an ever stronger desire, an ever stronger compulsion; it has burst into flame, expunging everything: it shall efface this book as well. Nothing shall remain of it save three letters, the first initials of three names; then the letters too shall pass and nothing shall remain of them, only the bare earth.

On that day when the rabbi told the story of the two goats, on the day of the fast, M. did not write his name in the book of the living. By the end of the year, he was dead. And Péter, until the very last hours, could not take in what was happening. 'I'm sure he will recover,' 'What's important for him now is to regain consciousness,' 'When we all feel ready, we will really have to talk about what happened during those two months'—that is how he spoke.

Towards the end of the winter, M., without any particular bodily exertion, grew so short of breath that he was obliged to curtail still further what could hardly be termed an active life. He would remain at home for days on end, and if he did go outside, feared that the lift would break down again by the time he returned, forcing him to climb his way up to the sixth floor. Péter's mother, who despite the onset of partial osteoporosis worked as hard, perhaps even harder, than years before, not only at her job in the chemical lab but at home as well, taking on extra work, observed the worsening of M.'s state with growing impatience, as she had felt for a long time that his continual low spirits, shortness of breath and constant need to urinate were depriving her of something that should have been her right, that she deserved for having endured a crippled life, one grown insensible to joy. As she felt old age approaching, Péter's mother—ever more embittered and malcontent—yearned for all she had missed. Péter observed this process with a cool impotence. As he saw it, his mother was the kind of person who needs to become complicit in their own torment and misery; eliciting indifference in others, encircled by it, the feeling of commiseration nurtured towards their own selves grows ever stronger, allowing them to regain a belief in their own value not otherwise offered by life. All of this did not mean that his mother, in her own indirect way, was indifferent to the pleasures of life. Indeed, the opposite was true. Nearly every week, she bought a new jacket, blouse or shirt, every time proudly announcing how little she had paid for it. Then, clattering away at the sewing machine, breaking a new needle in the fabric every ten minutes or so, bits of thread dangling between her lips, reproving her own clumsiness, saying she was capable of ruining clothes that didn't even suit her to begin with. How many times, in previous years, had the family heard from Péter's mother that she would never be able to travel abroad now, let alone go to the theatre or the movies, because she didn't want to go alone, although maybe she just had to make up her mind, like this or that one of her old girlfriends, but just look at M.—could you take him anywhere? There was still work to keep her busy, but who knows, she wouldn't give the firm even half a year before going bankrupt; there was the damned TV, which she would be more than happy to toss out the window. Around M., a suffocating need for clear and honest speech amassed and grew within everyone, creating on all sides obstacles both in front and behind him, from the fear of the effects of both speech and muteness. Only injury could penetrate these obstacles, words that were slipped softly towards another; or insults thrown in someone's face, which were not only irreparable but meaningless and despairing, so that the obstacles and hindrances grew and grew. At the same time, however, everyone could take these hindrances growing out of the feeling of being strangled as evidence that they still had something to say to each other, and although they didn't know what it could be, it would certainly not be meaningless.

In December, Péter's mother succeeded in convincing M. to stay overnight at the hospital for a medical examination. The doctors did not consider surgical intervention necessary, given the risks involved. The lungs, after examination with the speculum, showed significant dilation; one section of the coronary arteries had dried out, the right atrium was dilated—yet the female cardiologist, whom M. had from the beginning trusted unconditionally as a saviour, felt that a quiet lifestyle, medicine and reduction of bodily weight within reasonable limits could possibly contain the damage.

Time passed as before. We take each other by the hand, and we depart in succession. To look up at the sky once more and to say, The sky is blue; to look once more at the trees in the courtyard and say, Autumn has arrived.

At the end of June, Péter went to Lake Balaton with his wife and two children for a holiday. Owing to road work on the motorway, there were numerous detours; the wheels of the huge trucks roared half a metre above their heads, the lights of the oncoming cars were refracted in the raindrops on the windshield. For the first three days, they could walk along the lake front only in their raincoats. Péter ran races with his son in the grassy strip of land on the shore, threw pebbles into the lake and fenced with reeds fished out of the water. The colour of the water was exactly the same as that of the clouds. Only a few points of light were visible on the opposite shore; water beat against the steps. Péter sat on a stone bench with his son and explained where rain comes from, what creates mist and fog, and that there are certain sentences which are precisely the same if you read them backwards as well as forwards. Say one, his son asked. A man, a plan, a canal—Panama. His son repeated the sentence after him, both of them taking pleasure in the word game.

Three days later, the sun came out. The water still had not warmed up, but you could go boating, even take a brief swim; the children built a sand castle girded with stone walls on the beach, making drawbridges from broken scraps of reed. Péter dribbled sand onto the castle, making a tower at the foot of the bridge. Water was routed into the interior of the castle through a system of canals, which had to be continually deepened and cleared of debris, because the sand on the castle ramparts grew damp and crumbled down.

When Péter and his family returned home, M. was experiencing much pain in the area around his abdomen. The skin was red and inflamed, and he had not undergone a bowel movement for days. It was impossible to get hold of the doctor at the district clinic; as usual, they said he wasn't in. The doctor on duty prescribed painkillers and castor oil. Péter and his wife reassured M., saying that you can't turf up such a tough old stump so easily, in a few days he'd be feeling better. Only Péter's mother realized the seriousness of the situation. M.'s body was like a sack stuffed to bursting; the sheets on the bed bunched up beneath him, drenched with sweat; there were wide craters pressed into the mattress's springy upper layer and the pillows stacked up high. In the entire room, there was a sour unwashed smell. When M. wanted to get up, Péter reached with one hand under his father's armpit, supporting his back; with the other, he grasped his shoulder, while M. clutched at his son's neck, puffing and blowing. With trembling hands, he pulled himself into a sitting position, so that he could then probe with his feet for the slippers placed somewhere next to the bed, sliding the tips of his feet into them; and with his son's help, to try to stand up. There was a moment when M.'s stomach and chest were completely pressed against his son's, who still held his hand against his father's back; only now, however, it was so that if his father happened to lose his balance, he could prevent a fall. As he felt the touch of his father's body on his own, the scent of the sickened torso through the dark-blue sweatshirt, Péter extricated his hand from under M.'s arm and stood up. He let his father—shuffling and partially leaning forward, as he could not straighten up completely from the pain—make his own way. Then Péter's mother stepped over to M., grasping his wrist from below, and helped him along to the bathroom.

One morning, after a lengthy series of telephone calls, the ambulance came for M. The two paramedics in their red coats—a bearded older man and a bored-looking youth—stood in the room beneath the pendulum clock and kept looking at the time. The patient should, they clearly felt, have been ready to leave by the time they got there. Péter and his mother accompanied M. into the bathroom, and helped him to shower. The bathroom door remained open; the two paramedics watched with curiosity what was going on inside. M. could hardly lift his leg up to step into the bath. His stomach resembled a heavy sack ready to burst at any moment. Péter's mother sprinkled water on the stomach with the shower head and soaped his torso. Péter marvelled at the smoothness of the procedure: there was no exaggeration in the contact, no pain, nothing shameful. He would have liked to have known what the paramedics thought of it. How did they see those weakened hairless legs, those emaciated thighs, that caved-in chest, those spindly arms? What were they thinking, below the pendulum clock, of M.'s nakedness? Getting him dressed went more quickly. Péter's mother found a clean sweatshirt and T-shirt and gave them to M., pulled the trousers up onto his legs, then the socks, tied his shoes, and the three of them followed the two paramedics as they left the flat. Downstairs, M. asked Péter if he was coming in the ambulance with him. Péter said no, he was busy, but that he would come round to the hospital in the afternoon.

L et this be another resting place in this book. I will tell—but not to you, not to the book, rather to the fire—the story about the disciple. One day, the disciple who had been asked (so long ago that he couldn't even remember when) by his master to write down a dictation which his own hand in its great weariness could no longer entrust to the paper—one day the disciple was asked by his son why he had cast the Book of the Night and the Days, which he had written with such attentiveness, into the fire. By way of an answer, the disciple told a story. 'Once upon a time, there was a poor fisherman, who one day caught so many fish that his net nearly burst from their weight. Night began to fall and he pulled his boat onto a nearby island. That evening, he suddenly saw that more and more fish were swimming towards the shore. He had already prepared his net when the fish cast off their scaly robes and, stepping onto the shore as enchantingly beautiful fairies, danced until dawn. The fisherman was captivated by one of the fairies and he hid her dress of scales; then he concealed himself and pretended to sleep. When the dawn came, the fairies again turned into fish and swam off. All except the one fairy, who could not find her dress anywhere. She asked the fisherman, who happened just then to be awakening, if he had seen it. The fisherman replied drowsily that he certainly hadn't seen a dress of fish scales anywhere at all. With that, he sat down in the boat, pulled up the oars and was about to set off when he turned to ask the fairy if she wouldn't like to come with him. The fairy consented. The fisherman then released all of the fish gathered in the boat, so there would be room for the two of them. For many years, the fairy and the fisherman lived happily together. But they were never married. Since there was no church in their village, they decided one day to set off in their boat; at the first island with a church, they would drop anchor and be lawfully wed. When they passed the island where the fisherman had first glimpsed the fairy, the fisherman began to boast. 'Still, I did the right thing,' he said, 'when I hid your dress of scales.' 'What dress?' asked the water-sprite. The fisherman wanted to make sure he hadn't been dreaming, hence they went to the island. There he brought forth the dress of scales, the water-sprite looked at it, turned it over, then suddenly slipped into it. She cast herself into the water and swam away. The fisherman had only a spear at hand, which he threw after her. The water became flared silver, and the fisherman realized that he had fatally wounded the water-sprite.'

The X-ray showed that after the bowel obstruction of a few days earlier, the colon had perforated; excrement was being emptied into the stomach. General sepsis, the doctors said; a life-saving operation became an immediate necessity. The fear that Péter saw in M.'s eyes at that moment was totally unknown to him. His mother began to arrange things in the hospital room. She raked out the slippers from the sports bag, positioned the transistor radio and the eyeglasses in the drawer of the small cupboard next to the bed. M. was taken into the operating theatre at five-thirty in the morning. It was doubtful as to whether or not his heart could bear the stress; there had been no time to prepare, and the medication employed since the onset of thrombosis to prevent blood clotting could cause further complications. In the course of the operation, it was discovered that a large quantity of pus had been collecting in M.'s stomach; the blood tests had indicated nothing of the sort. Péter waited with his mother in the corridor; they watched as one of the nurses, one knee perched on a chair in front of the window, sipped tea from a mug.

The operation was successful. M.'s stomach was pumped and a gastrostomic incision performed in the intestine. That morning, the attendant in the intensive-care ward said that five days might be necessary for the intestinal activity to begin functioning, perhaps more. M.'s state was stable, but in the evening his stomach, incapable of removing its own gas, became inflated, thus pressing down upon the diaphragm muscle; the patient began to choke. The hospital was filled with the scent of disinfectant and motionless bodies. The day after the operation, M. was awake for a few hours. He seemed cheerful, winking if he wanted to drink; he sipped water through a straw from a white mug. He was happy to receive visitors and tried to nod if some-one asked him something. You see, he whispered in undertones, the family is still together in times of trou-ble. And when no one else was looking, he motioned Péter aside and said, don't write about my stomach. That night, M., heavily medicated and in a deep sleep, was connected to a respirator. The next day, it seemed that his heart would not be able to bear the burden. He was put on an intravenous drip, a tube inserted into his coronary artery in preparation for the possibility of further surgical intervention. His lungs continually produced fluid, which from time to time was siphoned off. The tea which trickled to his stomach via the surgeon's probe did not come back, proceeding onwards into the intestine; peristalsis, however, was not heard at all. As for the incision, it was inflamed, but not so much as to require anything beyond external treatment. No medication could be used to keep down the fever, only cold compresses. M.'s face had not yet fallen in. His son, daughter-in-law, wife stood there beside the bed and spoke to him, hoping that their voices and the touch of their hands could penetrate through the stupor imposed by sleeping pills and pain.

It was possible to regulate the beating of M.'s heart with potassium. The indicator displayed a regular sine curve, with no additional cardiac activity. While holding M.'s moist, swollen hand, or stroking his arm and speaking to him, Péter's gaze often strayed to the clock-like machine, evenly beeping, the green lines running in zigzags, the flashing green numbers. If the number remained somewhere in the vicinity of ninety, and did not go as far as hundred or higher, that was good. For Péter, his father's life became this number. He grew bored and imagined himself talking to the body below the sheet, telling him all about the story of how once, long ago, there was a little boy whose father embraced him with his large hands, and that was reassuring; and the number stayed below ninety. It bothered Péter that if he shifted his weight from one leg to the other, or took a step, the little plastic sacks pulled on over his shoes—which all visitors had to don before entering the sickroom—made loud crinkling noises.

On the fifth day, intestinal activity commenced, and the doctors grew hopeful. The breathing machine was lowered by several degrees, the coronary support withdrawn. It then turned out that the kidneys were no longer capable of expelling the toxic substances accumulated in the blood, thus necessitating dialysis every other day. M.'s blood flowed through a rubber tube into a cupboard-sized box mounted on a wheeled stand, on the top of which red and yellow lights flashed; below it stood ionized water in white enamel basins; coloured sticks were placed inside the basins, and from the other side of the appliance the cleansed blood flowed back into M. The hue of the clean blood was lighter. The poisoned blood was darker. It seemed as if inside the machine, a screeching wheel were turning, not too fast, not too slow, with a soothing evenness.

M. was awakened from his drug-induced sleep. For ten days, he had lain motionless under the white sheet. The functioning of the respirator was reduced; he could now take eleven breaths by himself every minute. His left arm was noticeably thin; his hands were swollen and he could not move his shoulder. He tried to speak, poking agitatedly with his tongue, pushing aside and thrusting out the tube inserted into his throat, but he soon gave up. The nurses, using paper towels, wiped up the mucus trickling out of his mouth and dribbling onto his chin and chest. M. was shaven every other day, every morning wiped with damp cloths; if the bed sheet was stained with blood and pus, it was changed. For this, one nurse held from the front and one from behind, the ill-smelling colossal body, even more weighty in its powerlessness and ready to topple over any minute onto the soft bed. From the necklace worn by one of the nurses dangled a medallion made from a golden one-pengő coin; the low cut of the white uniform and the contours of the nurse's neck framed the likeness of the elderly Emperor Franz Josef, his side-whiskers, his balding pate. Péter recalled that when he was a small child, his mother had worn a similar locket. He would be lying in his bed, his mother leaning over him, covering him with a soft quilted blanket, and the locket brushed against his face. He didn't know who this old man was but he could tell that he wasn't just anyone. A king, a heroic commander, a wise sage. This nurse allowed M. to caress her arm with his right hand, which he could still move, and pull her by the elbow a little to his side. Later on, when his consciousness was muddled even while awake, from the painkillers and sedatives, the nurse asked him what he wanted. M. replied, 'You.' At the same time, he claimed, in front of the attending physician, that Péter's mother was his fiancée, she had been so for a long time now.

M. could no longer be taken off the respirator. He was incapable of coughing up the mucus that had collected in his lungs, threatening him with asphyxiation. At the same time, it was necessary to avoid having the machine breathe for him for too long a period of time, as his spontaneous respiratory reflex would be severely weakened. For that reason, a small incision was made in his windpipe and covered with gauze, so that when necessary the covering could be removed and a rubber tube routed into his lungs. From this point on, M. was silenced until the end. He whispered without a voice, rasped soundlessly, ever more irritated and disgruntled that no one around him could read his lips, repeating day after day, I don't understand, please tell me again, I don't understand, and if someone tried to guess what he wanted, he would receive a glass of water when his back was itching, or his forehead be wiped when he wanted the blanket removed from his leg.

From the beginning, Péter's mother was afraid that should M. recover, she would never be up to the task of caring at home for a man already half dead, one whose consciousness would perhaps never be intact and could turn aggressive at any moment. She shook her head and, within earshot of M., repeatedly asked Péter, standing on the other side of the body, if he too saw that his father's condition had worsened. M. would stretch out his arm and, supporting his wrist across the back of his son and his wife's neck, tried to stimulate the circulation in the shoulder that he could still actually move. At times he pulled Péter's nape down to his chest with startling force and Péter let him put his face next to his own. But these moments brought little comfort. M.'s gaze followed the nurses' movements and appeared to be tranquil only when the medallion of Franz Josef appeared in the neckline of the white uniform, and when the black-haired nurse began to busy herself around him, bringing medications, adjusting the settings on the machine, wiping down his neck; even more so if at the same time Péter's wife stood next to the bed. M. had used to call Péter's wife 'my little ladybug'.

Time passed. Due to damage inflicted upon the nervous system or to the protracted time on the respirator, M. could no longer swallow properly. The incision in his windpipe was enlarged, so that breathing could be accomplished with the help of the larger tube now placed in his throat. In the meantime, bedsores began to appear, bleeding and festering, on his heels and hips. Péter sometimes slipped his hand underneath the body to scratch and rub down his father's hips. He felt how the skin, the knotted grimy bedclothes, the plastic mattress cover underneath them, were being pressed together into a single pulpified substance beneath the body's weight, and that now, separating the layers of this material, it fell to the movements of his fingers to revive slightly the patches of skin around the festering sores, half as large as a hand. The parts of M.'s body where his skin was exposed to the air—his legs, his forehead—on the contrary, were chapped and dry; Péter's mother applied moisturizer daily but in vain. When Péter touched his lips to his father's forehead, he felt the paper-like aridity below the receding hairline, and was grateful for the coolness of the surface without moisture.

The lower section of the stomach incision was continually inflamed. Every second or third day, a coffee mug's worth of pus was drained from the wound. After brief improvements in M.'s state, causing hopes to rise, he always plunged into the same critical condition. Everything depended on whether or not he had enough strength within to impel him back towards healing. One time, Péter's wife arrived at the hospital with an alphabet board. She showed the letters to M. in succession and his task was to indicate the next letter in the word he wished to spell out by nodding his head or giving another sign of some kind. This method, however, proved to be far too arduous. M. composed only one word. The first letter was *m*, the second *i*, the third *s*. Péter's wife tried to guess what word M. wanted to express. She tried different words but did not say the word she was really thinking. M. hissed ever more impatiently with his mouth, with his tongue: *e*, *r*. Péter's wife finally took mercy upon him. Misery? M. raised his eyebrows and angrily—because it had taken too long to pick out the letters—nodded. That was it. Misery.

After a few days of uncertainty, the doctors decided on the necessity of a new operation. Their hypothesis was that an abscess had formed in the vicinity of the previous operation. After the procedure, M. was judged to be in stable condition. The next day, the medication used to stimulate his blood circulation became unnecessary, his breathing improved and the kidney began to function, if only minimally. M., however, grew more and more detached from what was happening around him and to him. His eyes open, he stared at the empty air. It's all from the hospitalization, the doctors said. There was nothing to do but stand beside him, holding his hand, talking to him, watching the lines on the screen, the flashing numbers, wiping the mucus from his throat as it dribbled out from below the bandage. Outside, in the meantime, summer passed; it began to rain. Every day, Péter's mother rubbed skin cream on her husband's leg and tried to trim his nails but this visibly caused M. pain. In the course of the puncturing, a full half-litre of water was sucked from the thorax.

In mid-September, they were able to sit M. up on the edge of the bed a few times. The nurses called the surgical attendant to help. M., supporting himself with his fists against the bed, sat for ten minutes, twenty minutes, then whispered that he wanted to go home. The doctor laughed. The time will come for that, he said. Then the fever came back, inflamed spots began to form here and there in the stomach, and the bedsores continually leached poison into the organism. The prospect of another operation began to be discussed, more extensive and involved than the previous one, but it soon became clear that there was no real sense to it. In the final days, it was evident that M.—there was no telling for how long—was somewhere else. He didn't recognize anyone any more, and he acted crazy, wanting to drink from the stub of the respirator tube. To spare him greater discomfort, he was plunged in a drug-induced sleep; he awoke no more. Slowly, the circulation of the blood ceased. The body turned black, as the blood failed to reach the legs and then, higher up, the loins, the hips. To take leave of the body. To say that it is good to feel the touch of a hand, it is good that warmth, as in a living landscape, can still flow through another body; but get ready, it's time for you to go now.

Between the artificial-stone fronts of the portico columns, the rainwater was turning to diluted mud. The person leaving the building stopped and looked at the glittering lights reflected on the water. The air had a scent of moisture. But on the edge of the sky, the heavy clouds, about to break apart, were tapering off into thin smoky veils, as if the penetrating autumn sun had consumed them in fire. There was in all of this a certain tranquillity, as yet unknown, as yet unfelt.